# ETCHED IN STONE

## PETER M. WRIGHT

PublishAmerica
Baltimore

Softcover 9781606107836
PUBLISHED BY PUBLISHAMERICA, LLLP
www.publishamerica.com
Baltimore

Printed in the United States of America

*There is no solace on earth for us-for such as we-*
*who search for a hidden city that we shall never see.*

—John Masefield

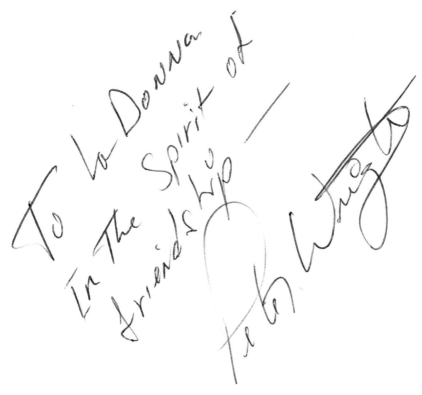

*For Connie*

# CHAPTER 1

## *The Stone*

Mike Zorka reached down to his bleeding left forearm and deftly withdrew the one-half inch sliver of Carrera marble that had imbedded itself as it pierced him missile-like off the blow of his two pound iron mallet and sculpture point. He stood for a moment watching the tiny sliver hole bubbling red, then wiped the blood away with a hand towel.

Looking at his forearm he could see a number of tiny white spots invading the usually sun-browned arm. He was used to being stabbed regularly by high velocity slivers of marble. Wearing an apron or long-sleeved shirt for protection didn't seem to work for him. Binding up in sleeves seemed to inhibit his creative notions and natural vigor. Protective goggles were his only concession to the typical sculptor's uniform donned around the world; most sculptors usually wore an apron, long sleeves, goggles and dust mask. Mike had read too many stories about one-eyed sculptors to take any chances with his own vision. The goggles he wore were irksomely pitted from those needle-like marble projectiles sky-rocketing off his Italian points. But so far, after several years of marble sculpture, his eyes were fortunately intact.

As was his habit he picked up a small piece of chipped marble and ran his tongue over the rough edge and then smiled at the familiar taste of sea salt. His love for marble was engrained in his soul, and in his very character. He refused to ever again sculpt in wood, he had in the past during his formative sculpting years. Wood was all too impermanent for real sculpture. A few granite pieces adorned his house but granite had gone the way of wood being too brutal to work and without the life-giving character of marble created over the millennium from shell fish and sea creatures. He felt that marble was alive and that it contained shapes and images that simply needed to be released. He often referred to his effort as simply releasing the forms from their metamorphic captivity. As he stood evaluating and considering this new piece of Carrera marble he knew deep down that his projected sculpture of '*Lovers*' was already inside the stone and it was his job to set them free. His projected idea for *Lovers* would be a young man and a woman their arms around each other and gazing of into the unknown future.

Feeling the sun heating his back fetched him out of his musing and he picked up the fine imported Italian point (chisel) that marble required and went to his electric grinder lightly rolling the tip against the whirling grit wheel. Satisfied he went back to the sculpture bench, retrieved his iron mallet from where it had dropped to the ground following the sliver attack and then stood gazing trance-like at the 300 pound block of marble. Krista Coleman, a Carmel by the Sea art gallery owner, had frequently asked him why he spent so much time standing inert in front of a project. "Settling it in my head," he always told her. Her typical reproach was,"Why?" But then he usually struggled to find and appropriate answer.

Mike Zorka could stand in front of a block of marble for hours envisaging where he was going with a new project but Krista Coleman enjoyed teasing him about it. Mike always took her jesting with that legendary '*grain of salt*' because he was in love with her, even though to date, he had never told her so.

"Well Michael," he said aloud, "time to get to work. Yeah, then what's stopping you?" Then he heard his house phone ring. "That's whats stopping me." Reluctantly he put his tools down and went into the house. "Mike," he more or less barked into the phone."

A long silence, then a woman's voice, "Michael, did you forget something?"

Mike said "Oh hell," half under his breath and then, "Sorry Krista. I'm an idiot, I know."

"You're not?"

"Krista, is that a confirmation that I'm an idiot or a denial? Am I or am I not an idiot?"

Mike could hear a slight snicker on the other end of the line. "Idiots have no tangible consciousness, Michael. However, you do have a little, at odd moments."

"Glad you noticed," Mike teased.

"Go figure! Looks like I'm having lunch by myself today."

"Sorry love but I've been distracted the past couple days."

"About? Or should I say what's her name?" Krista said.

"Wouldn't you like to know?"

"No I wouldn't and what about this seemingly elusive lunch?" Krista asked.

"Well first off, yes we will do lunch today and second off, I've a new commission."

"First off," Krista Coleman said, "I might have lunch with you and I might not, and second off, what's the commission?"

"Well first off you damn well better have lunch with me and second off, Mario commissioned me to do a 300 hundred pounder he wants to call 'Lovers'. Of course it'll only weigh a coupl'a hundred when I'm done chipping, grinding, and sanding."

"Okay, let's drop the first off and second off stuff while you tell me about our Italiano friend Mario Lucca," Krista said.

"Five grand up front with fifteen to follow when complete...and happy. Well more specifically, when Isabella Lucca is happy."

"For her...what?" Krista said.

"Garden in the Carmel Highlands. And Mario is not Mafia as you often speculate."

"You'll never convince me," Krista said.

"Krista sweet, Mario loves you like a daughter...ease up on him."

"I know, he's your benefactor. Yeah, he is difficult to resist. All Italian charm."

"At times," Mike said.

"Well Vincent Van Gogh had his brother Theo, so I guess it's customary to have a sponsor."

"Van Gogh was a painter," Mike said.

"No kidding? Gee I didn't know that. The professors at the Oakland Art Institute didn't mention Van Gogh."

"Krista, don't be a smart ass. I'm a sculptor. It's different. I can't whip out a sculpture in a day or two like that Van Gogh guy or Monet could paintings; Picasso included."

"Oh Michael you're just a Stone cutter," Krista teased.

"You've sold my stuff in your gallery. So don't call me Stone Cutter."

"Oh Michael you're just a rock quarry worker with dust on you and chips in your hair."

"Michelangelo's step-father was a stone cutter. Why are you being an ass Miss Krista?"

Long quiet pause. "Because you forgot to call me...Stone Cutter!"

"We stone cutters have hearts of stone," Mike promised.

"Tell me about it," Krista said.

"I'll pick you up in front of the gallery at 11:30 sharp."

"Yeah, right."

"Cross my icy stone cutter's heart."

"In that *Jeep thing* of yours?" Krista asked.

"Yeah, in my beautiful Jeep thing."

"That thing you call...what? Old Jeepie? Or is it Creepie?"

"Get it right Miss Coleman. I call my jeep Old Blue. Because it's blue! Have you ever noticed?"

"I'll walk to Caballo Blanco. It might save my life, and Carmel dignity."

"Suit yourself. Dignity?" Mike said, imagine Krista's flashing dark eyes.

"Alright Stone Cutter, 11:30 sharp. Not one minute late. And yes, in that damned Jeep thing, Old what's its name. And yes, dignity. I'm a local businessperson. Remember?"

"As our former Gov might say, hasta La vista, baby. But gosh, dignity?"

He heard Krista click off before he'd finished. He looked at the phone and shook his head, then went back to his sculpture bench and picked up his tools. He was nodding and smiling.

"You know," he said to the marble, "I just love that Krista girl, but sometimes I wonder why. I can't believe she doesn't like my…Jeep Thing. Yeah, Old Blue."

A Fine mist of chips and fragments began showering off the marble as he worked with a renewed zeal. "Yes, he said aloud, "my very own *dignified* girl, Krista Marie Coleman."

Those earlier dark cumulus clouds had crept in off the Pacific Ocean hiding the early morning sun and bringing in a light mist-like rain falling and beginning to dampen the Carmel Valley and the back of Michael Zorka's neck and shoulders. He shrugged into the mist and went into the house and put a pot of coffee on. "Time for some caffeine and a boost to Michael Zorka's energy," he said aloud. "Miss Krista Coleman will expect you, *stone cutter*, to be entertaining and full of life, vim, and vinegar. Yeah, my natural fun loving self."

He poured a large cup of steaming coffee into one of his Vietri mugs brought recently back from a trip to Positano, Italy and sat under an giant Home Depot umbrella on his flagstone courtyard watching the mist blowing in from the direction of the Pacific Ocean and carefully studying the huge block of dripping Carrera marble sitting abandoned on his massive work-bench. "Fascinating stuff, marble," he mumbled aloud. "God's gift to sculptors the world over. Or Mother Natures' gift? No, it's God's gift. Mother Nature doesn't always provide gifts that a person might want. Yes, she can really screw up a life when she feels like it. So be it."

He sat sipping his coffee while keeping a wary eye on the time. "Wouldn't do to stand Miss Krista up for lunch. Nope, really wouldn't." He thought about the origins of this magnificent stone called *marble*, if that is what it really is, *stone?* The metamorphous of fishes? Yeah, conceivably? No maybe what-so-ever about it. Fishes to stone? Yes!"

In the long run, he thought, marble is a rock resulting from the metamorphosis of sedimentary carbonate. Boring evolution, that. Then he thought about pure white Carrera Marble and how that species, if you will, is the one sought mostly by sculptors the world over. Such as? He asked himself. Well Michelangelo for one, Donatello for two, hell even Picasso loved the stuff from the Carrera Mountains. Why Carrera? Well because Carrera is the result of very pure silicate limestone or dolomite protolith.

Mike grinned and sipped his coffee. "Shit," he said aloud, "I could be a professor of geology. Yeah right, Zorka, you home-grown American with the Greek name. Well hell, Greeks were the first master marble sculptors in the world...well as far as history goes. Yeah, something like the discovery of cult sculpture on Greek Islands as early as 920 BC; Venus de Milo for instance. It's gotta be the Greeks. Yeah Zorka, the only kind of professor you could ever be is one of the bull shit variety. So true, so true. "

Please speak your mind, Mr. or Miss Student. Well yeah Professor Zorka what about marble that is not pure, you know, with those poopy streaks and teenage blemishes. That's an easy one for Doctor Zorka, impurities such as clay, silt, sand or maybe even chert end up in the limestone. Limestone? Yeah, the birth vehicle of all marble. Really? Yeah, a few zillion years of marine organisms dying and falling to the sea-bed and then laying there crushed under enormous pressure and heat for myriad ions of time. Gee, this is good Professor Zorka. Yeah, sometimes I amaze myself. Wait, *chert*? What's chert? Damned if I ever really know."

The rain intensified on the courtyard umbrellas suddenly jolting him out of the reverence for his astounding knowledge of the stone he loved. He looked at the time and said, "Shit, time to jump in that, what does Krista call it? That Jeep-*thing*, and run to her.

# CHAPTER 2

## *Cabello Blanco*

The Cabello Blanco (White Horse) Traitoria ponged of its usual warm ambiance. So very Italian. So very honest. So very convivial. A person could dine at Cabello Blanco and be directly removed to a traitoria in a hill-top village in Umbria, or at a street-side café in Florence, or in a country-side diner along the highway in Tuscany and recognize beyond any uncertainty that he has come to the *warmth of Italy.* Strange name for an Italian traitoria? The lore was that when Mario Lucca first arrived in the United States an aging Italian farmer in the area gave the fresh off the-boat immigrant a noticeably over-the-hill white horse to sell as a fresh start in California. Mario never forgot the three hundred dollars he received from the sale of *Cabello Blanco* to a riding stable in the Carmel Valley. Those three hundred dollars fed him during his first few months in Carmel.

Music from the Three Tenors, Luciano Pavarotti, Placido Domingo, and Jose Carreras, floated softly and appropriately in the background while nattily dressed waiters and waitresses flowed efficiently through a myriad of cozy individual dining rooms and those few intimate nooks designed for the covert pairings of no more than two contented diners. Flickering candles and petit vases of flowers adorned each table while the adjacent walls were artfully decorated with paintings and photographs of the stunning Italian countryside, hill villages, and very much celebrated cities.

Mike and Krista were seated by Mario Lucca in their favorite nook. Mario Lucca was the ever-present host and owner of Cabello Blanco. Mike had recently began to appreciate the subdued lighting in the quiet two-person nooks because he felt that it sort of leveled the ever annoying and tiptoeing crinkles around his eyes and the outwardly new lines that were menacing the immediate areas around his cheeks and mouth. While too closely pushing forty he felt good and hoped that he looked, well, okay, but knew those halcyon years of flawless youth were fading rapidly into the not so distant past.

However Krista Coleman, some 10 years younger than Mike, had no need for subdued lighting or any other kind of enhancement or disguise for her striking features; large brown serious eyes, an oval Madonna-like face that was crowned with a strikingly haloed head of auburn hair that frequently conflicted itself in an array of bouncing curls and waves that habitually reached more than half way down her willowy back. Krista Marie Coleman was a self-made woman who began her professional life as an art major at the Oakland California Art Institute but soon discovered that her real talents lay with marketing. It quickly became quite natural for her to migrate into the art-selling business, a resolve that led her to Carmel by the Sea, known wholly as one of America's key creative sites in the entire country. Carmel has been home to a revered plethora of America's ultimate artistic minds for more than a century; artists, sculptors, and writers have drifted easily to that stunning village beside the sea. For the individual with an artistic mind Carmel by the Sea is still the epitome of a nurturing place to live and produce. One of Mike's much loved quotes was by Henry Miller, "*To paint is to love.*"

Mario, being his usual self, greeted Mike with a double handshake and kissed Krista on both cheeks and took advantage of the opportunity to hug her mightily. She blushed when Mike jested Mario with "back off Wop and unhand my girl."

Mario backed off and stood admiring Krista. "She loves the touch of a real man. Only Italians are real men." Mario stretched to his full height of five-feet eight and grinned, his all but bald head shining like a friendly beacon in the nearby candle-light.

"Mario," Krista said giving him a light shove, "give me a break."

"Oh sweetheart," Mario said, "look at those hands of his, they are all beat to hell. And his arms are all corded with those ugly swollen muscles. And he shaves only once in a great while. The man is a bearded barbaric. He has no finesse. No gentleness. Look at these hands of Mario. The hands of a gentleman, caring to the touch of a woman's skin, sensitive…skilled."

"Would Isabella agree Mr. Cabello Blanco?" Krista jested. Mario shrugged, raised his eyebrows, and threw his hands up Italian-style, his dark eyes squinting shut. "Hmmm," he whispered, while putting a finger to his lips.

"Krista," Mike said, "I think we'll eat somewhere else."

"Mario laughed and punched Mike on the arm. "Sit my friend. Sit and shut up and allow me to serve this beautiful woman-girl…this so bella senorina."

"If we must," Mike said. "That is if you have anything that's edible."

"Today," Mario said, "the wine is on me, but only if you drink Italian vino."

"Bribery will not make me like you Mario Lucca," Mike said. "Oh Michael Zorka you know you love Mario and Mario loves you, even though you have that ugly Greek name." Mario reached up and slapped Mike gently on his cheek Italian-style.

# CHAPTER 3

## *Mario Lucca*

Mario Philippi Lucca had hailed from Venice, Italy some twenty-five years before, Landing on the piers of San Francisco Bay with nothing more than the clothes on his back and a very crumpled and very precious United States twenty dollar bill pinned safely to his shaggy two-week dirty underwear. With the twenty dollar bill still unspent and now stored in his ragged laborer's coat pocket he went straight to work making himself a millionaire within the first five years of residence. That same twenty dollar bill now stood framed (in a frame that cost far more than the twenty dollar bill it enshrined) above the desk in his office at Cabello Blanco. Mario loved telling the story of that twenty over and over and each time it became more and more embellished. Above his office desk hung a 24 by 24 oil painting in a rendering of his so much loved and remembered White Horse (Cabello Blanco).

Mario's rumored Mafia connections were legendary and the source of Carmel rumors and gossip around the group table at the Pine Inn over coffee and croissants many mornings, but a horde of investigators were collectively unable to unearth anything with which they could accuse him. They eventually and mutually said, "To hell with it." One of Mario's favorite lilts was to say something like, "Youse betta treat'a me right or I'll call in'a my friends Louie Da'Louse and Big'a Vinney to take youse for da ride down by da river," and then roar with laughter.

The truth about Mario Lucca was that he was a self-made man without the influence or interference of any organization, legal or illegal. However, due to his great success in diners and real estate the rumor persisted but in reality he enjoyed the suspected notoriety. He had often been heard to quip in public that "Yes, I am truly Carmel's *mystery man.*

Mario married Isabella Constanza two years after he set foot on US shores and the ensuing intervals produced six off-springs; 3 girls and 3 boys. Presently they ranged in ages 5 thru 17 and yes, were collectively spoiled. Annabella, the oldest girl, drove a Porsche Boxter to school and her brothers and sisters rode four thousand dollar bicycles like their two cycling heroes Tour de France winners Lance Armstrong and Greg LeMond. The children's rooms at Mario's Carmel Highlands eight thousand square foot mansion were the stuff most kids only dream about; giant flat screen televisions in each room, complete entertainment centers with Around Sound CD players and of course, their very own bathrooms with swimming pool sized tubs and showers with multiple heads. Oh yes, of course the tubs were Jacuzzi-style. Could a poor child expect less? Well for sure not the Lucca kids.

Tough guy that Mario Lucca tried to project failed miserably in the presence of Isabella. Isabella ruled the roost at Mario's Castillo de Amoroso, *Castle of Love.* However she did find herself in serious contest by her two oldest daughters; Annabella and Carmen were strong headed young girls who wanted their own way one hundred percent of the time. Castillo de Amoroso rang regularly with the so-Italian shouts of three strong-headed women trying now to out-shout the each other and absolutely have their own way. During these feministic brawls Mario often fled in his coal black Hummer to somewhere safe such as Clint Eastwood's Hog's Breath Inn in Carmel or some local testosterone-imbued watering hole. Escape was critical.

Mario Lucca took chances while on his road to riches. He began his odyssey by borrowing five thousand dollars on an array of credit cards and investing that money in a run-down former office building. He remodeled the building with his own sweat and, some would say, stolen material, and rented it out as an business office to a realtor. With the new equity in that building he was able to borrow enough to do another office and so it went for the next few years until he was wealthy enough to branch out into the restaurant business and so now you have a very rich Italian immigrant living in the style he would say in his own words, "The style I preserve." Until someone convinced him the English word was *deserve.*

"Mario…" Krista said, "You can't help but like him."

"Yeah, but he thinks he's the *Italian Stallion*," Mike answered. "Isabella says different."

"She does?" Mike asked. "Yeah, she says he's a puppy-dog around the house. Says the two oldest girls own him."

"Well we know he likes girls," Mike acknowledged. "Insists on having his feet rubbed at night."

"How would you know?" Mike asked. "Isabella has lunch with my group of girls every Wednesday."

"Oh, you mean the Burka Babes?" Mike said while avoiding Krista's eyes. "Mike, you ass. We're not the Burka Babes. We're a clutch of business women who like to dine and discuss business."

"And men?" Mike said with a grin. "We don't talk about men. Well not much."

"You talk about me?" Mike whispered. "The girls ask."

"About?"

"Oh nothing serious." Krista said as she avoided Mike's eyes. "About?"

"Well about your work and your former wife."

"What about my former wife? Yes, Barbie Doll Zorka. The one-time Diva of Carmel by the Sea."

"Well, you know, what happened."

"Nothing happened."

"She divorced you."

"I divorced her."

"Syntax." Krista said, shaking her head. "Call it what you like."

"Don't worry."

"I don't."

"I haven't discussed your sordid past with the, what do you call them, The Burka Babes?"

"Barbara was a scientist. I'm an artist. We didn't mesh."

"So you divorced."

"Yeah, no kids, no mess, no collateral damage."

"Good enough…I guess. But she kind'a cleaned you out money-wise?"

"All of everything we'd earned more or less together. She didn't need it though with her super rich Daddy watching over her. However, it was worth it."

"So she was kind enough to leave you, what?"

"My books, sculpture tools, the grand sum of three hundred, twenty-two dollars and seventeen cents, and my Jeep. That Jeep Thing as you call it."

"Messy life, Zorka."

"And you Miss perfect, your marriage and divorce; somewhat chaotic, untidy, muddled, hectic and frenzied I think, when you sent Bobby Coleman on his way. Or using that so-common cliché…*split the sheets*."

Krista looked out the window, thought for a long moment and then shook her head. "Bob was a drunk…a violent drunk. Sixteen months was all I could tolerate of him. I got pretty tired of explaining my bruises to friends as falls in the tub or down the stairs. Shit, they all knew the truth. Eventually several of my girlfriends cornered me clandestinely at a coffee shop and insisted that I do something…call the police or run and hide. I called the police, had him arrested and charged and then ran and hid until court time"

Mike reached across the table and took Krista hand. "I know. I'm sorry. This isn't really great lunch-time talk, so, do you think it'll rain?"

"Robert Coleman is history now. He's in some county jail up north for beating up his girlfriend while in one of his drunken rages. And… that is where he belongs. Bar none. And I hope to whatever Gods that may be that I never see him again. Yeah, I have nightmares still."

"If he ever bothers you I'll crack his head with my sculpture mallet…the old one."

"Michael Grow up," Krista said while shaking her head.

"Well I will," Mike assured her. "Yeah, I'll use my genuine Italian mallet made in…China."

"You know he has a daughter that he abandoned when she was just a child?" Krista said.

"Yeah, you've mentioned that."

"Becky was a cute little girl and eventually a very pretty teenager, at least she was the last time I saw her. I'm hoping that drugs and booze and unwanted pregnancies didn't enter her life. I saw some potential in her character."

# CHAPTER 4

## *To Touch*

Krista Coleman stood in a light rain under Mike's outdoor floodlights watching the rain drops misting like tiny stars as they drifted down through the arch of light. Through the floating drops she was admiring Mike's huge block of Carrera marble. Mike was standing with one arm around her shoulder and holding a snifter of brandy in the other. Krista moved to the marble and ran her hands over the glistening wetness.

"My God its beautiful stuff," she said," just to touch it feels magical. Is it Colorado Gray or something from Portugal? If I'm gonna hang out with you I've got to learn my marble."

"Carrera from Italy," Mike said." It's the easiest marble to work. I love it. Portuguese marble is probably the hardest to shape. Especially Portuguese Rose. Tough stuff."

"Have you been to Carrera? That's a dumb question, I'm sure you have," Krista said. "Yeah, me and Barbara went there for our so-called second honeymoon. I couldn't believe my eyes as we drove toward the Carrera Mountains. That is before I went alone to study in Italy"

"Because?" Krista asked. "We thought the mountains were covered with snow, and it was mid-summer, but when we got up there the '*snow*' was marble. An entire mountain of marble. Work crews with giant machines were cutting monster blocks of the stuff. Blocks the size of school buses; houses. Pretty fascinating. Those mountains are heaven to a marble sculptor"

Krista leaned close to the marble. "It looks like you've already started *Lovers*."

"Some. A few preliminary chips here and there. It's still not totally settled in my head. Sometimes I have to simply fool around with a piece before I really start cutting into it."

"Are you really looking at a year? That seems like a long time on one piece."

"Six months minimum. Could go a year. But Lucca wants the damn thing in his garden by summer."

"You mean Isabella?" Krista said. "Well yeah, Isabella. You probably know Michelangelo took years to finish some of his Stuff, and a bunch that he didn't finish. He took so long on one commission that his sponsor, Piero, a Medici, didn't live long enough to see it. But heck Piero wasn't very bright so it didn't matter a whole lot. History makes claims that his sunroof had a bad leak."

"That's not nice," Krista said.

"I do mean Isabella. She's the catalyst in the Lucca family."

"Yeah, when she can out-shout the girls," Krista said. "Let's get in out of this rain." Krista hesitated. "Does the weather affect marble?"

"It can, and will," Mike said. "Worse thing is pollution. You know auto fumes, smoke, and extreme temperature changes; rain, stuff like that."

"Yes," Krista said, "when I was in Greece some of the ancient stuff looked pretty damn bad. Lots of it broken-up too."

"The environment," Mike said, "has destroyed numerous marble artifacts. When most of this stuff was created we didn't have the pollution we do now. Of course World Wars One and Two took their tolls. Michelangelo's David was sand-bagged from head to toe to protect it from the bombings. Thank God those people there in Florence at that time and the rest of Italy were smart enough to safeguard ancient artifacts."

"In Athens I saw some of the sculptures that had been buried for centuries and then dug up. In that category they were fairly pristine except for breakage; arms and legs missing; the head. The Venus de Milo looked pretty good. She was dug up around 1820."

"The Renaissance sculptors learned their art by studying the early Greek and Roman stuff," Mike added. "A large number of those pieces were excavated out of ruins and as you say, were still fairly pristine. The Greek-style sculptures you see in Italy were mostly copies. Some Italian sculptors merely made copies of the Greek stuff. It seems that the wealthy Florentines needed lots of decorations for their homes and gardens. Of course the German's looted some areas of Greece for art works during their occupation of World War Two, but luckily some have been repatriated. The Greek government has recently taken Germany to international court over some of the missing artifacts and succeeded in their return."

Krista went back to running her hands over the dripping marble. "Shaping it is the hard part, I guess. It looks brutal to me with all that pounding with the mallet. No wonder your hands are beat up, but oh so strong." Then she turned and grinned at Mike.

"Not really," Mike said, "finishing the piece is the hard part."

"Such as?" Krista asked. "Using the side-grinder for final shaping, sanding with half a dozen different damp and dry grits, wet sponges, smoothing with steel wool, and then of course waxing. Using the grinder is the worse because you can ruin a human figure, or animal form in seconds. Abstracts aren't quite as chancy because you can usually adlib with offbeat forms. My granite sculpture called *Friends* was planned to be called *Family*, a man, woman and child, but when the child accidently cleaved off I had to rename it. Always disappointing when something like that occurs, especially when the piece, after months of work, is almost finished."

Mike and Krista went back into the house and sat before a roaring fire in the hearth. They had fixed dinner together and the dirty dishes still sat on the dining room table.

"We'll do the dishes in the morning," Mike said. "First we'll watch this fire burn down and then it's to bed for us."

Krista looked up at Mike and squeezed his hand. "What makes you think I'm spending the night?"

"You're too drunk to drive."

"Bull shit, Zorka."

"Friends don't let friends drink and drive," Mike said.

"That's a stupid time worn cliché and as a matter of fact I'm not even faintly tipsy."

"And?" Mike asked.

"And...I'd stay anyway."

"God I love it when you're firm about something," Mike said," however, you have to do the dishes in the morning."

"Don't hold your breath Zorka."

"Yeah?"

"Yeah!"

# CHAPTER 5

## *Legal Tender*

While finishing the dinner and breakfast dishes Krista stood frowning at Mike. He saw the look on her face and said, "What?"

"What's bugging you?" Krista said. "I know you're not hung-over."

"What makes you think I'm bugged?"

"Because I know you…have for a year or two," Krista said.

"That pal of yours, Mario Lucca, that's what."

"Okay, what has Mario done now?" Krista asked.

"His check bounced," Mike said. "You can't trust that man with money matters."

"That's news? I thought when he wrote a check the bank bounced," Krista joked. "No. It's pure Mario."

"How much was it for?" Krista said. "Five thousand bucks."

"As a down payment on the commission for *'Lovers?'*" Krista guessed.

"Smart girl."

"How much on completion?"

"The remainder of twenty thousand," Mike said," that is if he's happy with it."

"You mean if Isabella is happy with it," Krista offered.

"Correct."

"Call him," Krista suggested. "Mario has tunnel vision sometimes and lets things go."

"I will call him. I need that money. And…it's gonna have to be cash this time."

"Well work on *Lovers* and try to relax," Krista said. "Mario is just being Mario. He'll come through. You've gotta give Mario credit for what he's done with his life since immigrating to the US. You know he showed upon our shores with only twenty dollars in his pants."

"So the legend…or myth goes. However, I'm gonna call that Italian Mafioso bastardo right now," Mike growled.

"Michael," Krista said," no bastardo stuff."

Mike went to the phone and dialed Mario's number; it rang half a dozen times before Mike spoke up. "Answer the God damned phone Mario. I know you're there." Mike imagined Mario snoozing or smoking an expensive cigar at his desk below his beloved painting of Cabello Blanco…and ignoring the telephone.

Krista scowled. "Michael, use a little tact, Isabella might get wind of your wrath."

"Yeah, what'sa matter you Michael?" Mario more or less yelled into the phone rapidly retreated to the imagined safety of his Italian accent and purposely mangling the English language.

Mike looked at Krista and nodded. "He knows."

"Mike, what'sa matter you?"

"You know what's the matter you Mafioso bandit." Krista was shaking her head. "Michael! A little tact."

"Another of your checks bounced. Mario, I need the money. I eat and pay rent you might know."

"It did?" Mario said trying to sound innocent, the accent disappearing.

"It did. You too damned busy to go to the bank?" Mike said.

"Michael, it's my CPA. She's fucked it up."

"Don't kid me Mario; you're no micro-manager. You know what's in the bank and what ain't. No money, no sculpture. Work stops."

"Michael my friend you'll get your money," Mario promised.

"I repeat, no money…in cash…or no sculpture."

Silence followed for a long moment. "Mario," Mike said," are you still there?"

"Who the fuck you think you are, Michelangelo?" Mario said beginning to sound annoyed.

"I know I'm no Michelangelo, Mario. But hell, he had to eat too."

Long quiet pause. Then heavy breathing.

"He was gay," Mario said, "but alright Michael, I'll bring the dough out to you in the morning."

"Cash or cashier's check," Mike said, "and no later than ten."

"That'll ruin my whole day, Michael. But if Krista is gonna be there it'll be worth it."

"Yeah, why Krista?"

"So I can look at her," Mario said while chuckling.

"She'll be thrilled that the so-called *Italian Stallion* like's her looks."

"That Krista is heart-breakingly beautiful," Mario said.

"I can't guarantee she'll be here, but you'd better be, and bring Isabella."

"Get to work on my *Lovers* Michael. Arrivederci. Oh, and remember who loves you…Mario Lucca."

"Mario loves Mario," Mike said and hung up.

Krista stood shaking her head at Mike.

# CHAPTER 6

## *Mona Lisa Bartalucci*

Krista left an hour later and Mike began work on *Lovers* with a little less than abundant fervor due to Mario's bounced check.

"Damn it," he said to the marble, "I know better than to trust that Godless Mafioso." One of Mike's sculpturing practices had been to speak to his stone as he worked. He felt that talking to the stone helped it understand what he was trying to accomplish; his mood that day, his nous of vigor. He'd always intuited that the stone listened to him and cooperated. "I know you *lovers* are in there, so what do you think? You what? You'd rather not belong to the cheap-skate Mafioso. Can't say I blame you. But, well, heck, Isabella Lucca is a wonderful lady. It'll be okay. Mario is no art lover anyway. He'll never give you a second look."

Abruptly Mike got the stimulus he'd been looking for. These mysterious notions often came forthright out of the shadowy recesses deep in the isolated parts of his mind. When he felt that he was good and ready it would surface with a 'bam' right out of that cryptic place called the subliminal mind. The embryos still hidden in the marble had already been christened *Lovers* but this fresh concept would have the them hugging with arms around each other and silently peering deep into the unseen events of their coming lives together.

As Mike worked his mind drifted off to his early years when he was still trying to acquire the art of sculpture. Having never been the kind of person who liked being told what to do or follow directions he had opted to teach himself sculpture via the study of the great masters, copious reading, and experimentation. During those years he'd traveled to such far off places as Greece, Spain, and of course all those other related European countries that claimed artistic histories. In Europe he'd taken great interest in the French, the Italian, and Eastern European artists but his most enlightened times and experiences were the three months he'd spent in Italy. Rome had breezed by as well as Milan, Venice and Genoa, but the most satisfying and productive time was the months he'd spent in Florence studying Michelangelo, Donatello, Leonardo de Vinci and those other remarkable Renaissance artists.

In Florence he'd secured a small second story flat over-looking Palazzo della Signoria, the same palazzo where Michelangelo's seventeen foot tall *David* is exhibited along with a lesser number of his other pieces both finished and unfinished. Mike's days in Florence were halcyon with mornings and afternoons haunting the numerous museums and sidewalk cafes in the palazzos and back streets of that city of that once glorious Renaissance. At night Mike searched for new dining experiences but had fallen into the habit of lunching daily at a small cafe on a back street called Traitoria Donatello. As a sculptor, the name Donatello appealed to him. At Traitoria Donatello he quickly became enamored with a young beautiful Italian waitress who had begun serving him little extras without charge. After each lunch a delightful desert mysteriously arrived at his table followed by a small glass of grappa followed by a cup of coffee with no extra charge. Mike spent considerable time pondering this joyful phenomenon and coming to a hopeful conclusion. This young Italian girl was strikingly beautiful…or *bella*, as he was consciously trying to think in Italian.

On the day of his seventh or eighth visit to Traitoria Donatello for lunch the young waitress was not there. Mike felt disappointed and had even considered going somewhere else to eat when she suddenly appeared in street clothes, walked up to his table smiling, pulled out a chair and sat across from him.

"Buongiorno, "she whispered, "come va." (Good morning, how are you?)

Mike sat there with his mouth open for a long moment before he recovered his senses. She was smiling beautifully while tilting her head to one side. A magnificent array of curls and waves cascaded over her shoulders and down her back.

"Good morning," Mike said in English, "I'm fine...but?"

"May I join you?" She asked in near perfect English.

Mike searched his brain for what Italian salutations he could remember. "Come si chiama?" (What is your name?)

"Yours first," she said.

"Mike...Michael Zorka." He reached across the table and took her hand. She didn't pull her hand away after the obligatory shake. Mike felt slightly weak.

"I'm...you can believe it or not...Mona Lisa. Mona Lisa Bartalucci."

Mike grinned. "Wow, I've come to Italy and what happens? I meet Mona Lisa."

"Enough Michael," she said. "It is my father's fault. He was fascinated with that damned Leonardo da Vinci painting and the whole bizarre mystery of it. He thought da Vinci was God-like. And that mysterious Mona Lisa smile inflamed him something terribly"

"He was," Mike said. "Da Vinci was a genius. Your father must be a fascinating man."

Mona Lisa looked away and then back at Mike. "He was."

Mike thought he could detect sudden moisture in her dark eyes. "Is he gone?"

"Yes, recently," she said without looking directly at Mike.

"I'm sorry."

"So am I. Are you Greek?" Mona Lisa asked. "You don't look Greek."

Mike shook his head. "No I'm not Greek. The name was a result of a second marriage by my mother. Precy Zorka was Greek and he adopted me. He was a good man."

"What happened to your father?" Mona Lisa asked.

"Killed in a useless war," Mike said bitterly. "Vietnam!"

"Are there any useful wars?" Mona Lisa asked.

"No Mona, there isn't."

"You haven't answered me," Mona Lisa said. "I asked you if I could join you."

"Oh God, of course."

So began a love affair that would never be forgotten by either. For the next two months Mona and Mike spent every spare moment together. Mona worked lunches six days a week at Traitoria Donatello but on her days off they rented cars and explored the Italian countryside enjoying little cafes along the way or packing picnics. Mona lived with her mother on the fringes of Florence but began spending most of her nights with Mike. Some evenings Mike was invited to dine at the Bartalucci house. Soon the widowed Anna Bartalucci expressed a fondness for Michael Zorka and wasn't at all bashful about letting the two lovers know she was hoping there was a future for her daughter and the would-be American sculptor. Mike soon learned that Mona's professional dreams lay in the field of clothing design and staging. Together they felt like soul-mates with parallel passions for art and creativity.

The days and weeks of Mike's stay in Italy sped by all too swiftly and before they realized it the time had come for Mike to board an airplane and return to the United States. Their last night together was spent cuddled in each other's arms with Mona Lisa sobbing sporadically and begging Mike not to leave and if he did, to "please, please, please return to her as soon as possible."

And...that was the final arrangement. Mike would go home, work for a year, or less, save every penny and return to Mona Lisa Bartalucci for the remainder of his life. He could think of nothing more nourishing than to be in love with Mona Lisa Bartalucci and happily spending the rest of his life with her. He had begun to feel that Florence was that *hidden city* that he'd thought he would never see.

Parting with Mona Lisa had been heart-wrenching for Mike while leaving her standing on the curb in front of Traitoria Donatello looking forlorn, dejected, and in tears while the taxi cab pulled away taking Mike to the airport and a long lonely flight home.

In the beginning Mike and Mona had talked on the phone weekly and written frequent passionate letters but as in all absenteeism the communications dwindled until long periods of silence and then within the first year Mike had received a letter from Mona Lisa telling him that she was planning to marry a successful architect and that she had finally resolved that Mike was not coming back to her. A desolate Michael Zorka had lost himself in a transitory variety of girl-friends and bar room pick-ups while depleting his diligently earned and protected *return to Mona Lisa money* until that momentous and mostly chance meeting at a Carmel Art Association meeting with the very recently divorced Miss Krista Coleman. He soon realized that her presence in his life had centered him and he was quickly becoming the kind of man he had had always wanted to be. Mona Lisa Bartalucci quickly faded into that mysterious place in the soul where memories lurk and sometimes surface during the darkest hours of the night leaving the beneficiary just a little morose and filled with an unquenchable longing for that *'something buried and evasive.'* However the memories of Mona Lisa Bartalucci remained mostly dormant somewhere hidden in those elusive *windmills of the mind.*

# CHAPTER 7

## *Cash*

Krista was making coffee with an eye on the frying pan where eggs were bubbling beneath a layer of cheddar cheese. Mike was standing at the kitchen window considering his block of Carrera marble waiting patiently for his daily approach with point and mallet. A light rain was falling and the stone looked glistening in the subdued morning light.

"They are in there, you know?" Mike said to the window.

Krista looked up as she snapped the coffee maker on.

"Huh?"

Mike turned to her. "The lovers."

Krista returned to the eggs. "The who? Or whom?"

"The lovers."

"Where?"

"In the stone."

"Oh, those lovers," Krista said while turning the omelet.

"Yes," Mike said to the window," those lovers and my job is to set them free."

Krista went to the window and put her arms around Mike and kissed him. "That's beautiful. And try to remember Mr. Michelangelo, I love you."

"Krista, I'm no Michelangelo. Remember the other day? I was just a stone cutter; a mere stumbling quarry worker."

"Tell me about it," Krista said.

"Mike frowned. "About what?" Krista gave Mike a little shove. "No, not about Mona Lisa Barta-whatever her name was, but about the report that you jumped over a rope in Florence and touched a Michelangelo sculpture."

"Yeah, I sure as the hell did. Idiot that I am."

"And they arrested you?"

"Again, they sure as the hell did."

"Was it worth it?"

"Cost me hundreds, no thousands of Liras and it was worth every penny. You remember that former Italian play money?"

"And how much would that be in Euros or U.S.?"

"About a hundred bucks. That was before the Euro."

Krista poured two cups of coffee and dished out the omelet and buttered toast.

"Your Mister Pop-up does a good job," she said.

"Mister Pop-up?" Mike asked.

Krista grinned. "Your toaster. Mister Pop-up. That's what I call my toaster."

"Here he is," Mike said.

"Who?"

"The Mafioso. Mario Lucca the so-called *Italian Stallion.*"

"Just in time for breakfast," Krista said. "And come on Mike, he's not really Mafia."

"Oh yeah?"

"Yeah, just because he's Italian and successful everyone has to think he's tied to the mob."

"You have intimated that Mafioso theory a time or two yourself Miss Perfect."

"Pure jest."

"Coffee," Mike said, "nothing else for the *Stallion.*"

Mario had stepped out of his coal black Hummer and was standing in the rain looking at the house. Mike opened the door and yelled. "Quit stalling, Mario."

Mario came in and hugged Krista. While Mike shook his head no about the proffered handshake. Mario scowled and shook his head. "I was just admiring this antebellum mansion of yours, I wasn't stalling."

"The cash?" Mike said.

"Michael try to be nice," Krista said frowning.

"I gotta check," Mario said," I ain't a gotta time to go to the fucking banka."

"No checks Mario. And you can drop the Italian inflection. You ain't no poor immigrant Wop any longer."

Mario turned to Krista. "Bella, so sorry about the F word."

"I've heard fuck before," Krista said, grinning.

"Yes, but those beautiful ears of yours shouldn't have," Mario said.

"They're just ears," Krista said, "one on each side."

"Yes," Mario said, "But look what they are attached to."

"Enough Mario." Mike said. "All right, Krista and I will go to the bank right now and cash this damned thing. If it ain't good, I'm done with you."

"Michael, you still don't'a trust me. Who you think I am? J. Paul Getty?"

"That's right Mario, my friend, my used to be best friend."

"Ah Michael, my friend forever. You know'sa Mario loves you like a brother."

"Yeah, starving brother. Mario, the inflection."

Mario turned to Krista. "Krista, mi bella, bring this grouch to my house tonight for dinner. Seven sharp."

"Does Isabella know about this?" Krista asked.

"It's no problem. Renaldo my chef will take care of everything. Margaretta will set da table and do da cleanup."

"You sure?"

"Mi Bella, my Isabella hasn't washed a tea cup in years."

An hour later Mike and Krista strode out of Bank of America with fifty brand new one hundred dollar bills. Krista walked to her *Changing Paths Gallery* on Ocean Avenue to start the morning with her part owner cousin, Carolyn Stewart, and Mike drove home to the

Carmel Valley and his block of marble. On the drive Mike glanced in the rearview mirror, grinned, and said aloud, "Got you didn't I Mario 'The Italian stallion' Lucca? You would-be Mafioso."

# CHAPTER 8

## *Krista*

Krista Marie Coleman specialized in originals and prints by such notable painters as Henry Valentine Miller, Georgia O'Keefe, Freda Kahlo, Diego Rivera, Winston Churchill, and a variety of others less known but decidedly sought after. At times Krista would disappear from Carmel for days or weeks scouring the western United States for originals or prints by conservatively modern or abstract-experimental artists. Her favorite site was, and always had been since her early days in art, Santa Fe, New Mexico, where she could be found haunting the art galleries or dawdling away hours at Georgia O'Keefe's Ghost Ranch or in the sidewalk cafés.

Krista's *Changing Paths Gallery* did very well in the opulent economy of Carmel by the Sea, and those affluent non-conformists happily sequestered in the hills, ridges, and deep forests of Big Sur. Carolyn Stewart, Krista's first cousin, ran the day to day operations of the gallery leaving Krista time to search for art and socialize with the elite of the surrounding communities. She felt that a visible presence at social functions and weekly lunches were her best marketing tools. Krista relished the optional time she could spend with Michael Zorka at his Carmel Valley house, where she had quipped the first time seeing it, "It's so old," and then followed that with her newly learned Spanish, it's a Casa Viejo, *Old House*, and the name stuck. She loved the spontaneous freedom they felt when planning impromptu lunches, picnics, hikes on the beach at Point Lobos, or the quiet foggy afternoons often spent cuddled in Mike's king-sized bed with its picture window view of the Carmel Valley.

Krista Coleman had always felt that the *art life* was the *only* life for her, and that her link-up with Michael Zorka was a result of indisputable fate and divine celestial soul-matching. Orphaned at 10 when her parents died in a boating accident while on vacation in Maine she was quickly rescued and raised by her maternal aunt and uncle who loved and cared for her as if she were their own daughter. Her Uncle Frank soon realized that Krista had a serious desire for a life in the art world and caringly paid her four years of tuition at the Oakland Art Institute in Oakland, California. Walking off the stage four years later receiving her Bachelor's in Fine Arts Degree Krista had come to the practical conclusion that she was not a painter or sculptor but did want to join the art world in some way. The following year after vacationing in Carmel by the Sea and spending days haunting the abundant and diverse art galleries decided with considerable and boundless enthusiasm and resolve that she would connect with the art world by marketing those painters and sculptors she had learned to admire and respect. She felt that her training at the Art Institute provided her with the know-how she needed to acquire and sell art with an adequate amount of competence. During her years at the Art Institute she had discovered that her tangible passions lay with the a diverse group of artists like Si-Chen Yuan and an assortment of reproductions from the nascent works of Henry Valentine Miller; Big Sur's creative icon from those halcyon days of the Big Sur Tarkington Ridge faction. Her love for arts was, as one might say in Italian, *mixta.*

After her few days in Carmel and the sudden exuberance she felt about the chance of opening her own art gallery in that extraordinary city her Uncle Frank graciously advanced the start-up money by telling her that she must begin paying it back with the *first* installment due in 30 years. In as much as her Uncle Frank was in his mid-seventies at the time he was telling her that the money was a gift.

Ever a diligent person Krista had pursued her prospective business by haunting the myriad of art galleries in Carmel. She loved what she saw at the Zantman Gallery on Ocean Avenue, fully realizing that she didn't have to *reinvent the wheel.* With dozens of successful long-term galleries in Carmel she appreciated that the competition would be fierce but also knew that what *they* were doing had made them successful. She had learned at the Oakland Art Institute that selling art in the business world was no easy thing and that she would need fresh and innovative ideas in order to excite the art buying public. The Avalon Gallery provided impressive ideas for the display of her own chosen works and she'd focused intently on that particular gallery owner's practiced skill of a quiet and unobtrusive reception when a prospective customer wandered in.

Their practice was not to override the potential buyer but to let him or her enjoy the merchandise without undue interference. She had experienced early on in her art pursuits that when visiting some galleries the employees could be so attentive and aggressive that she'd flee in frustration without having completed-her assessment of the exhibition.

In her private life Krista had always been a champion of literature while focusing on some of the past-time greats; Hemingway, Fitzgerald, Steinbeck, Margaret Mitchell, and that iconic genre of unforgettable writers. The fact was she had been so enthralled with Mitchell's *Gone with the Wind* that she had named her Carmel Highlands house *Tara* after Scarlett O'Hara's Civil War plantation. She often giggled at her memory of the time Japanese tourist we're visiting her gallery and observed a photograph of her house and commented about the name on the frame's brass plate *'Tara'* and how one commented that the name of her house was straight out of *'Gone with the Window.'*

Krista had secretly dabbled with her own artistic bent but mostly with pen and ink. She saw herself as a person who loved all imaginative constructions, however with painting and sculpture standing securely at the forefront. Her pen and ink sketches seemed painfully amateurish and she kept them carefully stashed out of sight of Mike Zorka or anyone else who might query her covert labors but the commonly recognized desire to be an artist in her own right. Her attempts at art were a carefully closeted desire that she chose to keep hidden.

Krista had met Mike Zorka one evening two years earlier when they'd attended a meeting of the Carmel by the Sea Art Association and Art Council. After the meeting Mike told Krista he would like to discuss the possibility of showing a few pieces of his smaller marble sculptures in her Changing Paths Gallery. After the meeting adjourned they had walked to the Pine Inn and literally lost the evening in conversation about the myriad arts, literature, and gazing longingly into each other's eyes. Their fate was sealed that evening when Mike invited Krista up to the Carmel Valley for the next day to see his outdoor sculpture studio and to follow that with a lengthy alfresco-style lunch at the Carmel Valley Corkscrew Bistro. Krista quickly quipped, "Are you sure it's not to see your nude sketches?" Mike had quickly rebounded with, "Whatever it takes to get you there. You can have my sculpture, nude sketches…or hell…me in the buff." She'd bounced right back with. "Butt naked, please."

However, several months passed before Krista saw Mike 'butt naked'.

Krista Coleman saw herself as person who loved all art in general. Painting and sculpture came first, then poetry and the ages old classics in literature; *The Sun Also Rises, The Old Man and the sea, For Whom the Bell Tolls, A Farewell to Arms, War and Peace*, Edna Ferber's *Giant,* and of course Margaret Mitchell's classic Civil War novel, *Gone with the Wind*. She found herself very pleased while perusing Mike's book-shelves to see these same favorites embracing a distinctive mantelshelf all their own.

On their second date with Mike knowing about the *Tara* theme for her house and her passion for *Gone with the Wind*, and after asking her if she wanted to see him again, and while she purposefully hesitated, humming and hawing, he quipped, "Well frankly Krista, I don't give a damn." That is when she laughed and told him about the Japanese tourists calling the book, *Gone with the Window*. Followed by, "Frankly Mike, I do give a damn." And Mike trailed that with, "That means you want to see me again?" Krista answered him with a long passionate kiss and a lasting embrace that clearly answered his question and put his pending heart-ache to rest.

However, in the question of reading, Krista was no snob. She also read thrillers, crime, romance, and history novels. Her present reading for the past few months had led her toward the works of and author often referred to as *Carmel's Man of Letters*, Mike Swain. She had read several of his books and was just finishing his *A Time to Cry*. Swain had lost his life a couple years before while scuba diving on a sunken Japanese freighter just off the Big Sur Coast. His most recent novel *Islands in the Mist* had been recently made into a film starring Owen Wilson as Gary Buffet and Rachel McAdams as Monica Murray.

# CHAPTER 9

## *Mike Zorka*

Michael James Zorka had been in the recovery faze after a nasty divorce at the time he and Krista Coleman met and she'd readily expressed her apprehensions that he was merely rebounding from a gloomy situation and that she was an available standby for the camaraderie he'd known with Barbara Zorka the former Barbara Millhouse of the Millhouse and Satchman real estate Empire. Barbara Millhouse Zorka had faded from their relationship soon after the wedding and honeymoons (three subsequent honeymoons financed by Barbie's daddy). Mike's flight to Europe to study sculpture had been one of his getting over Barbara attempts making his acquaintance with Mona Lisa Bartalucci all that much more desirable. Barbara Millhouse Zorka had been absent from their marriage for more than a year before Mike 'more or less' fled to Italy.

Krista had insisted right away that the *'love and marriage'* words would not surface for at least a year. In far less than a month Mike Zorka knew he was in love with Krista Coleman and wanted to tell her so at every self-denying opportunity. However, that 'marriage' word remained verboten for the time being. Krista soon returned Mike's passion with something like, "Oh God, it was love at first sight for this girl Krista, and…Stone-Cutter-Man, you damn well knew it." As a result of this new and enthralling mutual admiration-pact with Krista, the former Barbara Millhouse Zorka faded without haste from

Mike's formerly circadian and nocturnal ruminations about '*the way we were.*'

Mike stood posed over his block of Carrera marble. In his heart he felt like a Roman Centurion postured to attack the Sicarii Jews ensconced atop Mount Masada. He stood with Italian chisel point and iron mallet in hand. Around his head a sweat-band had already begun to dampen. An unusually warm October day had settled early over the Carmel Valley and was promising to heat up as the day wore on. Today he wore his customary sculpting clothes; seriously frayed cut-off Levis and a shabby red tank top, mostly faded now to pink and white. With the beginning of each new marble carving he often felt that he was attacking the marble, or perhaps violating its ancient virginity. After all, how many years did it take to create this magnificent piece of metamorphic rock? Science believes that most marble was formed 500 to 100 million years ago, but the chronological age of marble varied as the world began to release its awe-inspiring secret; *metamorphic rock.*

Mike reflected that on the rare occasion he had chipped from somewhere deep in a piece of marble fish and crustaceans fossils. These fossils had been animated and living out their submerged reality ions ago and the earth had lastly put them to rest deep in its layers after a planet roofed mostly by oceans for millions of years deposited stratum upon stratum of dead sea creatures. And now, mountains of marble located around the earth's surface usually appeared to be snow-capped when viewed from a distant approach.

The very first cuts always seemed malicious; a violent intrusion into the quiet sanctity of the vanishing millennia. Those experimental chips taken the day the marble had been truck and hoist delivered had not been heated assaults on the stone but merely repeated and cautious tapings to search for clarity and those angry hidden fault-lines that could shear and destroy a nearly finished sculpture in less than a second. This customary and necessary testing provided a cultivated feel for the inherent density or softness of the metamorphic 'stone'. But on this overly warm fall morning Mike Zorka would cut and remove a lot of marble as he penetrated into its depth searching for his *'Lovers'*...probing in a very personal, passionate, and resolute effort to set them free.

As he worked chipping slowly and watching tiny flakes of stone popping off and gathering on his arms and in his hair he thought about all those times he'd been asked the question, "Why do you sculpt? It looks brutally hard. And with whom did you study?" His answers by now become pretty patented because in the beginning he really didn't know why he chose sculpture over watercolors or oils. Questioning people had forced him to examine is own motivations. His standard answer went something like this: "When I was a kid I always loved stones; stones of every kind, shapes, and sizes, and especially the stones on the beaches and along the river banks. I would walk the beaches for hours looking for stones shaped like animals or people or with just plain interesting forms. Eventually, when not finding something I liked on these walks I got the idea of buying myself some chisels and hammers and trying to shape them myself. My first experiments were by using a claw hammer and cold chisel. I worked on a big piece of granite and discovered I liked the feel of it and the hard work challenge it involved. I liked the feel of the steel and the rock and the hammer and the...well...the inherent blood, sweat, and tears it stimulated. It was a natural course of action for me to graduate into experimenting with marble and other kinds of material. In my very first marble effort I destroyed a fine piece of that nugget because I sure as the hell didn't know how to work metamorphic stone. I learned quickly with that blunder that you don't chip marble straight on at a ninety degree angle with your point. You always chip marble at a forty-five degree angle. Chipping the marble straight down stuns it deeply and when trying to finish the piece you can never grind or sand out those deeply penetrated spider-like veins. To sand or grind that deep would destroy the lines and integrity of the piece." The next part of the answer would go something like this. "I studied on my own. I read books on sculpture and I studied the greats; Michelangelo, Donatello, Rodin, da Vinci and one hell of a lot of my contemporaries, including the late and great Henry Moore." With that convoluted answer the questioner's eyes would soon glaze over and he or she would begin to look for a safe and inoffensive escape route; refill their wine glass or "Oh gosh, there's my cousin Bob," and scoot away in all too evident liberation.

When confronted with these inquisitive cocktail infused party-goers he would always remember what he'd learned in Florence, Italy about the great Leonardo di Vinci's estimation of sculptors. His brutal and demeaning opinion went something like this: "Sculpting stone is a laborer's work; his hands are rough and broken, his clothing tattered and unkempt, his hair uncombed and full of dust and chips, he is of a rough and obstinate nature, not a gentleman. Sculpture is merely a construction project." However, it is known that Michelangelo Buonarroti didn't agree and it is well documented that these two virtuosi made cruel sport of insulting each other on the streets and in the piazzas of Florence. Leonardo was known to criticize Michelangelo's *David* but it is known that he often spent time secretly studying that bravura sculpture and measuring it for detail and accuracy. However, no one could argue that di Vinci's *Last Supper* and Michelangelo's *David* are two of the greatest works of art ever known to man.

Mike had soon realized that he belonged to the Henry Moore genre of sculptors. Moore's celebrated philosophy of sculpture was that you should be able to roll a sculpture down a hill without breaking it. This viewpoint was very evident in most of his great mammoth figures seen in his *Nuclear Energy, Foto libre*, and *Reperes*. Moore was greatly influenced by a Toltec-Maya ancient sculpture called *Chac Mool* found in a Mayan pyramid in the jungle at Chichen Itza near Cancun. As well as some of the gold artifacts dredged up from the sacrificial well at Chichen Itza where research has disclosed that hundreds of young female virgins had been sacrificed along with a myriad of artifacts in order to please an array of mystical Mayan Gods, hoping for better weather, more food, and more than anything, to keep the boogie-man away. As the archeologists now know, it didn't work.

Mike was greatly influenced by Michelangelo during his months in Florence, Italy but soon learned that Michelangelo's male sculptures were always masculine and striking while his female figures were often crude in that the ideal of womanly beauty was usually absent as seen in his construction of the female breast. These feminine prettifications were often distorted and looked more like an abused soccer ball or badly warped watermelon. This disclosure left Mike wondering about Michelangelo's sexual orientation. Mike decided right away that if and when he did female figures they would predictably enhance the charm of the female form.

With Mike's question of Michelangelo's sexual orientation he felt that the great sculptor, painter, architect, and poet, undeniably enjoyed *divine intervention.* He felt that bearing in mind Michelangelo's era and without the benefit of today's modern power tools no mere human being without God's assistance would be able to produce the masterpieces he did. If an observer visits the Louvre in Paris and spent time studying the *Pieta* or spends time in Florence with his *David* he or she will understand this fairly universal assertion. It is all too evident in his works that Michelangelo had the blessings of an all-powerful and caring Divinity.

# CHAPTER 10

## Mario's Castillo Amoroso
## (Castle of Love)

Margaritta, Isabella's Mexican maid, answered the door chimes welcoming Mike and Krista to come in. Further into Mario's Castillo Amoroso the raised voices of Mario and Isabella, mostly Isabella, could be heard as they appeared to be embroiled in an argument of sorts. Krista looked at Mike and shrugged. Mike looked at Margarita and tossed his head toward the door as if asking "Should we just go?"

Margaritta chuckled. "Ah, ah. But you should have been here ten minutes ago. Mama Mia."

"Really," Krista said, "maybe we really should just go."

"Oh no," Margaritta said. "This is normal. They do this all the time. Tonight they're arguing about which wine to serve. Mario wants to serve Italian whites and reds while Isabella wants to serve Napa Valley Wines. So it is very clear…you'll been enjoying Napa Valley wines."

"Isabella always have her way?" Krista asked.

"Oh yes Miss Krista," Margaritta whispered.

Margaritta ushered Mike and Krista into the living room where a thriving fire was blazing in a huge walk-in style fireplace. Within a minute the sound of quarrelling voices quieted and Mario and Isabella came breezing into the room in all smiles and good cheer as if the dispute had never ensued. Chelsea, their four year old daughter, trailed closely behind. Hugs and cheek-kisses went around and then

Krista scooped Chelsea up and sat with her on her lap. Margaritta entered the room with a bottle of a Napa Valley Sauvignon Blanc and poured for everyone. She returned moments later with a second bottle of the same vintage and a large tray of unusual but tempting Italian hordourves; crackers, cheeses, nuts, and an assortment of fruit slices. Everyone sat and clinked glasses and sat quietly for a long moment savoring the wine and staring into the fire.

"Do you know why we always clink our glasses before drinking?" Mario asked.

"Friendship?" Krista offered.

"Good cheer?" Mike said.

"Marmi," Isabella said, "has all these strange ideas why we do what we do."

Mario giggled. "Isabella please don't call me Marmi in front of my friends. It's demeaning."

"It's my pet name for you…Marmi. You know you love it."

"I don't and if you insist on it I'll start calling you Issy. That which you hate."

"Mama don't like Daddy to say Issy," Chelsea offered, grinning up at Krista.

"That's right sweetheart," Isabella said.

Krista cleared her throat. "Mario, tell me why we clink our glasses."

"Thought you'd never ask," Mario said. "We clink our glasses for the music it makes. We clink our glasses to appreciate the approaching flavors, we clink our glasses for the blessings of abundance in our lives, we clink our glasses in love and friendship, and we clink our glasses for good luck."

"I like that," Krista said.

"Mario," Mike said, "I want to apologize for my attitude this morning. I was a bit of an ass."

"Oh yeah," Krista offered.

"Michael my friend, my very best friend, forget it. You know very well that Mario Lucca is a helpless fuck-up."

Isabella turned on Mario. "Marmi, watch your language in front of the baby. And Krista."

Chelsea was giggling from Krista's lap. "Daddy said fuck."

Krista made eyes at Chelsea and hugged her. "Sweetheart, that's not a nice thing for pretty girls to say."

Chelsea looked up at Krista. "Could I say it if I was ugly?"

"It is not a nice word for anyone to say. And besides, you will always be a very pretty girl."

"My sister Valerie says I'm ugly as a dog turd," Chelsea said with a giggle.

"Well that's not very nice, is it?" Krista said.

"See Marmi," Isabella said," your kids pick upon your language. Copy you. Sad!"

"Loosen up Issy," Mario said.

"Yeah Issy, loosen up," Chelsea said.

"Chels," Isabella said, "one more smart word from you and you'll go straight to bed."

"Krissy," Chelsea said, "do you ever use bad words?"

Mike giggled. "Hmmmm! Answer that one Miss Krista."

Krista hugged Chelsea. "Well yes, sometimes I slip and say a bad word, but I shouldn't."

"But you said pretty girls should never use bad words," Chelsea said, looking up at Krista.

"That's right, honey,"

"But you're a pretty girl."

Isabella stood up. "Off to bed with you. Enough is enough." Then she took Chelsea by the hand and led her toward the stairs. Everyone heard Chelsea say "Oh damn it" as they disappeared up the stairs, followed by what sounded like a whack on the butt. Mario shrugged and grinned. "That's my baby girl. She's her mother's daughter for sure."

Five minutes later Isabella sat staring across the coffee table at Mario and scowling severely. Mario pretended not to notice by reaching for a hand full of hordourves.

"Mario!"

Mario pretended to chew and examine the remains of an Italian cracker.

"Mario," Isabella repeated!

"Yes Issy," Mario said while grinning at Mike and Krista.

"Why did Michael apologize to you?"

"Oh nothing much. Just a little misunderstanding," Mario begged.

"Mario!"

"Yes, Issy."

"Don't call me Issy again. And…what kind of misunderstanding?"

"It was nothing Isabella," Mike offered.

"Mario?" Isabella said.

Mario looked at Mike and shrugged. "My check bounced."

Isabella's eyes widened. "What check?"

"The one to Michael," Mario whispered.

"The one for my sculpture?" Isabella practically yelled.

Mario shrugged again. "It was a tiny little book keeping error."

"It's not important now," Mike said. "I was just a little upset at the bank. I over-reacted later."

Isabella sat shaking her head and glaring at Mario. "It won't happen again Michael. From now on I'll write the checks and they'd better… Mario Lucca…be good."

"Not necessary Isabella," Mike said, "Mario and I are squared away now."

"Yes but I want my *'Lovers'* sculpture and I don't want you being distracted by my disorganized husband here…Marmi."

"Well whatever works for the both of you," Mike said.

Margaritta entered the room and announced that dinner was served.

Dinner was served on an Italian hand-crafted wooden table large enough to oblige 12 diners comfortably. Shrouding the table was a glorious tablecloth hand-made by weavers in Florence, Italy and shipped directly to Isabella through Mario's importing connections. The colors were a subdued combination of the tri-colors of the Italian National flag melded perfectly into a variety of wild-flower schemes and designs.

Margaritta served the five course dinner allowing enough time between sequences for the guests to talk and savor the diversity of the wines that were being served to complement each new course.

Mario danced around the table serving as the wine-steward, while not allowing Margaritta or anyone else to pour and usurp his closely defended passion based on his self-taught knowledge of wine making and viticulture. Mario considered himself an enologist of the first sense, second only to his self-proclaimed knowledge of grape-growing and the ever fickle vine.

"Italian wines are better," he was heard to whisper several times while serving. Followed each time by "Poor Marmi," from Isabella.

Hours later Mike and Krista drove back to the Carmel Valley in a rather uncomfortable state of an over-load of exceptional food and too many marvelous wines.

"Never again," Mike mumbled as they were getting into bed.

"Never again what?" Krista asked as she moved toward Mike and kissed his bare shoulder.

"Never having dinner at Mario's again."

"And why not? And why in the hell not?"

"Because I eat too much."

"And?"

"Drink too much."

Krista giggled. "Well, do you wanna…you know?"

Mike groaned. "Not tonight Honey, I've a headache."

# CHAPTER 11

## *The Engagement*

Two days after Mike cashed Mario's check he spent two thousand dollars on an engagement ring for Krista. He was nervous. Krista had warned him about that *marriage* word. Would she accept it? Would she runaway screaming? Would she…well…cry? He didn't know.

The day he bought the ring he lay away all night struggling with his decision to ask her to be his wife. He loved Krista and their souls were enjoined in their analogous love of the arts. In marriage he could continue with his passion for sculpture and she could continue with her art gallery. What could be better? He asked himself over and over. Well yeah, what could be better? Ask Krista. Krista may have ideas of her own for now and for the future.

How to ask her? How to present the ring? Where to present the ring? When to present the ring? Were all questions he struggled with? He knew that when he did ask her, he wanted it to be special, an exceptional time and place. God wouldn't it, he thought, be great to do it in Paris? The proverbial *City of Light*. A city he had learned to love during his hiatus studying sculpture in Europe. Paris, and for that matter Europe, were out of the question at the moment. Mike had work to complete and Krista had her gallery. Well hell, her cousin Carolyn could run the gallery for a week. Would Krista pack up and go on a moment's notice? Probably not. Would she be suspicious? Probably. Would she react in a terrified manor to that *marriage* word? Yes, she could and possibly will. Mike remembered that Krista felt she was merely a safety net from Mike's rhapsodizing over his loss of the one and only Barbara Millhouse Zorka.

Mike felt that now with Krista in his life he could think clearly about the former Barbara Zorka and that Italian seraph, Mona Lisa Bartalucci. After reviewing his and Barbara's lives together he'd realized that initially her daddy's money had been the launching and immutable damaging wedge. His first vision of Barbara Millhouse had been when she was wearing a deeply revealing summer dress and spiked heels with a mane of glorious golden tresses flowing beguilingly in the off-shore Carmel Bay breeze while seated in a brand new fire-engine red Porsche 911 on the day they met at a lawn party where one of Mike's early sculptures had been purchased via commission and then exhibited for the upper-crust to awe and ooh over. The Porsche had been Daddy's birthday gift to his darling little girl just turning 30. Mike had parked his open air Jeep Wrangler next to the Porsche where from his high seat he became the beneficiary of a rather spectacular view of the conspicuous and ample cleavage of the girl sitting smoking a cigarette in the fiery convertible sports car. Barbara Millhouse had looked up and caught his gaze, smiled sweetly, and blew him a kiss…and, with that enthralling gesture their fate was momentarily sealed. Hours later with far too much wine under their belts they wandered the Carmel Beach and viewed the fading sunlight lying together in the still warm sand in a half-nude devil-may-care fervent embrace. Michael Zorka should have been fair-warned…but he wasn't. During that joyful interlude between Barbara Zorka, and Krista Coleman, Mona Lisa Bartalucci had entered into his life for a few halcyon months and then that icy gulf, called the Atlantic Ocean (The Pond) had come between them and caused an unintentional and painful chasm. Even during his happy months dating Krista Mike had often found himself dreaming about Mona Lisa and their times together. Sometimes the dreams had been so real that he had expected to wake up with her sleeping beside him. In the aftermath of those dreams he found himself confused and secretly missing Mona. However, he knew that Mona Lisa Bartalucci and Florence, Italy were behind him and it was time for him to move on. He realized that his *life spirit* had flourished after discovering Miss Krista Coleman. There were those times when he wondered if some odd kind of fate was a play in his life, a fate that had led him toward creative women; Mona Lisa Bartalucci with her clothing designs and Krista Coleman with her love of the arts.

The Barbara Millhouse romance had continued for the next few weeks until Mike proposed marriage and with her family jumping immediately into the event, a wedding was planned, sans Mike's ideas, and they were family-style esteemed at the local Catholic church with Father Artimas Jones delivering the service (a priest that Mike refused to call 'father' due the minute fact that Jones was at least ten or fifteen years younger than he.) "Maybe I should call him son or junior, Mike quipped" and immediately began trying desperately to survive the 'you poor slob' stares of the entire family and then they were dually shipped off to Maui for two weeks of marital bless gratis Thomas Jefferson Millhouse the Second and his 'fucking' gold credit card.

One of Mike's far-most annoying remembrance of his relationship with Barbara Millhouse Zorka was when her father couldn't remember his name and referred to him while talking to his daughter as "that man you are married to."

# CHAPTER 12

## *The Perfect Setting*

Mike finally settled on a somewhat nefarious plan for popping the *marriage* question to Krista. It was a Sunday evening and he'd made sure that Krista had agreed to spend the night with him at his Casa Viejo. He'd carefully set the scene before her arrival; firewood stacked with kindling in the fireplace, bottle of iced Domaine Chandon champagne in the fridge, hidden from Krista's prying eyes of course, dinner to be delivered promptly at 7 from a local caterer, cell-pones disabled, and music from Frank Sinatra and Andre Rieu lined up and ready to mellow-out the mood while he and Krista were having her favorite before dinner drinks, the exotic and complex *Mojito*. The engagement ring would be securely fastened on the stem of a giant red rose that he would subtly produce with a well-rehearsed loving sentiment, followed by the discovery (hopefully) of the ring and then followed with "Will you marry me Miss Krista Coleman?" He'd thought about adding 'please' to the proposal but decided it rather echoed like *poor-boy* pleading.

Krista arrived in a huff. Mike took a deep breath, hugged her, drew her away and said, "What?" And at the same time thinking "God damn it, I knew something would go wrong."

Krista pulled away and sat down on the sofa. "I've been robbed."

"How so?" Mike said while thinking "Oh shit!"

"Check for a seven thousand dollar painting," Krista moaned.

"Yeah? That's not good."

"Yeah, non-sufficient funds," Krista said. "Crap, me and my enthusiasm to sell art."

"Not our beloved Mario, I hope," Mike said while shielding a grin.

"No, not Mario. But...I shipped the damned thing the same day of the purchase. Oh yeah, the so efficient Krista Coleman. Oh duh!"

"No credit card stuff?" Mike said while wincing.

Krista rolled her eyes toward the ceiling.

"No damn it. He was with his wife and kids...I guess they were... and he was driving a Porsche station wagon. So you know, it looked good."

"Where does this fine fellow reside?" Mike said, "I'll go kill him for you."

Krista looked away. "Michael, grow up."

"Krista, where did Robinhood and his band of merry men, well kids, go?"

Krista avoided Mike's eyes while letting out a huge huff of air. "Florida for God's sake, Miami Beach."

Mike laughed. "Why in the hell would anyone buy a Porsche station wagon?"

"Oh Michael, be serious. I'm pissed off...mostly at myself."

"Fool me once, okay. Fool me twice, shame on me," Mike joked. Krista more or less glared at him.

"I know, no more checks. I've been fooled before."

"Insurance?" Mike asked.

"I guess they'll cover it. Not so sure. Premiums will take a hit if they do. Probably fifty percent though, if anything."

"Who's the artist?"

"Gault! Andre Gault. Shit, I owe him fifty percent."

"Gault will not be a happy camper," Mike said while grinning with more glaring from Krista.

"No shit!"

Krista, there's nothing we can do tonight so why don't we mix up a batch of Mojitos and set a spark under the firewood?"

"Booze will make me feel a little better, but not much," Krista said while attempting a smile.

"Hungry?" Mike asked.

"Ah, not much," Krista said. "Appetite went along with the check-bounced notice."

"Oh shit," Mike said.

"Oh shit what?" Krista said.

"I said shit," he repeated.

"Why did you say that?"

"Just because."

"Michael, what's up?"

"Nut'in Honey."

"Michael? Speak."

Mike went to the kitchen, mixed the drinks and came back sitting down on the couch next to Krista putting his arms around her. Two tall frosted classes of Mojitos sat ignored on the burl-wood coffee table.

"What?" Krista asked again while squinting suspiciously at him. "Michael, you're acting kind'a strange."

"I'm always strange."

"Don't I know it?"

"Nothing."

"Ain't buying it. What's wrong?"

"Sit still," Mike said, then got up and went to the kitchen. He returned with the bottle of champagne and two frosted flutes. The Mojitos sat untouched and sweating. Krista narrowed her eyes again.

"Mike Zorka?" She whispered.

Mike carefully and with great ceremony undid the metal wire and tinfoil, wrapped a hand-towel around the champagne cork and popped it out, then poured the two flutes while pausing to let the foam settle. Krista sat with her eyes narrowed but with a very slight smile at the corners of her lips. After filling the flutes Mike went to his entertainment center, turned on a Frank Sinatra album with *Strangers in the Night* playing first and retrieved the single red rose with stem and went back to Krista and handed her the flower and sat down. Krista's eyes narrowed again as she inspected the rose and stem. Then she began nodding her head and reached up and kissed him. Mike took both of her hands in his and kissed then each one at a time, then slid the ring of the rose stem and slipped it onto her finger. Krista let out a long sigh and nodded again.

"Of course I will," she whispered.

Then the doorbell rang. The caterer was there. "Shit," Mike said.

Krista laughed. "Michael is that any way to respond to a girl that just said *yes?*"

# CHAPTER 13

## *Bob "Bubbles' Coleman*

Mike Zorka picked up the ringing house phone while removing his marble-dusted goggles. He'd noted the caller ID.

"This must be Miss Krista Coleman, my wonderful and beautiful fiancé."

"Michael, he's here." Krista's voice was off; strained.

"Let me guess who…whom. Clooney, Penn, Redford, the IRS man, the puppy-snatcher?"

"Mike, this is no joking matter."

"Sorry Honey!"

"Bubbles is in Carmel," Krista barely whispered.

"Bubbles?" Mike asked.

"Robert Coleman for God's sake. Bob, my Ex…thank the good Lord."

"Oh shit!" Mike said while drawing in a deep breath.

"Yeah Michael, oh shit."

"What's he want?"

"Oh duh Mike, me."

"Krista get packed. You're gonna come live with me until he goes away."

"Maybe! Half my business is conducted right here from Tara. And my puppy and kittens."

"Bring the little monsters," Mike said.

Long silence.

"Krista, you're not safe with him around."

"That's profound."

"Krista don't be a smart ass. You're in danger from this idiot."

"He's already talked to Carolyn at the gallery. Supposedly he did AA in jail and he's clean and sober. Scared Carrie half to death."

"And anger management, I hope," Mike added.

"That too, so he says."

"Bullshit Krista, haven't we heard that before?"

"Yes!"

"I'll call Sergeant Bob Duncan at the police department right now and give him a heads-up about this creep wandering around Carmel."

"Please do. Bubbles is for sure on probation or parole. Maybe Bobbie Duncan can do something about him. I just talked to Bobbie yesterday, but I didn't know then that Bubbles was here."

"What's this Bubbles crap?" Mike asked.

"His motorcycle pals nick-named him *Bubbles* in honor of his colossal daily consumption of beer…plus."

"Bob Duncan will roust him until he flees Carmel in dread. Bob Duncan has shot a few bad guys," Mike said.

"I know. He shot that guy right here on Highway One a couple years ago," Krista whispered.

"Bob's a good guy. He and I used to hang out some with that writer Mike Swain before he was killed Scuba diving. Bob use to regales us with his stories about shooting bad guys and some of his more gut-wrenching circumstances. Bob's a bold guy. He won't let us down. He did some rough years with the San Francisco PD before coming down here. Probably did too many years of homicide work up there. Says he still has nightmares."

"Yeah, I'm reading one of Swain's novels right now, *A Time to Cry.* Never met him though," Krista said.

"Bob drinks but he has every reason too; *post-traumatic stress.*"

An hour later Mike called Krista at the gallery. "Krista, I did some internet research on your Bubbles."

"He isn't my Bubbles," Krista said.

"Cost me a bundle."

"And what did you find out?" She asked.

"Krista, you don't want to know."

"Yeah I do."

"Alright, but it ain't gonna make you feel any better. He just finished a year in Shasta County Jail for domestic violence on his live-in. But it gets better, so-to-speak. His criminal record is as long as my arm…maybe leg. I'll just run down the list without dates, times, convictions, or sentences: attempted burglary, sexual battery, two DUI's, shop-lifting, suspected auto theft, assault and battery, CCW, that's for carrying a concealed weapon; doesn't say what; his arrest in your domestic violence incident with him is there…and on and on. Bob Duncan will run him through the DOJ and get a better rap-sheet than I got from a dubious Internet web-site."

"DOJ?" Krista asked.

"Department of Justice; state and FBI."

"Almost all of that is news to me." Krista whispered. "He has a daughter I got kind of close too, Becky. Poor kid was farmed out early in life by that son-of-a-bitch. But it probably saved her. Sweet kid but kind of nutty at times. Pretty girl!"

"That's sad. But Krista Honey, how'd you ever get mixed up with that guy?"

"Young girl me. He handsome, charming, sort of dangerous in a beguiling way, had money at the time, probably stolen, and spent it freely. Charmed me out of my socks. Terribly innocent girl makes a giant mistake. No babies thank God."

"He charmed you out of more than your socks Sweetheart, but you're forgiven."

"Carrie, in an innocent-like attempt, tried to find out where he's staying but he stormed out of the gallery calling her a sneaky little bitch. Then he came back, jerked the door open and yelled something about he'd be back. He's dangerous Mike. I think he's crazy enough to kill."

"Did he ever threaten to…well…kill you?"

"Yeah! Especially if he ever caught me with another man. Hell, he didn't even want me to talk to other men…not even his motorcycle pals. Yeah, as if I ever wanted to."

"But you got away from him.

"Barely with my life and body in one piece…sort of."

"How'd you manage it?"

"Stayed with my cousin Adam and his wife, Maribel up in Sonoma. When Bubbles found out where I was he began calling and riding is chopper by the house. Sometimes half a dozen of his dirt-bag pals would ride by with him. Adam finally bought a gun and said he'd shoot the, quote, un-quote, son-of-a-bitch. I finally had to leave Adam because it was causing him and Maribel too much stress. They have kids, too. That's when I came down here to Carmel by the Sea for the first time and fell instantly in love with it."

"Carmel affects people that way. Krista, get packed. I'll come get you right away."

"Nope!"

"You met Coleman after you graduated from the Oakland Art Institute?"

"Sadly so. I was celebrating my degree with a couple weeks in Healdsburg up in Sonoma County. Dumb, dumb, schoolgirl stuff."

"I'm coming to get you."

"Maybe tomorrow. I'm swamped with business right now."

"Tomorrow if I have to kidnap you and those damned puppies," Mike ordered.

"And kittens?"

"And those too. But can Carolyn can come lives with us too?" Mike asked with a very innocent tone.

"Zorka, you're skating on thin ice."

"Just being thoughtful. Carrie is just like a sister to me."

"Yeah, right."

"Well she is pretty," Mike said.

"Oh you've noticed?"

"Yeah and well…kind'a sexy."

"Zorka you're gonna pay for this."

"I bet I will."

# CHAPTER 14

## *Sergeant Bob Duncan*

Sergeant Bob Duncan was sitting at his office desk with Mike and Krista across from him. They were sipping paper cups of hours, maybe day's old police station coffee dregs.

"That's God-awful," Krista said after tasting the coffee. She sat the cup down on Duncan's desk, while making a sour face.

"Krista, this is good stuff," Mike said. "Ain't it Bobby?"

"Well, it's hot at least," Duncan said. Then he tossed a stapled pack of paper on his desk and pointed to it. "DOJ rap-sheet on Robert "Bubbles" Coleman."

"And?" Mike said.

"Well, legally you can't look at it but I can share it with you."

"Legally?" Krista questioned.

"Yeah," Duncan said with slight smirk on his face. "Krista Honey do you know the difference between illegal and unlawful?"

Krista shook her head. "Guess I don't."

Duncan grinned. "Unlawful is against the law, illegal is a sick bird."

"Oh Robert Duncan for God's sake," Krista said.

"Got'ya," Duncan laughed.

"He's for sure an asshole," Duncan said while scanning Coleman's rap-sheet by sliding a ruler up and down the page. "Mike your Internet version left out some pretty important details."

"Go figure," Mike said. "Such as?"

"Well FTPC, or failure to provide for underage children, and a burglary that was probably connected to shop lifting. Seems he had a daughter somewhere along the way and pretty much abandoned her."

"Yes, her name is Becky. That other stuff though was shop-lifting, is that the same thing as burglary, or maybe robbery?" Krista said.

"Yeah," Duncan said, "if the suspect entered the store and stole something when he actually had no money on him that means he had intent to steal. Any time you enter a building with the intent to steal it becomes a felony…burg in the first."

"Then what's a robbery," Krista asked.

Duncan grinned liking this sudden girlish interest allowing him the chance to expound.

"Robbery is the taking of personal possessions from another by use of force or fear."

"Fear?"

"Yeah, sort'a like I'm gonna kick your ass if you don't give me your wallet."

"Force?"

"Using a gun, knife, club or some kind of a weapon."

"Go on," Mike said. "Let's have some more Bubbles history."

Duncan cleared his throat and took a sip of coffee. "Well, this is the kicker. The asshole, excuse the A word Krista, got busted for exposing himself to little girls on a playground. He did time for it and is now what the law calls a 290 registrant. He's a Penal Code sex offender for life. He's on probation and he must have his PO'S permission to leave the county, that being Shasta County, and I'll bet a hundred dollar bill he didn't. I'm gonna call the Shasta County Probation Office and get the scoop on our boy *Bubbles*. I don't have to tell you his ass is mine."

Mike reached and took Krista's hand. "Honey, you really know how to pick them."

Krista looked at Mike and frowned. "Yeah, I picked you didn't I?"

Duncan laughed heartily. "Mike, my friend, my very best friend, you just put your foot in your mouth."

"Yeah, both feet," Mike said. "Sorry Sweet."

"You're forgiven," Krista said leaning over and kissing Mike on the cheek.

If I can catch up with Bubbles-Boy I'll have him in the slammer so quick his eyeballs will bounce. Shit, maybe I'll get to haul his ass back up to Shasta County. Be a little vacation for me. Actually though, I'll probably have to kill the bastard."

"Robert!" Krista said. "I don't want you to do that. It wouldn't be fair to you. Aren't you gonna retire in a year or so?"

Duncan grinned. "Krista Honey, killing the first time is the hardest."

"Oh God Robert!" Krista moaned.

Mike and Krista drove in his Jeep toward Tara.

"I'm even more scared now," Krista said.

"Bob will get him soon."

"I hope."

"Krista we're gonna pack you up and you're coming home with me. Carmel isn't safe for you."

"How about Carolyn? She has to run the gallery. Needs me there too."

"He's not after Carrie. She'll be okay at the gallery. Bob's got extra patrol scheduled for Ocean Ave. for the time being. They're alerted to possible trouble and they're looking for 'Bubbles' on Bob's say-so."

"I'll be okay at home," Krista promised," but gosh, we've got two Bobs going at each other."

"More like Bob taking care of Bubbles," Mike said. However, I'm not so sure you'll be safe at Tara."

"I've that pistol," Krista said.

"Ever shoot it?"

"Well, no. But I don't know if I could actually shoot someone."

You could if someone was after you with a butcher knife," Mike assured her.

"I guess! But I wouldn't want to."

"I'll teach you," Mike said, "but you need to live with me anyway."

"There's always Mario," Krista said.

"What about Mario?"

"Well he has friends. You know, rough types, the kind you see in gangster movies."

"Meaning?" Mike asked.

"Oh I don't know. Sorta like, well…hit men."

"Krista, you want Mario's Italian friends to take care of Bubbles? You want Mario Lucca to put out a contract on Bubbles?"

"No. I'm just fearful. Maybe they could just…scare him away. You know, like in that Godfather movie?"

"You mean like sort'a break his legs?" Mike asked with a tone less than serious

"No, no, I guess not," Krista whispered.

"Honey, Mario doesn't really have *those* kinds of friends. Mario is fictional Mafia. He likes people to think he has underworld connections. Trust me, he doesn't."

"I know. Isabella wouldn't allow it."

"Bob Duncan will more than scare him away."

"Yeah, but I'm afraid for Bob too…and you," Krista said.

"Me?"

"Yeah, you can become loose cannon at the drop of a hat."

"Not me, I'm just a big friendly pup," Mike said jokingly.

"Yeah, you're a Dr. Jekyll and Mr. Hyde character. Trust me!"

"Ain't not."

"Yeah, what about that guy you hit and knocked down the steps at Nepenthe in Big Sur?"

"Krista Honey, he walked by and grabbed your butt. He had it coming."

"He was drunk."

"That's no excuse to molest the girl I love. Fact is he's lucky he stayed down."

"Okay John Wayne, enough. Take me home."

"Okay…Pilgrim."

# CHAPTER 15

## *In Krista's Garden*

Krista's house phone rang. She ignored it for the fourth or fifth time. She had turned her voice-mail off fearing Bob Coleman would call and leave messages. She didn't want to hear his voice again. Within a minute it rang again. Exasperated she answered it. There followed a long moment of silence and then the caller clicked off. She felt chilled.

"Shit," She yelled. Standing there waiting for the phone to ring again she felt the hair on the back of her neck stand up. She had that feeling that she was being watched. She turned toward the picture window that in the daylight would give her a view of her delightful garden and courtyard. Through the window she could catch the occasional flicker of a car's headlights on Highway One as it made its way south through the Carmel Highlands toward Big Sur and beyond. In the absence of the flickering headlights the big window showed nothing but black and that space she normally loved, suddenly seemed threatening and cold. She moved toward the window intending to draw the drapes. As she reached for the cord she saw a match flare in the courtyard, then fade, leaving what appeared to be the glow of a cigarette. She watched as the tiny spark of light brightened and then dimmed as someone drew on a cigarette.

"Someone smoking," she whispered. Before she could draw the drapes the phone rang. She went to the phone and picked it up without answering.

"Don't pull the drapes Krissy Honey. I'm watching you...and I like it."

Fear shot through Krista like an electric shock. "God damn it Robert I knew it was you. Go away...I'm calling the police."

"Nah," Robert Coleman said, "this is the county. It'll take a deputy sheriff and hour to get here. You're mine tonight Sweetie. And my friends still call me Bubbles."

"I've a gun Robert and I know how to use it. And I'm not your friend."

"You don't have the guts and you know it," Coleman growled.

"The Carmel Police will come out here and you know it."

"Who, your fat-cop pal, whats-his-name? Dumkin? Sorta like Dumkin Doughnuts."

"His name is Duncan and he's one hell of a good cop. And...he's on to you. He knows you're on probation and he'll arrest you the minute he sees you...trust me."

"Nah, I'll kill his fat ass first. I got a gun too, Krissy Honey."

"Yeah, well your probation officer is on his way down here from Shasta. You're gonna have more than you can chew."

"Krissy, you really got a gun?"

"You'll find out soon," Krista warned him while trying to sound convincing.

"Ha, I think I'll come in and get it," Coleman said. "It'd be like taking candy from a baby."

Krista saw a set of car headlights illuminate her driveway. The lights suddenly went out.

Her cellphone buzzed. "Krista, this is Bob Duncan, you okay tonight?"

"Bob, where are you?" Krista practically yelled.

"In your driveway."

"I saw your lights. Thank god you're here. He's here in the yard."

"Bubbles?"

"Yes, he's been harassing me. Threatening to come in. He said he has a gun. Be careful."

"I'll find him. Don't worry. You'll see my flashlight."

"Bobby please be careful."

"Krista, I've done this before. I thrive on bad guys. I chew them up and spit them out."

Half an hour later Krista and Bob Duncan were drinking coffee in her kitchen.

"Son of a bitch fled from me like a rat leaving a sinking ship," Duncan said, grinning.

"How did you know I was in trouble?" Krista said.

"I had one of my old premonitions," Bob Duncan said. "I was drinking coffee at the P.D. waiting for this damned 3 to 11 shift to end so I could drink a beer or two at the Hog's Breath when this wave of alarm hit me. Something told me you were in trouble. This weird stuff happens to me all the time. Anyhow I jumped in the car and headed this way. Glad I did."

"So am I. Bobby, you're a prince."

"Nope! I'm more like the village idiot," Duncan joked.

"No you're not," Krista said.

The doorbell rang and Duncan reached for his pistol. "It's Mike," Krista said. "I called him while I was making coffee."

Duncan got up with gun in hand and walked toward the door. "I'll make damned sure of it"

# CHAPTER 16

## *Pfeiffer Beach*

"Bob Duncan is a jewel," Krista said as she knelt down and picked up a Star-shell from the sand on Big Sur's Pfeiffer Beach. She and Mike had parked the car at the end of the dirt Pfeiffer Beach access and were walking north along the beach. They'd packed a picnic lunch.

"He is," Mike said. "He's been a good friend for a long time. The guy would give you the shirt off his back if you needed it. He's had kind of a shitty life though, in some respects."

"Yeah, I guess so," Krista added. "Police work has kind'a troubled his mind some. That night after he scared Bubbles off he told me he has something they call *Post Traumatic Stress* over some of the stuff he'd done. Said he wakes up in the night sometimes in a sweat seeing dead bodies and stuff like that."

Mike stopped and pointed out to Sea. "Right there is where Mike Swain the writer, Carmel's Man of Letters, met his Waterloo just about fifty yards or so off shore."

"Spooky," Krista said. "I guess they never really found him."

"They found lots of his diving equipment washed up on the beach. His diving mask was busted and investigators found a shark's tooth imbedded in the rubber frame."

Krista shuddered, looking out to where Mike was pointing. "Ouch! I suppose a Great White shark got him."

"Yeah, a Great White. That shark is still probably out there right now looking for someone or something to eat."

Krista sat down in the sand with her back against a large drift-wood long. "Let's eat."

Mike sat beside her and retrieved a bottle of red wine from the back-pack. "Let's drink a toast to the memory of Mike Swain." He opened the bottle with a cork-screw and filled two plastic cups. They toasted while looking out to sea.

"Michael," Krista said, "why don't we have a little drift-wood fire?"

"Done," Mike said. He got up and gathered an arm-load of driftwood sticks and built a small fire.

"I love the smell of campfire smoke," Krista said. "It's so comforting. Sort of what you might call a primeval well-being. Comforts me after those threats from Bubbles."

Mike sat sipping his wine and staring out to sea. "Well excuse my French but fuck Bubbles. But now more importantly you know we here on the California Coast have the biggest Great Whites in the world. Africa has lots of Great Whites but they aren't as big as ours."

Krista was looking out to sea and thinking about Mike Swain. "They made a movie out of his last book, *Islands in the Mist*."

"Yeah, damned good movie. Big surprise at the end."

"When he was killed," Krista said, "he was diving on some old ship out there?"

"A Japanese freighter, the *Honda Maru*. Newspapers dubbed it *The Ship of Fools*."

"Because?" Krista asked.

"Legend had it that the captain flipped his lid and began beating sailors and locking them up without food or water for bullshit reasons."

"And?"

"And the crew finally had had enough and tossed his ass overboard along with the first mate. However, the first mate was the only navigator on board which directly led to the rocky coast of Big Sur. One sailor survived to tell the story."

"I feel kind'a creepy," Krista said. "What if Swain was alive and he's a bearded beach-comber now?"

"Yeah, we just might see a bearded, long-haired hippy-type walking down the beach with a gunney-sack full of conch shells." Mike offered.

"I hope so," Krista said, looking up and down the beach. "We'll ask him to eat with us."

"Bet he'd be real horny by now," Mike said, grinning at Krista. "I'd have to keep you out of his reach. But he'd be too old for you anyway."

Krista gave Mike a gentle shove. "Michael honey, they are never too old."

Suddenly Krista stopped talking and stared at a spot in the sand near her bare feet. "Mike look, there's a cross in the sand."

"Pop-top off a beer can," Mike offered.

Krista reached and brushed sand away from the object. The piece was attached to a chain.

"Wow," Mike said, "looks like someone lost their silver Cross of the Crucifixion."

Krista wet the cross with her tongue and then wiped it clean on her jeans. The cross was badly tarnished but brightened some with her effort. "It's not a religious medal," Krista said, "It's a Cross of Lorraine. It's French."

Mike reached and took the cross and chain from Krista. "You're right. The Cross of Lorraine was the symbol of the Free French underground during both World Wars One and Two."

"Oh my God," Krista said, "if I remember right from reading the bio of Swain's life he wore a Cross of Lorraine that had been given to him by his French mother. It was never found."

Mike looked at Krista. "Yip, this could be it."

"It's beautiful," Krista said. "I'll polish and keep it."

"It'll give you night-mares," Mike offered. "Swain might show up in your bedroom in the middle of the night looking for his cross."

"Or...well...something else," Krista said while grinning.

"Kristy, behave."

"Well you said he might be horny by now."

"And old and smelling like the sea," Mike added.

"Yeah...I know," Krista said, grinning.

"He's a ghost now Krissy honey. He'd scare the hell out of you. If that's possible."

"It won't. I heard Swain was an okay guy."

"Yeah, but when he died he was in love with a twenty-two year old girl named Lainy Swanson. She worked at the Carmel Kaffee. Owns it now."

"I know Lainy," Krista said, "nice person. Has a couple kids and happily married."

"Yeah but he was fifty something at the time," Mike said.

"And so what?" Krista said. "Like fifty is too old to fall in love?"

"I guess not," Mike said.

"Is love controlled by age?" Krista said.

Mike ignored her question. "Probably should turn the necklace in to the authorities."

"Bullshit Mike...when pigs dance."

"Krista, you're a ghoul but I love you."

Mike took Krista's hand and pointed out to sea with his other. "You've heard the stories I presume?"

Krista looked at Mike and squinted her eyes. "Stories about?"

"About the Japanese music people hear when they're out here at night or in the evening."

"Ah, yeah?" Krista questioned.

"Well some folks claim that when they are on this beach at night they often hear Oriental music coming from out there where the Honda Maru went down on the rocks."

"Yikes," Krista said, shuddering.

"Over active imaginations I would guess," Mike said. "Maybe too much booze."

"Maybe," Krista said.

"However, numerous folks had reported it. Even a deputy sheriff who was down here one night looking for a stolen car. Poor bastard probably got harassed over that. It'll teach him to keep his mouth shut. I think he's the same deputy that claimed he saw a UFO one night. Some guys never learn."

"Seems like he wouldn't risk his credibility with something like that," Krista said.

"Yeah, it seems the other cops began calling him Shogun or Admiral Tojo."

"Yeah, sometimes it simply pays off to keep your mouth shut about stuff like that."

"I've an airline pilot friend who reported seeing what looked like a flying saucer during the night on a run to Hawaii and did he catch a lot of hell and criticism over that? Just ask me."

"How about his co-pilot?" Krista asked.

"He saw it too. Other pilots began calling them both the Captain Nemo brothers."

# CHAPTER 17

## *Bubbles Coleman*

Krista told her cousin Carolyn goodnight and walked to her car parked on Fifth Street. It was late for her to be leaving the gallery; near six thirty. Along the way she was reminding herself that she shouldn't be walking alone in the dark and knew well that Mike Zorka would be manic if he knew. But still she gritted her teeth and made sure she had her car keys in hand. She could feel a certain ache deep in the pit of her stomach. Now she regretted Carolyn's offer to walk with her. The dark October streets were still busy with pedestrian and car traffic. Krista checked her windshield as always for the proverbial parking ticket, saw none and put her key in the car door. It opened too easily, making her slightly uncomfortable. "Hmmm," she mumbled aloud, frowned, shook her head and slid in behind the steering wheel. Suddenly a male voice from the back seat caused her to jump and she yelled, "Oh shit."

"Krissy honey, you dummy, you forgot to lock the car this morning."

"Bubbles," Krista blurted, her breath coming in gasps.

"Got'cha Krissy baby," Bubbles Coleman growled.

Coleman grabbed Krista by her pony-tail and yanked her head back.

"Let go of me you bastard," Krista gasped.

"Ah, ah, not 'til you talk to me."

"We've nothing to talk about. Now let me go."

"Nope, fact is we're gonna make love right here in the car, just like we used to," Coleman snarled. "You remember those days don't you Krissy honey?"

"Love? It was always rape with you. You don't even know the word love."

"You liked it."

"Don't make me gag."

"Bitch! I bet you're screwing some gorilla, or that stone-mason."

"Bob Duncan will get a report on this and he'll have your ass. Trust me."

Suddenly Krista felt the side of her head go numb as Coleman slapped her hard. Her right ear began to ring. Then she heard the car door slam as he left. She locked the doors and then sat there crying. Ten minutes later and after gathering her composure she called Mike Zorka on her cellphone and then turned the car around and drove to the Carmel Police Department. She was right, Mike had been something just a little less than disconcerted about her walking alone in the dark. "Why didn't you ask me to come get you?" He'd later scolded.

After making a report of the attack to the Carmel Police where photographs were taken of her injury and a detective had dusted her car for fingerprints explaining he was hoping to be able to physically place Robert Coleman in the car for evidentiary purposes, Krista drove to Mike's Casa Viejo and together they made a call to Bob Duncan. Duncan was at home but had sounded slightly drunk. He'd promised to see Krista and Mike first thing in the morning. Within an hour Krista's face had begun to swell and had darkened with an azure bruise beginning to color.

Mike fixed Krista a strong cocktail and put her to sleep on the couch wrapped in a thick quilt. Her sleep was restless and troubled. Mike sat nearby watching over her and listening to her almost silent whimpers. He was so outraged that had Krista not been there he would have taken his gun and gone looking for Bubbles Coleman. While on the phone Bob Duncan had cautioned him against taking just such an action.

The following day with Krista's statement and the police photographs Bob Duncan visited the Monterey County District Attorney's Office and filed a felony complaint against Robert 'Bubbles' Coleman for car burglary and felony assault and battery. He left with a warrant in hand.

# CHAPTER 18

## *Fire*

Three hours after Krista's confrontation with Bubbles Coleman she had roused from her much needed salvaged sleep and she and Mike were sitting in his living room drinking white wine while Mike tried to calm her and settle her rampant nerves. He had rather firmly informed her that he would be her shadow until Coleman was in jail… and he had added "or dead." Krista had quipped while finding a little humor, "Can I go to the bathroom by myself?" Mike had followed that with, "Maybe if you leave the door open." Krista had informed him quite firmly that that would only happen when "pigs ballet."

By this time Krista's eye was beginning to blacken and she'd readily voiced her anxieties that she would "Look like hell in the morning and would have to stay away from the gallery," Mike had told her she wasn't going to the gallery again until Coleman was neutralized, so she should quit worrying." And then he added," Little Miss Vanity."

"Do you think Bobby will catch Bubbles right away? "Krista said.

"Yeah, with that felony warrant someone will catch him. And for sure there's probation hold on him by now."

"Sorry I wasn't there Krissy," Mike said putting his arm around her."

"Probably a good thing you weren't. But had you been it wouldn't have happened. Bubbles is a coward…a woman beating coward. He's afraid of you."

"All the more reason I wished I'd have been there. I'm gonna shoot him on sight."

"Michael, you are not."

"Well then maybe I'll just run over him with my...Jeep thing."

"God, let us pray Bob will get him...tonight." Krista said. Then she stared at the front window with widening eyes and whispered, "What's that?" and then pointed at the window.

The living room curtains had been drawn for safety sake but now a mauve red glow could be seen penetrating through the fabric. Krista jumped to her feet.

"Oh shit," Mike yelled. "I don't know, but something tells me it ain't good."

Mike reached beneath a couch pillow and palmed his Colt Forty-five automatic.

"Michael!" Krista yelled.

"Sit," Mike ordered as he moved to a side window in a darkened corner where he could safely peer out through the partially closed blinds. "Oh God Krista, "he yelled, "Your car is on fire. Do 911."

Krista pulled her cell phone out of her purse and after fumbling shakily with the numbers made the call. The police dispatcher kept her on the phone at length necessitating informant information.

A minute later Mike ordered Krista to go into the bathroom and lock the door and stay there.

"No, Mike," Krista yelled, "I'm staying with you."

Mike turned to Krista," Don't argue, just go."

Krista made a face at Mike and then turned toward the bathroom.

With the pistol in hand Mike went back through the house and exited through a door onto his flag-stone patio and then crept around the side until he could see the burning car and feel the intense head emanating off the inferno. His first thoughts were that the gas tank would explode and set the house on fire. He grimaced when he remembered ordering Krista into a locked bathroom. His Jeep was safely out of the way parked in the backyard. Seconds later above the roar of the fire he heard a car start up on the street and speed away toward the west and the Carmel Highlands. "Bubbles you son-of-a-bitch," he yelled. Krista startled him when she touched his arm.

"You don't behave very well," he said.

"I wasn't going to let you face this alone"

"Bubbles," Mike said.

"Yeah, and I bet he's hoping I was in it."

"That son-of-a-bitch could have had us," Mike said. "Damn it, we've got to be more careful. I'm sure he has a gun…or guns. Shit, sitting in the house drinking wine and not being even a little bit aware. Shit, Zorka, you're getting slow. Guns?"

"They all do…all his motorcycle buddies. Brass knuckles, chains, switchblade knives, straight-razors, wrapped lead pipes, you name it," Krista said.

Sirens could be heard in the distance.

"Well that's the end of my BMW days," Krista said, "I can't afford another one."

"Insurance will replace it," Mike said.

"Yeah, how much of it?"

Mike turned on a garden hose and began spraying the roof and the exposed side of the house. "This old place could go up in flames easily," he yelled.

An hour later with the smoldering BMW surrounded by firemen and two fire trucks Fire Captain Todd Jamison told Mike and Krista what he thought had happened.

"There's an empty one gallon gas can lying in the ditch near the road with the lid off. There's some kerosene left in it. Smells that like it, anyway. The can is pretty greasy so the odds of getting fingerprints off it are likely nil. We found window glass on the ground outside Krista's car so it looks like whoever did this broke the window and poured the accelerant, *kerosene,* inside and tossed a match in. My guess the perp is what's his name? Robert Coleman."

"Yes," Krista said, "he's my ex-husband and probably wants to kill me. No, I know he wants to kill me."

A Monterey County deputy sheriff standing behind Jamison spoke up. "Well he isn't going to get you Miss Coleman. Either Bobby Duncan or we will get him first."

"I hope to God," Krista said. "Thank you for being here and supporting me."

The deputy sheriff pointed at the gun in Mike's waistband and said, "I can believe in and support that, Mike. Shoot him if he gives you half a reason."

"You can bet on it," Mike said. "This mess is reason enough in my book."

"Roger that," the deputy said.

"The gas tank didn't, or hasn't exploded, so stay away from the damn thing," Captain Jamison said. "Could be a bit of spark left deep inside the frame. But there shouldn't be. Hope not anyway. We'll get it out of here within the next couple of hours. The arson guys are finished and I think they've enough evidence to charge arson to whomever set the blaze. Probably your Ex, Krista. Seems he has that mentality, so I've heard. Bob Duncan filled me in on the situation at the fire house just yesterday. Yeah, Bob likes to hang out there and drink free coffee. That is my coffee. Typical freeloading cop."

"Can't be soon enough," Mike said.

"The arson team picked up a cigarette butt on the road near where the suspicious car was parked and they'll test it for DNA. Krista, I know your Ex has been in lots of trouble so I'm sure the courts have access to his DNA."

"He's a 290 PC registrant," Mike said. "I'm sure they have his DNA."

"Can they do that with just a cigarette butt?" Krista asked.

"Yes, they can, and they can get it off a coffee cup or even a straw. They can even get a certain kind of DNA from a single hair. DNA prosecutions are fairly new but it works. Some cold cases, very old cold cases are being prosecuted based on DNA evidence left at the scenes of crimes; rapes, murders, stuff like that. Even arsons."

The deputy sheriff stepped up to Mike and Krista. "Miss Coleman could you tell me all you know about your ex-husband; height, weight, hair color, tattoos, habits, anything that might help my guys nail him?"

"Yes," Krista said, "let's go in the house and make coffee. I'm sure you could use some."

"That'd be great," the deputy said. "You know there is an old saying about good cops."

"And that is?" Krista asked.

The deputy grinned. "They say a good cop never goes hungry, gets wet, or lacks for…well,…girls."

# CHAPTER 19

## *Gualala*

Bob Duncan sat his coffee cup down on Mike's kitchen table and looked squarely at Mike and Krista. "I've a suggestion. Why don't you two take off for a couple days? This car burning incident yesterday is an indication that our Bubbles Boy is escalating his violent behavior. He's already assaulted you once Krissy and the next time it might be fatal, or he'd make you wish it was. If you'd both leave for a day or two, or three, it'd give me time to, well, neutralize the asshole. Right now I'm worried sick about you, Krissy. If you leave that'd help me focus on getting him."

"I'm staying with Michael every night now and staying away from the gallery as much as possible. I think I'll be alright. I worry about Carolyn though; she's there all the time…and alone most of it. None of this is her problem but she' also paying a price. She's scared to death of Bubbles. But I may have to go back to Tara for a day or a night, I've stuff that's gotta be done there."

"In that case I'll stay with you," Mike said.

"If I go I'll ask Carolyn to stay with me…you know, girl talk and stuff like that."

Mike scowled. "Yeah, you two are a couple tough broads. Bubbles would be terrified."

"Michael, be nice. I have the gun."

"A real Annie Oakley," Mike said.

Duncan shook his head. "Not good enough. Do this for me." Then he reached around and patted the pistol hanging in his shoulder holster on the back of the chair. "It's gonna be violent when it happens and I don't want you, or Mike, to get hurt or even have to witness it. It ain't pretty. You guys are artists and this shouldn't be a part of your life. This kind'a shit is my life. Hell, you are both Renaissance people; creative. Get the hell away for a few days."

Mike took Krista's hand. "He's right Krissy. We' could take a run up to Gualala on the coast above the Sea Ranch area and hang out for a coupl'a days, give Bobby time to do his thing."

"You think?"

"Yeah! I know a great place up there that'll blow your skirt up. It's the Saint Orres Hotel and Inn. They've a great restaurant and the room I like best is a cabin in the woods called Sequoia Cottage. It'd be good for you. It's got a huge fireplace with a big picture window with a view of the Pacific Ocean and a King-sized bed that'll hold us both."

"How far?" Krista said.

"Four, five hours."

Duncan lit a cigarette. Krista frowned. "C'mon, you two, go."

Krista looked worried and reached across the table and took Duncan's hand. "Bobby."

"Yes Krissy."

"Will you…well…go easy on the drinking until this is settled? I worry about you."

Duncan grinned. "No more than it takes to settle my nerves."

"That's what I'm afraid of," Krista said.

"Don't worry Krissy, I'll be on my best hunting for bad guys behavior."

"Okay, we'll go but when I get back I'm gonna have to stay at Tara Manor once in a while. Again, I've got stuff that has to be done there."

"What kind of stuff?" Mike said.

"Girl stuff," Krista said.

"When you decide to spend a night there let me know ahead of time," Duncan said.

"I'll be with her on those nights," Mike said.

Krista scowled at Mike. "Yeah?"

"Yeah, Annie Oakley."

"Hmmm," Krista said, "there are those times when a girl needs to be alone. We'll see. I'm no feinting auntie, you know."

Mike looked at Krista and shook his head. "Yeah, you're a tough one alright."

"Well," Krista said, "I can be."

Duncan took time to light a fresh cigarette off the butt of the old one. Krista frowned and shook her head again.

"Terrible habit," she said.

Duncan grinned and blew out a huge puff of smoke. "I know," he said "but I can quit any time I want to. I know I can because I have at least a dozen times. I usually last about a week, sometimes a lot less."

"Your heart," Krista said.

Duncan grinned again. "Yeah, damn thing flutters sometimes."

"Do you ever have pain?" Krista said.

"A little angina from time to time. Nothing serious."

"Bobby," Mike said, "that is serious."

My medic, Doctor Feelgood, gives me a prescription for nitro and I gobble a few whenever that happens; smoke another cigarette or swallow a few shots of Jack Daniels. Always immediately feel better."

"Bobby," Krista said, "you need to take care of your health."

"Yeah, but Krissy, I like to smoke and drink and eat. Hell, what else is there for an old divorced guy with few prospects of love."

"A longer, happier life," Krista said. "And you do have a girlfriend."

"Well Krissy you know what Jack London said about life?" Duncan asked.

"Something like I would rather be ashes than dust. I would rather be a superb meteor, than a sleepy planet," Mike interjected.

"That's' pretty close," Duncan said, "and that's my philosophy too. I shall use my time."

"But Jackie London we don't want to lose you," Krista said.

Duncan grinned and said," Jack London, *my hero*! Now, back to your immediate exodus."

"Yeah, I guess we could," Mike said, looking at Krista. She frowned and shook her head no.

"Go long enough for me to get this guy off the street...or dead. Remember, I don't want him to hurt you Krissy, or this Michelangelo guy."

"I don't want to dump all my troubles on you Bobby," Krista said. "And I don't want you to be dead or hurt."

Duncan reached across the table and patted Krista's hand. "For Christ's sake Krissy, this is what I do. I'm a cop."

"Yeah," Krista said, "but I know you've been shot and a whole gambit of other hurtful things have happened to you."

"Caused a shitty divorce too," Duncan said, smiling.

"Common history for a lot of cops, I hear," Mike said.

"Yeah," Duncan said, "I also caught a bullet from a 211 guy, but got over it. Hell, he suffered a fatal bullet from me just as I was going down. I hit him right Square in the face with one round. Actually a lucky shot. Asshole was DOA when the paramedics arrived. But those sweet firemen guys took care of me first. Wasn't that nice?"

"A 211 guy?" Krista asked.

"Armed robber," Duncan said, "that's a Penal Code number. That's the way we cops talk; by Penal Code and the Ten Code. Hell, it's a second language for us. If we cops don't want you guys to know what we're talking about we use codes. Hell, we even have code talk for the sighting of a pretty girl."

"Like?" Krista said.

Duncan smiled at Mike. "Well we might say something over the radio like, Lincoln and Ocean, an *eight* on the prowl, or maybe with a real exceptional gal we might say check the number *ten* sitting in front of the library."

Krista shook her head. "You males are disgusting. An eight means what? An hour glass figure?"

"Yeah!" Duncan said with a grin and looking at Mike.

"And a ten?" Krista asked.

"Well...sort'a...well endowed, you might say."

"And what do our girl cops say?" Krista asked.

"They only bark when the see Clint Eastwood or Tigger on the street."

"Tigger?"

"Yeah, Tiger Woods"

"Do you know Clint?" Krista asked.

"Popped a few cool ones with Clint from time to time at his Mission Ranch or downtown at the Hog's Breath Inn. Clint's one hell of a good man; awesome. Clint would have made a good cop. Hell, I've met all the biggies in Carmel; writer Mike Swain, we tipped a few together before the sharks ate him, he was clandestinely in love with that girl at the bakery, Lainy Swanson, she owns it now. I can see why he was smitten with her, she' still drop-dead beautiful; Julia Roberts, Redford, Heston and others, etc. etc., I've met them all."

"Well Krissy," Mike said, "let's get packed to go."

That afternoon Mike and Krista drove north staying on Highway One after passing by the seaside town of Jenner by the Sea. Just north of Jenner the highway negotiates a sheer cliff area for 20 or 30 miles giving a neophyte driver something to think about other than the incredible scenery. Having never been in this area Krista was nervous while peering down several hundred feet into the surging Pacific Ocean and advising Mike to pay attention to the road and doing it all too frequently for his peace of mind.

Finally Mike said for the eighth or tenth time, "Krissy honey, I've driven this road one or two dozen times. Just relax and enjoy the ride…we'll probably make it. Come to think of it though, I did see a car go over once."

"I don't want to hear about it," Krista warned.

"Yeah? Well I'll tell you anyway. They were a couple sight-seers standing on a turn-out gawking at the sea lions below. Oh damn, you know what? They forgot to set their brakes. Car went into the drink with a big splash. I think it was a Porsche. I wonder if they float."

For the third or fourth time Krista asked, "How much further?"

"Fifteen, twenty miles," Mike repeated.

"If we get there," Krista said.

"Krissy, earlier today you told Bob Duncan what a tough broad you are."

"I'm afraid of heights and roads along sheer cliffs. But I'm not afraid of Bubbles Coleman any longer. And I'm not a broad."

"Krissy, your Bubbles is one hell of a lot more dangerous than this road. And my use of the broad term was merely a euphemism. You know I think you're an angel."

"Michael Zorka he is *not* my Bubbles. And did you say angel or angle?"

"Angel. But *Angle of Repose* was a great book by Wallace Stegner. You ought'a read it sometime."

Krista giggled. "I wish I was in bed right now reading it."

"I wish you were in bed too…with me and with no clothes on. And sans Wallace Stegner."

"Michael you creature. Pay attention to your driving."

"Well, that's what I'm driving at."

"Yeah, that's what you're driving toward. That's why you are taking me there, so you can take advantage of an innocent girl. Have me trapped and helpless."

"Well, yeah. God you're a bright lady. But helpless? Hardly."

"Yeah, but If I were really bright I wouldn't be hanging on this cliff-side with you."

"Where we're going will make it all worthwhile…Angle…Angel."

"I'd feel safer," Krista said, "if we weren't in this big wheel Jeep thing."

"Krissy, this Jeep…Jeep thing…is much safer than a passenger car. Heck, we can go anywhere in it with this four-wheel drive…even off road. I'll show you."

"Don't you dare," Krista warned. Mike laughed and reached and took her hand.

"Michael, both hands on the wheel."

"Yes mother."

Shortly after passing by Fort Ross, *the historical Russian fort*, and making a quick stop for coffee in the small but charming seaside town of Gualala, Mike abruptly turned off the highway and drove up a steep drive and stopped in front of the Russian domed St. Orres Hotel and Inn.

"Wow!" Krista exclaimed. "Is this it?"

Mike shut the engine off and sat looking at the Inn.

"Michael?" Krista said.

"Yeah, let's check in. I reserved a cottage in the woods for us called Sequoia Lodge."

After unpacking in the lodge Krista sat in the window seat sipping a freshly made Mojito and looking out toward the Pacific Ocean. Mike was down on his knees preparing the fireplace for their evening warmth.

"Michael, this is really nice. Just look at that view. I love it. And look, there's a small heard of deer down there in the grass."

Mike looked up from the fireplace, reached out and took Krista's drink and downed a large mouthful and then handed it back to her. "Yeah, they're Mulies. This country swarms with them."

"They're beautiful. Do they hunt them up here?"

"During deer season."

"That's should be a crime," Krista offered, frowning.

"They only shoot the Bucks."

"Why only the Bucks?"

Mike laughed. "Krissy, the Bucks can impregnate a dozen Does in a season, but the Does can only get birth once a year."

"Do they ever have twins?"

"I've seen Does up here with triplets."

"Hmmm," Krista said, "you've spent some time up here?"

"Ah, some," Mike said, not looking at Krista.

"All by your lonesome?" Krista asked.

Mike pretended to be busy piling wood into the fireplace.

"Michael."

"Yes Krissy."

"All by your lonesome?"

"Ah, not exactly."

"With who have you stayed here?" Krista said.

"You mean with whom?"

"You know what I mean."

"Now that's none of your business young lady."

"You've stayed here with whats-her-name? Barbie Doll?"

"Yeah, with what's-her-name, the very formerly Barbara Millhouse Zorka."

"Barbie Doll Zorka!"

"Yeah, and good riddance."

"Who...I mean whom else?"

"Krissy?"

"Whom?"

Mike reached up and took Krista's drink, tipped it up and drank the remainder and handed it back to her. She looked at the empty glass and scowled at Mike.

"In need of some giant killer, Mister Zorka?"

"A casual friend that came along to comfort me. Hell, I'd recently been divorced. I needed some tender loving care."

Krista pointed at the king-sized bed with the empty glass. "Did she comfort you in that?"

"Krissy!"

"Yes Michael."

"Well heck Krissy, I'm sure they've changed the sheets since then."

"Don't try to be funny Michael."

"How many more have you, let's say, entertained here? You know TLC kind'a stuff?"

Mike grinned. "Oh God I lost count after a while."

"Yeah, and how many more do you plan on engaging here?"

Mike grinned again. "Krissy honey would you like another Mojito?"

"Michael?"

"Hopefully dozens."

"You beast," Krista said while giving him a playful kick with her bare toes.

"Krissy honey, I love you and will not ever, never, never ever, be with any other female on the face of this planet again."

"Never ever again?" Krista asked.

Mike grinned. "Probably not."

"Michael, you're getting in deeper and deeper."

"Just kidding sweetheart. There will never ever be another girl for me."

"Cross your heart?"

"Cross my cold stone-cutter's heart." Then with his fingers crossed the left side of his chest.

"Michael, that's the wrong side."

Mike looked down. "Oh, so sorry sweet." Then he crossed on the other side.

"Well then," Krista said, "I guess I can forgive you for your indiscretions."

Mike stood up, leaned down and kissed Krista on her forehead. "And I damn well mean it."

Krista handed Mike the empty glass. "Another mojito please, Bartender."

"Coming up."

"Make two," Krista said. "And make them strong."

Mike took the glass, leaned down and kissed Krista again. "Party girl!"

That evening after dinner while they were walking through the woods back to the cottage Krista stopped him, hugged and kissed Mike and then took both his hands in hers. "We need to go back tomorrow."

"Okay Honey, but I've paid for two nights. And may I ask why the rush?"

"I'm worried about Bobby."

"I am too, but we can't help him deal with Bubbles. He's a cop and that's what cops do."

"But I feel like we've abandoned him to deal with our...my problems."

"Krissy, it is *our* problem."

"But if we're there at least he'll know we care. Here we are away having a great time while he's probably gonna have to kill...Bubbles. Or be killed."

"We'll head back first thing in the morning."

"Bobby drinks too much," Krista said. "Heck, he might even be drunk when he meets up with Bubbles."

"That's to be seen."

By nine the next morning they'd passed Fort Ross on their way back to Carmel. Krista had called Bob Duncan on her cell phone and he'd maintained to no avail that they stay away. Krista tried to make him promise to join them for dinner that night at Mike's, but he'd declined claiming his recent assignment to the three to eleven PM shift. She'd argued heartily that he could at least sneak away for a half hour or so for a quick dinner at Tara but he'd stubbornly resisted. Krista had remarked after the call that Bob had sounded a little hungover.

Mike had shaken his head. "Go figure."

"He's gonna kill himself," Krista said.

"I shouldn't tell you this Krissy but Bobby, from time to time, chats up the value of suicide. Especially when he's been boozing."

"That's so sad," Krista said.

"Yeah, "Mike said. "However, they tell me cops go that route all too often."

"The crap they live with I guess," Krista said.

"And…they are all wearing the means to that path strapped to their sides."

"All too convenient," Krista said.

# CHAPTER 20

## *Sergeant Bob Duncan*

"Well to hell with me," Bobby Duncan slurred. "God damned Duncan is drunk again."

Mike and Bobby Duncan were sitting at Mike's dining room table with a pot of coffee and two empty cups sitting in front of them. Duncan was smoking and red-eyed staring at the floor. Mike and Krista had been home from St. Orres' since early afternoon. Bod Duncan had clandestinely taken the night off and gotten himself thoroughly drunk. I t was 12:30 AM and Krista had gone to bed just before Duncan arrived. Duncan's coat was off and his automatic pistol was on a kitchen counter where Mike had put the gun after taking it away from him.

"You drinking heavy every day, Bobby?"

"Every God damned day," Duncan slurred.

"Do you know why?"

Duncan grinned through a cloud of cigarette smoke. "Yeah, the shrinks call it PTS; post fucking traumatic fucking stress. But I think that's just bullshit."

"I know you suffer from it, Bobby."

"Yeah?"

"Yeah, you sometimes bring it up when we're talking."

"Yeah, well I've got some I guess."

"Like the dead girl you found in a vacant lot up in Frisco."

"And?"

Duncan looked back at the floor and then up at Mike. His eyes were beet-red and looked damp. He made an attempt at a smile. "Raped and beaten to death by a monster."

"Talk to someone. Try to let it go."

"Shit Mike, she wakes me up at night. I've talked to the shrinks. Modern day shrinks have no idea what it's like to see something like that. That kid was only 21 years old and a living beauty. One hundred and ten pounds when the pathologist weighed her poor little body. Head of hair clear down to her lower back. She was due to graduate from her university in a coupl'a months. She made one hell of a mistake going out walking alone at night. We were looking for her because her roommates had called about her not coming home that night. Damnedest luck, I had to find her of course."

"The killer?"

"That's the crutch of the damned thing. He got away with it. Probably went on raping and killing girls. The bastard! I'd have gladly shot that son of a bitch."

"Maybe someone got him. Let's hope," Mike said.

"Buddy of mine up in Frisco shot himself after investigating a suicide by some 17 year old kid. Jack didn't want to live on this planet anymore. Hell, he did it while on duty and in his patrol car. Hell, sideways can be alluring at times."

"Sideways?"

"Yeah, that's what we cops call suicide. I have to tell you those skyscrapers in the city were alluring at times. You know, step out a window ten stories up; splat, end of problems. Even the old Golden Gate Bridge tempted me once or twice. But crap, *that icy water*! Then there's the ages old Smith and Wesson route. Messy though! Or the shotgun methods like old Nesto did p there in Idaho. Mean bastard did it where his wife would find him. Some suicides want to punish the family. I've see it more than a few times. I worked one sideways where the mom, right in the middle of opening Christmas packages, walked into the bedroom and put a gun in her mouth. Some of my hard-ass friend on the PD joked about it by saying, "Well kids, other than that how was Christmas?" Assholes say stuff like that to keep from going crazy."

"Nesto?" Mike asked.

"Yeah, Ernest Hemingway."

"Well Bob my friend you are staying here tonight."

"Naw, I ain't gonna intrude on you and Krissy."

"Krissy is sound asleep in my bedroom and you can use the guest room. No argument."

"Yes mother."

"Krissy will feed us like kings in the morning."

"In that case I will stay. I can't think of anything better than eating a great breakfast and looking across the table at Krissy. And…I'll be sober and being a good boy. Anything for Krissy."

"Alright, off to bed with you, Romeo."

"Can I take a beer with me?"

"I'll wake Krissy and tell her and you'll catch midnight hell."

"I guess I don't need another beer, but do you think Krissy would come in and kiss me goodnight?"

"Duncan you're getting in deep."

"Yeah?"

"Bobby, at least take a leave of absence and get some help for your post-traumatic stress and the boozing that follows it."

"Michael, like how, and well, like where?"

"Sit back down for a minute," Mike said, "Let's talk some more."

"About?"

"About you. Krissy and I care about you. Hell, Krissy loves you like a brother."

"Damn, I was afraid it was just brotherly-love. But okay, what'll I do?"

"There's a great Zen Monastery down in Big Sur. I've heard a lot about it. You can go there for a month or two for practically nothing. I'll pay for it."

"I've got some dough. But that's Buddhist, isn't it?"

"Yes, and they are great at getting people healthy and off whatever it is that's screwing their lives up. They'll feed you right and make you exercise. Bobby, you could drop a pound or two. Be good for your heart."

"I'll think about it, but I'm no Buddhist. Hell, when I die I'll go straight to Hell."

"You won't go to Hell Bobby, you haven't done anything wrong."

Duncan shook his head. "Yeah, how about those dead faces in the night?"

"Bobby, do you know what the Buddhist philosophy of life is?"

"Can't say that I do."

"Do no harm to yourself; do no harm to others; do no harm to the earth."

"I'll sleep on it. However, first things first."

"Yeah?"

"Yeah...our boy Bubbles."

"You have a plan?"

"It's up to Bubbles Boy to make the first move,' Duncan said.

"And he has," Mike said.

"Yeah. The asshole should'a never hurt Krissy. I may have to kill his ass for that."

"Off to bed, Dunk."

# CHAPTER 21

## *Sculpting In the Rain.*

Mike suddenly ripped the cloth face-mask off his face and tossed it aside. He spoke aloud to no one. "Damned thing makes me sweat underneath and I can't breathe through it and it gets in my way. I'd rather die of White-lung than wear those God damned things. Well hell, marble is organic anyway."

He stepped back and took a long appraising look at his work. A three foot by three foot block of Colorado Gray marble stood stoically on his sculpture table. The Colorado Gray stood snuggled up to his in-progress Lovers piece for Mario and Isabella Lucca. Mike had often found himself working on two separate pieces at one time in order to settle his mind and provide diversion and respite. He'd discovered that leaving an in-progress piece for a time helped the final design jell in his mind. He had recently made the seven hour round trip to a place in Oakland, California called Renaissance Stone where he'd acquired this new monolith of metamorphic rock and half a dozen grinder bits and a new Italian point (chisel). Just fifteen minutes earlier he'd missed striking the new point with his iron mallet and struck his left thumb. He'd cursed, examined the wounded digit, saw that it was red and starting to swell.

"Occupational hazard," he mumbled. "Krista will kiss it later and make it all worthwhile."

He continued to work throughout the afternoon failing to notice that a light rain had begun falling. By five o'clock he'd removed some twenty-odd pounds of marble and the earth around his bench was littered with small fragments of gray-white marble. His face and arms were covered in powdered marble dust turning gooey in the rain and his lungs, as they normally did, had begun to ache a little from breathing the fine white marble-dust mist emanating of his chisel after each careful and temperate blow of the iron mallet.

As he worked he occasionally spoke to the stone. "You aren't gonna be anything special, just a pleasing, I do hope, abstract form in the Henry Moore genre or maybe even something like the great Picasso might have hammered out. Weird guy, that Picasso follow."

He was so immersed in his work that he failed to hear the soft shuffle of footsteps approaching from behind. Suddenly he was encircled with strong arms. Reacting immediately he dropped his mallet and point and drew his right arm back for an elbow strike against his assailant.

"Easy does it big guy." Krista yelled, "It's only me, Monica."

Mike relaxed his arm. "Is that you Monica, I was afraid it was Sally?"

"Nope, actually it's Busty Betty," Krista giggled.

"Oh shit I'm glad it's you Betty, Monica is too fat for me and all she wants is sex, sex, sex."

Krista twirled Mike around and kissed him on his dust covered lips and cheeks. "Okay Stone-cutter, who are these Monica and Betty broads?"

Mike grinned and looked away. "Oh just two babes I know."

"Yeah," Krista said," well that's the end of it...understand?"

"Jealous?"

"Ha," Krista said, "and you're getting marble dust all over my blouse and pants."

Mike grinned. "Then take them off."

"Not here in the rain."

"How about my bedroom?" Mike offered.

"Hell of a deal," Krista said. "But it'll cost you dinner."

"You charging now?" Mike said, grinning.

"Yeah!"

"Oh forget it then," Mike said.

Krista giggled. "Gee if you're broke your credit is good."

"Hmmm, do you charge interest?"

"Not if it's paid in full within ninety days."

"Sounds like a deal," Mike said.

"But the offer is only good within the next hour...or so," Krista giggled while taking Mike by the hand and leading him toward the house.

# CHAPTER 22

## *Threats*

Arriving at Tara Manor after having worked long hours at her Changing Paths Gallery hanging a new show for an upcoming painter, Krista locked the door behind her and snapped on extra house lights. She saw the message light blinking on her telephone recorder. With a bit of apprehension she pressed the flashing button and stepped back as if whomever spoke might reach out and grab her. A voice came on causing her too flinch and draw in a deep breath.

"Shit," she yelled aloud and then reached to turn it off but knew it had to be listened to.

"Right Krista, you idiot, she said aloud, "should'a had Michael stay with me tonight. He wanted to."

"We had fun in your car the other night didn't we Sweetheart?" Bubbles Coleman growled. "You lucked out Krissy baby; I'll be back, count on it. Maybe you need to go live with that artsy guy, Zorka. But that wouldn't help. He's done a shitty job of protecting you so far. And that fat over-the-hill cop guy couldn't find his ass in the dark with both hands. I hear he's boozed up most of the time. He probably couldn't hit the broad side of a barn with a load of buckshot in his pistoli. Oh yeah, a few of my biker pals are coming down this way to join in the fun. You'll love them. You do remember 'Crazy Cal' don't you? He always liked you. Especially your butt. Terry 'Ratco' is coming too. Gosh he likes knives. Nastiest dude I ever knew. He just finished three years in the joint for cutting a guy up pretty bad. He got out early for good behavior. Can you imagine? Good behavior? Terry 'Ratco'? Well Krissy Sweetheart would you like to know what we're gonna do when we get together? It'll be just like old times in the sack. Well first off we're gonna…" Krista punched the off button but didn't erase the recording knowing it would be needed as evidence.

First she called Mike and within a half hour he and Bob Duncan arrived together at Tara Manor. Bob Duncan sat listening to the tape with a look of anger and defiance on his face. He copied the telephone tape recording as evidence. If Coleman was captured alive and tried for his crimes against Krista Coleman the menacing tape would help seal his fate. After the threatening phone call Mike and Bob Duncan had both insisted that Krista live with Mike or her cousin Carolyn. She refused, allowing that she would spend some of her nights at Casa Viejo but not because she was afraid of Coleman. She insisted she'd come to terms with his threats and potential for violence against her. Mike had accused her of being an overly independent hard-head. She quickly agreed insisting that Bubbles Coleman or no one else was going to intimidate her any longer. She'd said it was time for Krista to be a big girl. Secretly she was terrified but had previously allowed Bob Duncan to loan her one of his pistols. Mike had taken her out into the Carmel Valley Hills and taught her how to shoot. Krista turned out to be a natural with a gun and swiftly learned that she liked shooting and even contemplated taking it up as a sport and joining the National Rifle Association. Mike had jested that he'd probably created a monster out of his formally sweet and gentle Krista Coleman. Krista had come right back with, "It's that side of my dark soul."

# CHAPTER 23

## *'Bubbles'*

Sergeant Bob Duncan switched off the headlights on his unmarked detective unit and turned off Pine Ridge Road leading 50 yards up a paved driveway to Krista Coleman's Tara Manor. Minutes ago he'd been drinking coffee at the police station spending the last few minutes of his 3 to 11 PM shift, the one he called the '*Snoop*' shift. It seemed to him that on the '*Snoop*' shift a detective spent his evenings prowling neighborhoods and business districts armed with binoculars while trying to flush out bad guys and suspicious activities. He didn't like it but that was what Detective Captain Lewis had assigned him to do. On this shift he had rousted two drunks in an alley behind The Pine Inn, stopped a drunk driver on Ocean Avenue for the patrol officers, and sent a teenage boy and girl home after finding them naked in a parked car on Scenic Drive near Carmel Bay.

Fifteen minutes before his shift would end whereas he had planned on heading over to the Hog's Breath Inn for a beer or two he'd suffered another of his nagging premonitions. When this one struck, it struck hard, and try as he could he could not dispel it; drive the nagging angst away. The attached anxiety was pervasive and he knew beyond any doubt that it was trying to tell him something, or to warn him. It usually forced him to act killing any doubt or guilt it may have engendered. He'd always passed premonitions off as a cop's imbedded paranoid intuition. But nine times out of ten he had responded in some way to these portents and in most cases they'd proved to be painfully fecund. He knew from past hunches that he needed to act on them. Previously he'd often attempted to ignore them but soon learned he'd more often than not pay a price for his sloth.

And now because of this inherent paranoia he would not drink a few beers at Clint Eastwood's Hog's Breath Inn and the fact was he might not even get to his apartment on this somewhat evolving ominous night. However, as on most Robert Duncan nights, he would be alone there, leaning haphazardly on some bar and staring sullenly at his aging image in the back-bar mirror with his imbedded memories of Anna Duncan and *the way we were*. The nuptial had faltered from early on. Anna Duncan was not cut out to be a cop's wife. She cringed at the violence refusing to listen to him at the end of a particularly gruesome shift when all that he really needed to do was unload his deep-fried emotions with someone loving and accepting. Tell another cop? Not a chance. Bob Duncan had learned early on is his police career that you had to be *John Wayne-like* and never let your troops see you cry, tremble, cringe, and for God's sake, vomit. However, while still with the San Francisco Police Department and in uniform he'd clandestinely vomited after discovering a suicide in a closed-up car that had been sitting in the heat for 10 Days. The flies and the maggots in the car were enough to make any half-normal human being vomit, or run screaming down the street, not to mention the never ever or gotten sight of the rotting corps or smell of the decaying and oozing flesh.

In his bachelor apartment high up on Eighth Street in Carmel by the Sea he kept his memorials; Anna's letters and half a dozen photographs of the two of them together. He had loved Anna deeply, but that wasn't enough. Wedges had developed between them until the chasm was too great and then a tearful separation with Anna Duncan soon filing for divorce. It was then while lonely and feeling abandoned, that Robert Duncan, former Vietnam Marine, began his serious and debilitating drinking. A myriad of girlfriends followed but to Robert Duncan they failed the love idea miserably. It had only been recently that a new woman in his life gave him some hope of ever feeling love or loved again, but he recognized that his intemperance was already creating a chasm between them, a crevasse perhaps too deep to cross.

The premonition had persisted as unrelenting as a toothache at three in the morning. And now at eleven fifteen PM on a foggy Carmel night, he found himself inching his car up Krista Coleman's Tara Manor driveway instead of sipping a cold beer at The Hog's Breath Inn. The recent harassment of Krista by her estranged former husband had left him on edge. In more than a dozen cases during his 28 odd years in police work he'd seen his share of woman tormented, beaten and murdered by their husbands, boyfriends, ex-husbands, or psychopathic monsters. The scenario was all there regrettably imprinted in his mind and in his very depth. Krista Coleman and Michael Zorka were his good friends and he loved them both and he intended to protect them at all cost. In his secret heart he'd promised himself that if Coleman harmed Krista again he would hunt him down and kill him. Bob Duncan knew beyond any doubt that he loved Krista Coleman while realizing that the possibility of he and her together was a mere fantasy and that he would have to remain only her friend and at the same time wisely loving her from afar.

As he drew closer to the house he began to feel something was wrong. "The God damned premonition," he mumbled aloud. And now it loomed large and ominous. Then his cell-phone chirped. Struggling to get the phone out of his coat pocket he saw a light come on in Krista's garden and courtyard area. The light caused the hair on the back of his neck to stand up. He was aware that Mike Zorka had installed motion lights in the out-of-doors around Krista's house. Something in the yard had triggered the light; a rabbit, cat, bird, dog? Or Bubbles Coleman?

"Bobby, can you come up to Tara right away?" Krista whispered into Bob's cell-phone. "Something or someone is out in my courtyard."

"Krista, I'm here," Bobby said, "in your driveway. I saw the light come on."

"Oh thank God," Krista whispered. "The house lights are out. Bubbles must have cut the wires. The motion detectors are on eight volt batteries…thanking God…and Mike Zorka."

"He coming?" Duncan asked.

"I've called. He's on his way…at probably close to a hundred miles an hour."

"His Jeep won't go that fast, but sit tight Krissy."

"How'd you know I was scared?" Krista asked.

"One of my God damned premonitions. Cop paranoia, brain damage, mental illness, call it whatever fits," Duncan said.

"I love them," Krista whispered.

"You locked in?"

"Yeah, and I've got your gun right here in my hand. How do you say? Locked and loaded."

"Use it if you have to, but don't shoot me."

"Trust me," Krista whispered. "Bobby you're a wonder."

"Yeah," Duncan said, "some folks wonder what."

Bob Duncan parked the car and got out without shutting the door hoping to avoid announcing his presence. The detective unit had been modified so that the interior lights would not come on at night and the brake lights could be switched off via a toggle switch located underneath the dashboard.

Walking slowly toward the house with a five battery Kel-light in his left hand and his Colt Forty-five automatic pistol in his right he quickly squatted low as he saw the flare of a match somewhere in the shrubbery near Krista's courtyard. Watching intently he recoiled at the brightening glow of a cigarette as the smoker drew in a puff of smoke. "Now I've got you," he whispered beneath is breath, "You son-of-a-bitch. You know, or should know, asshole Bubbles, that you fucked around with the wrong man." Then he heard glass shattering on the driveway or in the courtyard. "Booze bottle," he guessed under his breath. My pal Bubbles is boozing tonight. That's in my favor," he grinned into the dark. "Glad I skipped the sauce." But he felt an ill-omen and a prevailing ache deep down in the pit of his stomach and realized he was struggling to subdue a slight trembling in his hands. "Fuck Duncan," he whispered to himself, "you're becoming an old lady. Maybe getting too old for this shit. Son-of-a-bitch gives me the slightest reason I'll shoot his ass," Duncan told himself over and over.

"I'll give you no quarter asshole." Then familiar thoughts intruded into his mind. 'Was Anna right? Am I a killer? Is it something I want to do? She accused me of being that way. Hell, I'm not. I've killed bad guys that threatened my life or someone else's. Yeah Duncan, seems you always declared that after the first one it became easier. Yeah well Detective Duncan, that's cop bullshit. It gets quicker, but not easier.

As Duncan walked slowly toward the house a dark figure suddenly appeared ahead and was slightly back-lighted by the courtyard illumination. Duncan crouched, aiming his pistol toward the apparition. Then the darkness was abruptly brightened by the chilling muzzle-flash and the deafening roar of gunfire. Duncan leapt face-first onto the pavement as he felt one side of his sports jacket jerked violently as a bullet tore through and exited. From the prone position he fired two times at the fading figure of the specter. Then he saw a muzzle-flash directed into the sky and guessed that the his antagonist preformed a reflex shot as he fell backwards after being hit. Duncan quickly illuminated the area with his flashlight as he rolled to one side into the bushes. The apparition was gone. He killed the light and lay waiting and listening with pistol ready and aimed in the general direction. He could hear his cell phone jangling in his coat pocket but refused to go for it, guessing it was Krista trying to find out what had happened.

In a minute Duncan thought he could hear sobbing, and then he was sure of it. Moments later a garbled voice broke the stillness. "I'm dying you son-of-a-bitch. I'm fucking bleeding to death." Then silence. Then, "For God's sake help me."

Duncan lay very still. "Not a chance Bubbles my boy," he yelled. "I think you said something about me not being able to hit the side of barn with buckshot. What do you think now, Bubbles Baby?"

Duncan laid there remembering a Hemingway short story where the hero had had to go into the bush looking for a wounded lion. "Not me, he mumbled, "I ain't no fool."

Within a few minute Duncan heard sirens and then following that he saw flashing red and blue lights coming in fast off Pine Ridge and turning up Krista's Tara Manor driveway. "Thank God," he mumbled.

"Do I love those guys? Yes I do. And thank you Miss Krista for calling 911."

Police car spotlights came on illuminating the area around Duncan and where the phantom had been. He remained still and oddly aware that he could smell the slow residue of gun smoke still drifting out of the still warm muzzle of his pistol. He sensed that somehow he liked the portentous smell of burnt gunpowder.

"This is Duncan," he yelled toward the police car spotlights. "Shots fired. Suspect down but armed. Stay safe."

"Ten-four Duncan," a deputy sheriff yelled from somewhere in the dark. "Where are you?…But stay put. Where's the bad guy?"

"In the bushes at the side of the driveway about 30 or 40 feet from the house."

"I'll turn the dog loose," the officer yelled. "You okay?"

"Not sure," Duncan yelled. "I think I took a hit somewhere on my bod."

"You hit him?" The deputy yelled.

"I'm sure I did."

"Go find him Jack," the deputy sheriff told his dog.

"Oh how I love those dogs," Duncan mumbled. Then the dog was on him. It growled, sniffed at him while Duncan said the dog's name. "Jack, go away, it's just me." Jack stood over him for a long second and then raced off toward the house. Seconds later he barked loudly and appeared to be hovering over something in the brush.

"Jack's got him treed" the deputy yelled. "Don't you shoot my dog, asshole. You do and you're a dead man." Then he moved cautiously ahead armed with a pump shotgun. Jack quit barking but remained hovering over the object in the bushes.

"All's quiet on the Western Front," the deputy yelled. "I think he's dead."

Two hours later.

"God it's awful," Krista said. "Poor Bobby has had to kill again and all because of me."

Mike and Krista were standing on her patio drinking coffee and gazing out toward the spotlights and flashing red and blue lights emanating from the site while investigators gathered evidence and photographs. Broken bits of glass sparkled on the pavers in the patio light. They could smell the residue of whisky on the cool night air. The Monterey County Coroner had already been there and had authorized the morgue people to haul Bubbles body away for an autopsy that would take place later that night or early the next morning. The coroner had assured Bob Duncan that the shooting of Robert 'Bubbles' Coleman was justified. After seeing Krista and Mike Bob Duncan had retreated to the Carmel Police Department to write his report of the incident and killing.

Krista had insisted that he come back later and spend the night with them. Later while writing his reports Duncan discovered a neat round hole in the left side of his sports jacket. As he fingered the hole skewering it with a pencil displaying it to other officers he couldn't help but mumble aloud," God is my co-pilot." Another officer quipped, "Naw Dunk, its Diablo, the Devil. Ain't no angel gonna follow you around. Too fricking dangerous."

Duncan laughed and said, "You think?"

# CHAPTER 24

## *Shooting Aftermath*

Mike and Krista were having lunch in the new addition at Restaurant Bicyclette on Seventh Street. Mike was sipping an Amstel Light and looking directly at Krista. She was drinking a cup of Green tea and gazing out the window into a rainy afternoon. Their lunch had been ordered. Mike moved his head around trying to get her attention. She continued to stare out into the drizzle.

"Gloomy," she said without looking at Mike.

"Hmmm," Mike said, "you've always been a rain lover."

"Oh it's just the stuff that's gone on this last week."

"Yeah?"

"Yeah, Bubbles virtually wanting to kill me and then poor Bobbie Duncan committing homicide for me."

"For me too," Mike said.

"Homicide…is that what it is?" Krista said.

Mike nodded. "Yeah, it means the killing of a human being by another human being. It doesn't necessarily mean murder."

"Is Bobby okay? I know he took a leave of absence after the… shooting."

"He didn't take leave of absence. When and officers kills someone it's automatic that he's put on administrative leave until the district attorney decides the shooting was justified or not. In this case Bobby was defending himself. Hell there was a bullet hole in his jacket. Your

Bubbles fired first. That was more than enough justification for Bob to defend himself with deadly force."

"He wasn't my Bubbles."

"Sorry. I didn't mean it that way. Bubbles would have killed you and me if he'd had the chance. He sure as the hell tried to kill Bobby. Again, that bullet in his jacket missed his bod by not more than an inch."

"I heard from Carolyn that Bobby has been drinking a lot and is chain-smoking again."

"Yeah, I know."

"He's gonna kill himself. He's overweight," Krista said.

"I've been in touch with him this week. He'll pull out of it. Why don't you call him? You know he thinks the world of you. In love with you I'd guess. He told me that when he dies he'll go to straight to Hell. I told him it would be more like *Purgatory.*"

"Mike, you didn't?"

"Yeah, just trying to lighten it up a bit. Heck, why don't you call him?"

"Should I?"

"Yeah, he might be thinking that you don't approve of what happened. Bubbles and you did have a history."

"Historical nightmare."

"Let's have him up to Tara for dinner," Mike suggested.

"But it happened there. Maybe your place would be better."

"Good thought!"

"How many?" Krista asked.

"How many what?" Mike said.

"Has Bobby killed during his police career?"

Mike looked out the window. "Krista honey, it doesn't matter. Quit worrying about Bobby. He's a tough old bird."

"How many?"

"Four or five," Mike guessed.

"God, that's awful. He has to live with that."

"Every case was life or death for Bob."

"What did they do with him?" Krista said.

"Who…whom?"

"Bubbles."

"Coroner had him cremated," Mike said.

"He had family."

"I know," Mike said, "but no one could be located."

"The ashes?"

"Stored at the morgue until next of kin can be located."

"He has a daughter somewhere, you know? Becky."

"I know."

# CHAPTER 25

## *War Stories*

"Bobby, you're a little drunk," Mike said as he opened his front door into a rain storm. Bob Duncan stood there leaning against a hand-rail and grinning. He was hatless and appeared soaking wet.

"Not ah little," Duncan said, "totally fucking wasted."

"Robert Duncan tell me you didn't drive here."

Duncan turned and looked at his parked car. "I can't fucken remember."

"You did!"

"Who gives a shit?"

"I do. Krista does. Your police chief does."

"Krista, Krista, beautiful Krista," Duncan slurred. "You are one lucky bastard...*Bastardo*, as Mario Lucca would say in his Italian lingo."

"Come in here before you fall down and kill yourself. You need about 30 or 40 cups of coffee."

"Thank you my friend, my very best friend," Duncan said as Mike grabbed him by the arm to hold him upright."

Mike half carried Duncan to a couch in front of the flickering fireplace and went into the kitchen to make coffee and telling Duncan to "Stay put."

"Yes boss," Duncan giggled.

Mike came back in a few minutes later and handed Duncan a large cup of coffee. "Drink up."

"I was hoping Krista would be here," Duncan said.

"Good thing she isn't. She's been worried about you. This wouldn't help."

Duncan tipped the coffee cup up and drained it. "Shit," he yelled, "that was hot."

Mike poured him another cup out of the pot. "Drink."

Duncan looked directly at Mike. Mike thought he could see moisture in the eyes. "Krista thinks about me sometimes?" he whispered.

"Yeah dummy," Mike said, "she thinks the world of you."

"Yeah?"

"Yeah, she does," Mike assured.

"I can't ask for anything more than that," Duncan whispered. "Can I?"

Mike shook his head while reaching over and touching Duncan's arm. "Poor bastard," he thought.

Duncan sat quiet for a long moment staring into the fireplace then said," I sure as the hell killed that son of a bitch, didn't I?"

Mike put his hand on Duncan's shoulder. "You had too, Bobby. You know he would have killed *Krista. You saved her life.*"

"Yeah. I sure love that Krista girl."

"I know you do Bobby. She thinks the world of you. Loves you like a brother."

"Really?" Duncan said while tears began sliding down his stubble cheeks.

"You dumb shit, haven't you noticed?" Mike said.

"No."

"And you know damn well that your new girl Babs love you."

"You think so? She's only been my sort'a girlfriend for a few weeks. But she ain't no Anna, that's for God damned sure," Duncan slurred.

"Yeah, she told Krista she loves you. But Krista and I know you still ache over the loss of Anna."

"I ain't known Babs very long."

"Love at first sight, Bobby."

"She's a Montana girl. Good pioneer stock. I'm gonna buy her an engagement ring this week."

"Well you'd better start saving your money and stop this poor little me bullshit."

"Yeah? You think? Duncan said.

"Yeah! Bads doesn't want to be married to a drunk. But Dunk, don't rush into it out of loneliness."

"Yeah? Well you know me, I'm and impulsive bastard. Hell, I even shoot...kill people on impulse."

"Plan on staying here tonight, my friend," Mike said. "You are too drunk and it is too stormy out there."

"You can't make me," Duncan said, grinning. "Yeah," Mike said, "watch my dust."

"I give up," Duncan said. "You'd better, or I'll call Krista and she'll put you right." Duncan laughed and then appeared to think for a minute. "Michael, you ever hear the one about Sir Lancelot?"

"I guess I haven't but I'm afraid I'm going to." Duncan drained off another cup of coffee. Mike poured him another."

"Well it was a real stormy night, much worse than this one. Sir Lancelot had heard that a dragon was terrorizing the locals so he went to King Arthur and asked for a horse so he could go out into the storm, find and slay the son of a bitch. King Arthur rang up the stable guy and was told all the horses were sick, hoof and mouth disease or some shit like that. So the dog kennel guy was summoned and he arrived with a great big dog and told Lancelot that he'd have to ride the dog. King Arthur immediately objected and said, *'I wouldn't send a knight out on a dog like this.'*

Duncan laid his head back and laughed hysterically and repeated, *I wouldn't send a knight out on a dog like this."* Get it?"

Mike rolled his eyes up at the ceiling. "I got it. Sergeant Duncan are you carrying your gun?"

"I think so," Duncan said. "How in the fuck am I gonna shoot myself if I don't got my gun?"

"You're not gonna shoot yourself," Mike said, "give it to me."

"Aw, it's in the glove box in the car. I'm bullshitting you. I'm too chicken shit to off myself. Lots'a cops do though. The constant shit-work can do that to a guy. They call it PTS; post traumatic stupid. Or some shit like that."

"Yeah Bobby, and they become drunks too. Have you…noticed?" Duncan rubbed his eyes, wiping the tears off his cheeks with the back of his hands. "Sorry pal."

"Police work can be a killer…huh?" Mike said. Duncan sipped his coffee and seemed to think about Mike's question. "Well yeah, in some respects, but we had fun too. I remember one time when my partner and I found a four story department store open in the middle of the night with no one around. We checked it out and called the PD to have the God damned manager rousted out of bed and get his ass down there and lock the joint up. Well we were kind'a bored you know, three in the morning and not much going on. Hell, bars closed and drunken husbands home now and all finished beating their wives and passed out in bed, so we went upstairs to the women's lingerie department and decided to have some laughs. My partner put this great big woman's bra on and was parading around while I put a flimsy nightgown on. Hell, I looked pretty damned good in it. But suddenly I saw my partner freeze and turn snow-white. I took a look at the door and there stood the manager, watching us. I turned back to my partner and told him to take his bra off, it wasn't his color. Shit, we used to climb up on the top of buildings during the night and drop firecrackers in the alleys behind the officers walking beats. When we didn't have firecrackers we'd drop metal trash can lids. Shit, you ought'a see how many trash can lids ended up with bullet holes in them. We used to back our patrol cars out of sight in the alleys at night, lights out, and when the beat man came walking along we'd suddenly lay on the siren. Most of those guys had to go home and change their pants after that. Yeah, we had some good times. Hell we'd go up in the park during the night and shoot at rabbits. Bunch 'a crazy assholes, that's what."

"For God's sake Bob, I just lost all my faith in patrol cops."

"Yeah, but we got the job done."
"Bed time Bobby."
"I think you're right…Mom."

# CHAPTER 26

## *Bobby Duncan*

"Krista," Mike whispered into the phone. "Yes Michael, and why are you whispering? Are we telling secrets?"

"Krista, listen. I've got some bad news."

"Real bad?" Krista asked. Silence for a long moment. "Sad, Krista."

"Okay," Krista said, "I'm sitting down."

"Bobby died this morning."

"Oh God, no," Krista cried. Long silence. Mike thought he could hear Krista sobbing. "You okay, Honey," Mike whispered. Still silence then," No!"

"The Chief called me this morning."

"No," Krista said, "it can't be. I just talked to him yesterday evening…invited him to dinner."

"I did too."

"Oh God, how'd it happen?" Krista whispered. "I guess he was shaving this morning when he had a heart attack. His new girlfriend Babs tried over and over to call him with no answer so went by to check. Found him on the floor of the bathroom."

"Oh God, poor Babs," Krista said, "I'll see if I can help her but I hardly know her."

"Yeah, you know Bobby was in love with her and already talking marriage. He was a lonely guy."

"I know Bobby had a daughter somewhere. I hope they can find her."

"Babs could use some help now. She just moved here from Montana and doesn't really know many people."

"Chief Davis is gonna put a memorial together for Bobby. He's already called the Marines hoping to get some kind of military ceremony. Bobby was a Vietnam vet."

"Kind'a my fault," Krista whispered, "but I could see it coming."

"No. That incident with Bubbles was right up Bobby's alley. Don't even think that for a moment." Mike told Krista he would be with her in a few minutes and hung up. He knew she was crying quietly.

## Three Days Later

It was raining. It had been since the day Robert Duncan died. The Monterey Cemetery was sodden. It smelled damp and the dampness was carried on a chilling breeze coming in off the bay. The seven uniformed Marine honor-guards were getting their dress-blues soaked. Krista and Mike stood under an umbrella while a Marine Corps bugler played-out the final notes of taps. The sound echoed forlornly through the cemetery and surrounding hills. Opposite the Marines a police honor guard stood at attention saluting Bob Duncan's casket. More than 40 police cars and fire trucks lined the cemetery entrance road with red and blue lights flashing. The column of police officers and friends had followed the funeral procession from St. Patrick's Church where a Marine Colonel had delivered the eulogy. *Eulogy:* "Staff Sergeant Robert Paul Duncan was a Marine's Marine. He was one of the few survivors of the Ia Drang Battle. He came out of the jungle with a Purple Heart and a Bronze Star. Near the end of the Vietnam War he was offered a commission as a second lieutenant but refused. Seems Sergeant Duncan had this idea that he wanted to be a cop more than a Marine officer. We'll try to forgive him for that. Bob went on to a successful career as a police officer, spending many years with the San Francisco Police Department and then with the Carmel Police Department. He spent a ton of years as a homicide investigator and was known around the State of California as one of the best. It is well known that other police agencies often called him for advice.

In closing I want to say that society owes Bob Duncan a big debt of gratitude for his labors as a Marine and as a police officer. Sergeant Duncan…you are truly one of the *few good men.* Semper fi Sarg."

# CHAPTER 27

## *Santa Fe*

"I'm going to Santa Fe for a few days Michael, why don't you come with me?" Krista said. Mike turned away from his sculpture and put his sand-paper down. "The gallery?"

"Carolyn will run it. She does 24-7 anyway."

"Your cousin is a sweetheart. Pretty too."

"Careful Zorka. I'm watching you."

"Gee, maybe Carolyn and I can get together while you're gone. You know, dinner, dance, a walk on a moonlit beach."

"I'll murder you both."

"Who first?"

"You."

"C'mon Krista, there ain't no one else for me."

"Don't say ain't."

"I ain't gonna say ain't no more."

"Oh God Michael, you're incorrigible."

"But you love me."

"You think?"

"Yeah!"

"And why must you go to Santa Fe?" Mike asked. "Oh duh, buy stuff for the gallery. Come on Michael, go with me."

"Why?"

"We'll site-see and have romantic dinners in some of those heavenly Santa Fe restaurants. Sit by a roaring fire in the evenings and drink wine and then…we'll you know."

"Devil woman! You're trying to lure me into your snare."

"Ha, you don't take much luring. Usually you are the lure-or and I am the lure-ee."

"You love it."

"I do. And you've never seen Georgia O'Keefe's Ghost Ranch. It's something to see."

"Can't go."

"Yeah, why not, Stone Cutter?"

"Mario is bugging me about this chunk of stone. Wants me to finish *Lovers* so he can have it in his garden for some big festivity he's planning."

"I'll handle Mario," Krista said. "And besides its Isabella, not Mario."

"Mario Lucca, your soul-mate. The self-proclaimed Italian Stallion," Mike said. "We speak the same language," Krista said. "Huh? He's Italian and you're and English babe trying to speak Spanish."

"My Spanish is okay. My Italian is a bit rusty."

"You speak Mexican, not Spanish," Mike offered. "My gardener understands me. And this is California and it belonged to Mexico before you gringoes stole it from them."

"God bless the Bear Flag." Mike said, grinning. "Enough Zorka, come on, go with me," Krista pleaded. "I'm at the stage of sanding and polishing this thing. If I spend a few more serious days on it, I'll be done. Then Mario and Isabella can have the damn thing and I can have my final check."

"Obsessive artist."

"Nope! Starving artist."

"Tunnel vision," Krista suggested. "Discipline."

"I'll feed you," Krista said. "Food? I thought our relationship was based on wild sex."

"Love!"

"I'm not a kept man, Coleman."

"Yes you are."

"How so?"

"I'm gonna keep you forever."

"From what?" Mike asked. "From that Italian siren Mona whats-her-name."

"Yeah, gee, I think about her all the time."

"Michael, you ass."

"Kidding love, I never think about her…much."

"You're getting yourself in serious trouble, Zorka."

"I want the truth Miss Coleman, why are you leaving me? Another man? One of those Indian savages in New Mexico?"

"Maybe."

"I'll scalp him right after I neuter him," Mike promised.

"Yeah? Well George Custer tried."

"Leave Georgie Custer out of this. He was a war hero."

"Yeah," Krista said, "Custer ended up wearing arrow shirts."

"Funny girl," Mike said.

"So you won't go?"

"Can't."

"Can't, or won't?"

"Can't."

"Well then remember one thing," Krista said. "Yeah, what's that?"

"I love you and always will."

"Krista honey, you are coming back?" Two days later Mike drove Krista to the San Francisco International Airport and kissed her goodbye. Driving back to Carmel by the Sea he cut over to the coast deciding to drive Highway One. Periodically he would look at himself in the rearview mirror and shout something like, "Zorka, you idiot, why didn't you go with her? Dumb ass!"

That evening he called Krista on her cell-phone but didn't get an answer. He left her a voicemail saying something like, "You're probably out with whats-his-name, Sitting Bull, so dump him and call me. You're in serious trouble Miss Coleman."

Three hours later Krista had not called back so Mike called her again, left her another message, waited another hour and tried again, but still no answer. He sat for a long time starring at his cell-phone and hating it for its worrisome silence. Near mid-night he reluctantly went to bed but sleep eluded him. While in a semi-conscious state reoccurring images of Krista kissing him goodbye crowded his mind, followed by the sound of her voice as she practically begged him to go with her. Then the lone image of her waving goodbye and throwing him a kiss as she hurried off to her boarding gate. He remembered thinking then that she had never looked more beautiful.

At three AM he gave up the notion of sleep and called Krista's cousin Carolyn and woke her up. She too had been trying to reach Krista without success. With the new dawn just lighting the sky Mike was startled out of a semi-slumber by a loud banging on his front door. Mario and Isabella Lucca was standing on the steps with their arms around each other. Both were crying openly. Mike drew in a deep breath. "Mario…what?" Mario tried to control his sobbing and then looked at Isabella and shook his head. "Krista."

# CHAPTER 28

## *Carolyn Talks*

The following day after she learned of her cousin's death Carolyn Stewart went to see Mike. She found him in his bedroom packing a suitcase, his eyes red rimmed and moist. He smelled of alcohol.

"Santa Fe?" She asked. "Ah huh," Mike whispered without looking up from the suitcase. "I thought you'd go," Carolyn said, "your wedding was just weeks away. Krissy will be smiling in Heaven when she sees you coming for her."

Mike sat down on the edge of the bed and said, "I just don't know what to do. I'm lost. I keep expecting Krista to call and tell me she's alright. I'm afraid, Carolyn. I'm afraid to go to Santa Fe. I don't want to see Krista dead. I want her to be alive. I want the phone to ring and hear her voice. Carolyn, I still have her on my voice mail. If I don't see her dead then maybe I can always pretend she's alive."

Carolyn reached and took Mike's hand. There were tears in her red-rimmed eyes. "You need to erase it Michael. Hearing her voice over and over will just make it worse."

"I know, but that's the only real thing I have left of her; her voice. In a way she can still speak to me."

She loved you Mike, you can always be sure of that. But you, *you and I*, have to go on with our lives. Krissy would want that. One of the very last things she said to me before she left was that she hated the idea of being away from you for three or four days."

Mike nodded. "Yeah, and God damned me, she wanted me to go. But hell no, I had too much important stuff to do. Important bullshit, that's what."

"Michael she understood that you had work to do. After all, she was going to Santa Fe to do Changing Paths Gallery work; buy paintings and crafts."

"I know, but still. You know I could have been with her during those last moments. God how I wish I had been."

"I know."

"I'd be with her right now."

"She is with us."

"What about the Gallery?" Mike said. "Well, it belonged to Krissy and I, so I'll continue to run it just as we always did. It still belongs to Krissy. Changing Paths Gallery was her dream. You know she took to heart the very essences of Poet Carl Sandberg's belief in life."

"And that was?"

"*First a dream.*"

"She was like that."

"And she'd want you to continue providing me, she and I, with your sculptures." Mike shook his head. "Don't know if I'll ever pick up a mallet again."

"You will. Remember, Krissy will be watching."

"You think?"

"I know so."

# CHAPTER 29

## *Bringing Krista Home*

Mike flew to Santa Fe to bring Krista home. As the commuter plane approached the end of the runway he looked down and could see a large burned area near the beginning of the tarmac and what looked like a clean-up crew removing remaining bits of aircraft wreckage. The sky had darkened as the airplane approached Santa Fe and Mike could see veins of rain streaming back over the wings and windows and believed that this storm was probably a remnant of the one that had brought Krista's airplane down short of the runway in a violent hail-storm.

At the morgue in Santa Fe the coroner asked Mike to identify Krista's remains. In near shock he stood rock-still while a cover was removed from '*something*'. When the form was exposed that '*something*' did not resemble Krista Coleman. Krista, the beautiful Krista he had known and loved was not there. Perhaps some of the vehicle that had carried her through life was there, but Krista Coleman was gone.

After a few minutes the coroner seemed to become agitated. "Well?" he suddenly blurted out. Mike stared at him for a long moment. The coroner looked away. "Yes," Mike whispered, "my Krista."

The coroner turned back to Mike. "How so? Think you can be sure?" Mike looked at the coroner with an increasing degree of hatred in his eyes. "You did DNA I assume?"

"Well yeah, tried but we didn't have a comparison yet. Her Carmel doctor is sending it."

"So what more do you need from me, Mister Coroner?" Mike said roughly. "We like to have the NOK do identification for our records," the coroner said. "NOK?"

"Next of kin."

"I'm not her kin, I'm her fiancé."

"And?"

"The ring." Mike pointed to the ring on Krista's burned hand. "This is our engagement ring."

"I guess you want it?" the coroner said. "It's yours. Must'a cost some big bucks." Mike stared at the coroner. The coroner avoided his eyes. "No, I want Krista to have it forever. See that it stays put."

"Suit yourself," the coroner said, shrugging. "and…I'm no thief."

"Can you leave us alone for a few minutes?" Mike said. "Ain't supposed to, but I guess I can. I'll be back in a couple." The coroner left leaving the door open. Someone else came by and closed it. As the door to the morgue closed Mike pulled a chair up to Krista's sheet-covered body and sat next to her. He reached out and laid his hand on the sheet that covered her and began to cry. An hour later he walked out into a cold rain.

Mike staid in Santa Fe an extra day making arrangements for Krista's body to be sent back to Carmel by the Sea.

## Four Days Later
## Eulogy to Krista

It was one of those clear days along the California Coast. It was one of those days that Krista Coleman always called *halcyon*. Looking out at the Pacific Ocean from the hillside cemetery you could not see a wave, not even a riffle. The sea was calm with little wind and the sky high up was clear with an azure blueness, and there was a friendly almost cuddling warmth on the sea-breeze. A Monterey Peninsula winter day…but, yes Krista…*a halcyon day*.

Krista's casket had been placed over the grave-site by six pall-bearers just minutes ago. Mike Zorka stood near the casket, facing the others. Krista's cousin Carolyn stood by him holding his trembling hand. Mike cleared his throat, wiped slightly at his eyes, and recited the homage he'd written and memorized for Krista: *"When we are conceived we gather a number of minerals from the Earth. When we die we must give them back. Krista Coleman would be very pleased could she be here today knowing that she was replenishing the very Earth she loved. Why? Because Krista was a giver, and never a taker. If she could speak to us today...and to me, she'd smile and say something in the Spanish language she so loved,...something like "Hasta la vista, amigos, et Buena suerta, or, in English, see you soon my friends...and good luck. So Krista, my friend, my love, my joy, and my inspiration, I'll say goodbye with this fitting but so humble a thought; Some people come into our lives and all too quickly go. Some stay for a while leaving joyful patterns in our hearts and souls, and we are never, ever the same. Via con Dios my Krista...go with God."*

# CHAPTER 30

## *Shadows of the Night*

The Carmel valley seemed to darken and it wasn't just the overcast or the intermittent rains that had fallen for weeks following Krista's funeral. Most mornings Mike took quiet walks along the Carmel River and frequently spent an hour or so sitting on a granite boulder at the water's edge. His habit was to sit quietly listening to the river and animal sounds. There were times when he enjoyed this collective harmony but then there were those shadowy days when the same wild-life clamors and voice-like watery riffles incensed him and he often thought or said something aloud like, "Don't they know Krista is dead? Why is the river so happy; so bubbly? Why are these animals so joyful? Don't they know life is supposed to end now?" Then he'd take a quick look around hoping no one had heard him. With these flare-ups he gradually began to think that he was readily losing control. He knew, and was chagrined, that whiskey had become a regular part of his daily life, and that alcohol would continue, in some measure, to dull the relentless torment he felt over the loss of Krista, and falsely trusting that if given enough time the drinking would cauterize and heal his deep-seated emotional wounds. Mike knew he was suffering from an unyielding guilt for having not gone to Santa Fe with Krista. That demanding onus lingered continually in his waking thoughts and in his dreams. All too clearly he saw that his alcohol-infused path to a cloudy recovery was at best poisonous and fatal but lacked the strength or even the desire to come to terms with it. A sundry of his friends including Krista's Cousin Carolyn Stewart and both Mario and Isabella Lucca had tried to reason with him while their heartfelt efforts fell unheeded on deaf ears; *Michael Zorka felt that he was more than ready to die.*

On this particular morning Mike took his place on the granite boulder and looked east toward the rising Sun, shook his head and said aloud, "I've lost my morning Sun." He sat silently as the morning Sun crept toward him along the river bank crowding out the shadows of the night. His meditations reworked over and over the emotional trepidation of that first night alone after learning of Krista's death. He remembered he was lying awake and staring into the gloom when he thought he heard Krista's voice whispering, "Michael, come to me." And then he remembered her words of love just before leaving. "Michael I love you and always will."

That murmur had carried him sitting upright on the bed, searching and staring into the gloom and feeling that somehow Krista was there with him. Then in a matter of seconds the room was filled with the scent of her favorite perfume. He got out of bed and frantically searched the house calling her name over and over. The house was hallow-cold and very empty. All too quickly her scent faded leaving the house hushed and vacant, the rooms where she might have been were dark with their emptiness. He went back into the bedroom and was sitting bleakly on the edge of his bed with his head in his hands and sobbing openly when he abruptly looked up toward the ceiling feeling a sudden chill, and that a light had suddenly gone on, and yelled, "Yes, of course," now clearly understanding why her scent had emanated throughout the house; *Krista was sending him a message of love; a message that said, "Michael I'm okay."*

"Bless you Sweetheart," he said into the gloom. "I should have known you would try to comfort me."

Then he heard her whisper gain, "Michael come to me." Mike lay back on the bed and pulled a blanket over his chilled body. "I'm coming Sweetheart, I'm coming. Please wait for me." Then he said, "I'll find a way to be with you, Krista. I'll find a way."

# CHAPTER 31

## *The Help*

"You need's help, Michael," Mario Lucca said quietly. He was gazing at Mike over the rim of his coffee cup. Mike and Mario were drinking coffee on Mike's flagstone patio. It was raining and it had been for three days. A palpable sadness hung over Mike's Casa Viejo. They were sitting under a big umbrella. Mike ignored Mario and picked up a pint bottle of Jack Daniels whisky and poured another dollop into his coffee, and then pushed the bottle toward Mario as if to ask, "Do you want some?" Mario frowned and shook his head no.

Mike turned away from the table and stared toward his sculpture bench where his tools lay abandoned and rusted. A 200 pound block of Portuguese Rose marble sat wet and slightly mossed. Isabella's anticipated sculpture '*Lovers'* sat silently abandoned and fragmentary.

"What kind of help?" he said, still looking away. "And why?"

"Michael my friend, my very best friend, you are a sick man. You are killing yourself. You need to see a grief counselor."

"To help me what?"

"Michael, Krissy is not coming back. She, and Isabella and I, want you to get well. We want the old Michael Zorka back."

Mike got up and walked out into the rain to his sculpture bench and placed his hands on the wet marble.

"Mike Zorka is gone," he said. "At least, what did you call me, the old Mike Zorka?"

"I refused to believe that, Michael."

"I'm the real Mike Zorka now," Mike said. "The one that is finally the drunken sort he always thought he'd be."

"Michael, stop that."

"Is there any point on going on?" Mike whispered. "Any point on me attacking this piece of marble or hell, even getting up in the morning?"

"Yes."

"Why?"

"Carolyn Stewart needs your work for the Changing Paths Gallery. Isabella and I need you. Isabella is hoping to see her 'Lovers' finished soon. Krissy wouldn't want you to abandon her cousin and the gallery. You owe it to Krissy to get back up and, what was it Frank Sinatra always liked to sing in his *That's Life* song? *"Get back up and get back in the race."*

"My life is a race toward the end now."

"Michael, that's nonsense."

"It's the way I feel."

"Michael, why don't you give Mona Lisa Bartalucci a call? It might be good for you."

"Can't," Mike whispered.

"Why not?" Mike.

"Just...because."

"You know she loved you. She told Isabella and I that when we saw her in Florence. Even had tears in her eyes."

"She did?"

"Yeah."

"Sweet, lovely girl," Mike whispered. "Beautiful is more like it," Mario said. "Beautiful heart too."

"See a counselor right away and if that doesn't work Isabella and I will pay for you a good long stay in that Big Sur Zen Monastery. That one up on Tarkington Ridge."

Mike shook his head. "I'm not a Buddhist...but I could be. Krissy talked about Buddhism sometimes."

"Today Michael, call and make an appointment with a counselor for tomorrow. Don't wait. Isabella expects you for dinner at seven tonight. Come and be with us and yes...be sober."

"I'll be there," Mike said,"...and sober."

Mario got up and kissed Mike on both cheeks. "That's my pal Michael Zorka...the sculptor."

Later that day Mike was perusing the yellow pages looking for the number and address a local grief counselor.

"Hell, I don't know who...whom," he mumbled in confusion, looking at an entire page advertising grief counselors and psychologist specializing in counseling. All addresses showed Monterey locations. "I sure as the hell don't want to waste my day...days...driving over there," he said aloud.

Eventually his eyes and fingers stopped at the name of a psychologist that specialized in grief counseling and addictive behaviors. Doctor A.J. Howard, MS, PhD, 991 Pacific Street, Monterey. Mike wrote the number and address down on a Post-It and then sat at his kitchen table trying to decide whether or not to call. Twice he picked up the Post-It and began to tear it up but stopped short and stuck it back in front of him on the table. He knew very well that if he went to dinner tonight at the Lucca's he would be questioned...no...grilled. That thought encouraged him to make the call while thinking that he could always cancel the appointment.

After Mario had left that morning Mike had taken a long nap and then forced himself to go jogging. Coming back to the house he'd taken a shower, and then a hot tub, and then another long nap. Surprisingly for the first time in weeks felt half human, but reluctantly had to admit he was dying for a stiff drink. The nearly empty pint bottle of Jack Daniels lay abandoned in the kitchen trash, but he was very aware of its location and it seemed, he thought, that it was calling to him.

"Nothing doing Zorka," he'd told himself aloud before dialing the phone number of Dr. A.J. Howard, MS, PhD. A soothing woman's voice answered his call.

"Arlene speaking, Doctor Howard's office.

Mike briefly explained that he wanted to talk to Doctor Howard about the death of a loved-one. Arlene made him an appointment for eleven the very next morning. Mike had quipped saying that that didn't leave much time for him to cancel.

Oh Mr. Zorka," Arlene argued, "don't cancel. Dr. Howard will be very open about helping you."

"Yeah," Mike said, "I bet he needs the money."

"Now Mr. Zorka, don't be mean."

Mike smiled in spite of himself. "Sorry, that's just how I feel right now."

"That's why you're coming here," Arlene said.

# CHAPTER 32

## *Dr. A. J. Howard*

10:45 the next morning Mike parked his Jeep...*his Jeep thing...* in a parking lot next to the Howard Building beneath a sign that read Customers Only-All Others Will Be Towed Away At The Owners Expense-followed by the Monterey Police Department's phone number.

Mike sat there in his Jeep thinking "Am I a customer or am I a patient?" Then he thought about driving away but said aloud, "No Zorka, you sure in hell need to talk to someone. Yeah, the most interesting things along the way were the God damned liquor stores."

Bracing himself he got out and walked in through a set of double glass doors. A young red-headed woman sat behind the receptions desk and smiled as he walked in.

"I'm Arlene and this this must be Mr. Michael Zorka," she said. "And right on time."

"Reluctantly," Mike replied.

"Now, now," she said, while handing Mike a clipboard with several medical history forms attached. An ink pen dangled from a string. "Please sit and answers these questions and Dr. Howard will be with you shortly."

Twenty or so minutes later a backroom door opened and a tall, rather thin fiftyish man came into the waiting room. "Can't be Dr. Howard," Mike thought, "no suit and tie or wing-tipped shoes. Customer?" Faded Levis, plaid shirt, worn on the outside, and what appeared to be hiking boots walked directly to where Mike was sitting and put out his right hand to shake. Mike took the proffered hand while standing back up. The grip was firm but not over-done. Mike thought he caught a whiff of cigar whiff.

"Adam Howard; you're Mr. Zorka I presume."

Mike directly felt a slight sense of partiality toward this so-very-different appearing *Shrink*.

"Yes, Michael Zorka…but Mike will do."

Howard pointed toward his office door. "Well Mike come on in and let's BS a bit. Arlene Sweetheart, hold my calls…and Mike's calls too. We're going into my Man Cave and do macho stuff."

Arlene Browning grinned at Mike and shrugged her shoulders.

They entered the room and before sitting down Howard pulled off his plaid shirt tossing it into a chair and leaving exposed a rather faded and frayed T-shirt with the words "I survived Kathmandu" printed across the front. He directed Mike to sit in a large over-stuffed chair and sat himself next to it in an exact duplicate. Mike took a moment to survey his surroundings. Howard's wooden desk sat directly in front of the two chairs but showed very little business; no scattering of papers, no half dozen pens and pencils with the most dominating feature being what appeared to be a family portrait that revealed a smiling Howard, a very pretty blond woman and a somewhat toothless two or three year old boy or girl; hard to tell which. Mike realized right away that this was not your typical scientist's office with the seemingly obligatory bare walls and whole regiments of gray filing cabinets with desks and tables piled high with a myriad of what-so-ever papers. Howard's office was that of an artist, or art lover. Abstract paintings in the Jackson Pollack genre lined the walls and on various tables were assembled what seemed to be a mix of African, Mayan, and Chinese artifacts of one kind or another. On the wall directly behind Howard's desk hung an African spear and a double bladed rather primitive looking leather-handled knife. Just below these artifacts hung a photograph of Howard in jungle garb talking to what appeared to be two Masai men and two shaved headed women. Both women appeared to be holding babies wrapped in scarlet blankets. The only other noticeable thing on Howard's desk was a very attractive wooden box with the word *Cubans* stenciled on the kid.

Howard saw Mike looking at the photograph. "Kenya, East Africa, a Masai village. I was bargaining with the chief...and his wives...for the spear and knife. Got one hell of a deal."

"I was right," Mike said.

Howard smiled. "About?"

"The aroma of cigars."

Howard reached over and patted the box. "My only weakness," he said smiling. "Well, actually my wife might not agree with that *only weakness* assessment. But they aren't Cuban. JFK ruined that for us stogie smokers with his embargo. You know, the Missile Crisis fiasco."

"That he did. I do a stogie from time to time," Mike said.

"My Dad always said that you can't trust a man that doesn't drink or smoke stogies," Howard said, grinning.

"Smart guy, your dad," Mike said.

"Well one of my heroes smoked stogies every day of his life and lived to be 87. Proves they're okay," Howard said.

"Who's that?" Mike asked.

"Greatest fighter pilot and top ace of World War Two," Howard said.

Mike nodded. "None other than Joe Foss."

"Right on," Howard said. "So, let's smoke a stogie and talk."

Mike turned and looked toward the closed door of the reception room.

"Arlene won't squeal on us," Howard said.

"Old Smokey Joe would be proud of us," Mike said.

"That was Joe Foss's nickname on Guadalcanal. But you knew that, Mike."

"Since reading about him when I was a kid. He and Eddie Rickenbacker."

"True Americans," Howard said while opening the cigar box and handing one to Mike. They sat silently while lighting their cigars with kitchen matches.

"Never light a cigar with a lighter," Howard admonished through a cloud of smoke.

"Almost blasphemous," Mike added. "This is my first Partagas ever. Lovely!"

"Lighter fluid taints the rich tobacco," Howard said. "My old dad taught me to smoke cigars and how to light them. Actually you're supposed to light a small slice of cedar with a match and then light your cigar from that."

Mike puffed on his cigar and grinned through a cloud of smoke. "I would never have guessed seeing a shrin...(he quickly corrected himself) counselor could be this pleasant. Should have started it long ago."

"Well cigars aside, "Howard said, "we should talk about what's bothering you."

Mike nodded slightly in partial agreement. "If we must."

"When did Krista die?" Howard suddenly asked.

Mike quickly looked up from the examination of the tip of his cigar. "You know about Krissy?"

"Yes."

"You knew Krissy?" Mike asked.

"Nope. But look around my office and you might guess how I knew about her...and you."

Mike surveyed the room again. "Changing Paths Art Gallery, Carmel."

"Right," Howard said. "I know Carolyn Stewart, Krista's cousin, from my visits to the gallery. Two of these Jackson Pollack look-alikes were purchased from Carolyn, and Krista...of course."

Mike began nodding. "Of course...now I recognize one of them."

"That one over there I bought from Carolyn two, three years ago. That one there more recent."

"Yeah, that's the one I recognize now. And somehow I stumbled onto you. Hell, I spent hours perusing the yellow pages before deciding on who...whom to see."

"Fate," Howard said. "I've always believed that things happen for a reason. You know, the *Great Plan Theory*?"

"God's will?"

"Nothing like that. Actually, "Howard said, "I'm agnostic. I hope that's okay with you. But what I'm saying is that I really don't know if there is a God or not. But after having done charity work in Ethiopia and watching hundreds, no thousands, of beautiful children starving to death…really causes me to wonder."

"Causes me wonder too," Mike agreed, thinking of Krista's horrific and abrupt death.

"Now Back to Krista…no…actually back to Mike," Howard said. He paused to relight his cigar. "Life over?" he asked bluntly.

"That's the way I feel," Mike said. "Far as I'm concerned the sun doesn't ever need to come up again."

"That's normal," Howard said," but like Ernest Hemingway penned, *the sun also rises.*"

"Yeah…but."

"But what?"

"I can't shake it," Mike whispered. "Krissy's been gone for months."

"It will come," Howard said. "Don't try to rush it. You're trying too hard."

"It's turned me into a drunk."

"Do you feel guilty when you discoverer you haven't thought about her for a while? A day perhaps? Minutes even?"

"Yeah, I think so. I'm so afraid she'll think I've forgotten her."

"You have to allow yourself to have moments, hours, even days when you forget about her. Understand, that when you do, you really haven't forgotten about her. She knows that. She knows you still love and miss her. But she doesn't expect you to think about her all the time."

"I'll try," Mike whispered.

"Mike, do you ever consider suicide?"

"Some days I just want to, be you know…gone."

"Self-destruction via gun, bridge, or booze is a long-term solution to a short term problem."

"I know. Heck, I've close friends who've offered to pay for a few months in a Big Sur Zen monastery. Maybe I should take them up on it."

Howard smiled. "I think that's a great idea, Mike."

"You think?"

"Yes I do. Mike, you're depleted. You don't look well. You're not an alcoholic. You drink to help cauterize your emotional wounds over losing Krista."

Mike raised his cigar up and studied the long ash. "No stogies in a Zen Monastery."

"And no booze," Howard said. "But lots of meditation, exercise, quiet, and wholesome chow."

"Sounds right," Mike said.

"Has she visited you?" Howard asked.

Mike looked up from the examination of his cigar tip. "Yes."

"In what way?"

"In the night sometimes."

"How?" Howard said," tell me about it."

"Once she filled the house with her perfume at midnight. Hell, I searched the house for her. I was sure she was there and her death had been just a bad dream…nightmare."

"And?"

"Her scent disappeared as suddenly as it had appeared."

"Do you know why that happened?" Howard asked.

"I've thought a lot about it, but not really."

"Krista is telling you she is okay and for you to quit worrying… and crying, and this self-destruction bent."

"You really think that, Dr. Howard?"

"Adam. And yes I know that. That is Krista's way of telling you goodbye. She is finalizing the relationship for you. She wants you to go on with your life. Krista would even be happy if you found a new love. Trust me, she would. Krista doesn't want you to be lonely. Can you believe that?"

"I think I can. I'll try."

"The best way for you to honor your relationship with Krista is to let her go. You know Mike, if you really, really love someone you have to be able to let them go."

"Adam."

"Yes Mike."

"Damn it all…you're helping."

"I'm glad and now I'm gonna recommend that you take that… vacation…at the Zen Monastery."

"Will I see you again? Need to?" Mike asked.

"Well this is gonna cost me money but I want what is best for you. Go! However, we will smoke a stogie or two together in the future. I want to come up to your place and see your sculpting projects. Heck, I might even buy one."

"I'll look forward to it," Mike said. "The Carmel Valley is a wonderful place. Come up Sometime and I'll treat you to lunch at one of my favorite bistros."

"Yeah?"

"Yeah, the Corkscrew in the valley," Mike said.

"Call me when you get back from Big Sur," Howard said. "We'll do cigars and you can enlighten me about that Monastery so that I might recommend it to a future patience, and buy me that lunch… with wine of course."

"I sure will," Mike said.

"And remember Mike, you should live every day likes it's your last, because sooner or later it will be. The past is gone and the future is nothing more than smoke and mirrors."

# CHAPTER 33

## *Rebecca Coleman*

In the weeks that followed Krista's death Mike had compelled himself to start sculpting again. However he knew his heart was not in it but at times the work allowed him some moments of serenity; a calmness that caused him alarm while thinking "how could I forget about Krista even for a second?" Those brief moments of peace caused him to feel some guilt. Most days he felt rather depleted because he continued to drink himself to sleep at night. His myriad of friends continued to council him but he always managed to say, "Yeah, you're right," and then continue with his head-long self-destruction.

Doctor Howard had made good sense but practicing what he'd recommended was not coming easily. The nightly drinking and morose thoughts continued to intrude but had receded only marginally.

Mario and Isabella Lucca continued to pursue him doing everything they could to get him to stop drinking and get back to sculpture. Isabella continued to tell him that Krista was not coming back and that she would want him to go on with his life. She told him repeatedly that he was being disrespectful to the memory of Krista by trying to destroy himself. The Lucca's, being very aware of Mike's new inclinations toward Buddhism, again volunteered to pay for a few months of therapy at a Zen Center in the hills of Big Sur. Mike had steadfastly resisted anyone's efforts to help him. Carolyn Stewart had repeatedly begged him to produce new sculptures for the Changing Paths Gallery, hoping that his work would someway jolt him out of his depression. She had called a psychologist making an appointment for him that he promptly cancelled telling Carolyn that, *"he didn't need a Shrink."* The final reality was that Dr. A.J. Howard had provided him with a semi-direction toward his recovery. Yet, he still steadfastly resisted moving in that direction, still feeling blocked by the dreadful finality of Krista's death and his fateful decision to not accompany her to Santa Fe.

On this cloudy morning he had approached his sculpture bench unwillingly but with some remnant of his former work-ethic. He'd sat staring at the piece of stone for more than an hour while drinking strong black coffee attempting his regular morning ritual of recovering from a previous night of heavy alcohol consumption. Finally, but reluctantly, he got to his feet, head throbbing and eyes burning picked up his mallet and point and began chipping lightly on the formerly intact stone, and now and then pausing to pick up a fresh chip and run it across his tongue. He loved that familiar salt taste and it caused him to smile faintly. Then he tossed the chip over-head and flapped it away with his hand much like a baseball player hitting a ball away, shook his head in an now very unfamiliar 'yes' motion, and went back to work on the stone just as a fragment of the morning Sun broke through the overcast. "Might just be an okay day," he whispered aloud. The tools felt good in his hands.

The doorbell rang and he looked up into the mixed sky and said aloud, "Oh, shit." He put his mallet and point down and went into the house to answer what had become a persistent doorbell. A very pretty girl of 20 years or so was standing on his steps; her eyes reds and swollen as if she'd been recently crying. Mike took a deep breath and thought, "What now?"

"Good morning," Mike said, suddenly aware of his unkempt condition; shower-less days, hang-over breath, faded and rather ragged Levi's, overly dirty and scruffy T-shirt, and sporting several weeks of untrimmed and increasingly graying beard now partially filled with marble splinters and naked arms speckled with snowy dust. Immediately that thought about his moldy appearance entered his mind, "Hmmm, that's interesting, I haven't given a shit how I look for weeks now…a pretty girl will do that to you."

"Mr. Zorman," she whispered? "Zorka," Mike said. "Mike Zorka."

"Oh I'm so sorry," the girl said. "I've your name written on a piece of paper but the writing isn't very clear. A policeman gave it to me."

"A policeman," Mike said, "I'm in trouble?"

"Oh gosh no, but people had said that the police department would know how to find you."

Mike grinned. "Yeah, I guess I'm one of those guys they try to keep track of."

"Oh it's nothing like that."

"Well Miss, if you'd have given me some notice I'd have cleaned up a bit."

"Oh Mister Zorka you look just fine."

"You're just being nice," Mike said, "but you can call me Mike."

"Okay Mike."

"And?" Mike said. "Huh?"

"You must have a name." She looked away, then back at Mike. "I'm not so sure you really want to know my name."

"Try me. I've an open mind, that is what's left of it."

"Okay, here goes," she whispered, "Rebecca…"

"Nice first name. Rebecca what?" The girl looked away and took a deep breath. "Coleman. Rebecca…Coleman."

"Ah, yes," Mike said. "Krista told me quite a bit about you. She said that you are pretty; she was right."

"She did?"

"Yeah, she did. She even said that she was very, very fond of that… what…bratty teenager Rebecca."

Rebecca laughed. "Yeah, I guess I was…kind'a. But she really didn't know me too well because my Dad sent me off to live with relatives when I was a kid…sort of. I didn't get to know Krista until she and Dad were dating. Then not much because Dad didn't want me around interfering with his life-style. He claimed he was afraid his motorcycle buddies would take advantage of me. Yeah, right."

"Could'a dumped his pals," Mike said. "I would have."

"His pals were his life." Rebecca said.

"I can guess you want to talk about...Bubbles?" Mike said. "Yeah, that's why I'm here bothering you. And I hated that crummy Bubble name."

"You aren't bothering me," Mike said, "It isn't every day I open my door to a beautiful young woman."

Rebecca blushed and looked away. "You're embarrassing me. I'm not...beautiful."

"Well Rebecca I think you are but you need to come in and give me ten or fifteen minutes to clean up, then we'll have lunch on my patio. You can make sandwiches, can't you?"

Rebecca rolled her eyes. "Oh gosh, I live on them. I'm an expert. But my friends call me Becky."

"Well, seeing as we're friends...Becky it is." When Mike returned freshly showered, shampooed, and wearing fresh jeans and long-sleeved shirt, Rebecca was in the kitchen making sandwiches with Rye bread, tomatoes and ham. She'd filled a water picture with tea bags for ice-tea. She turned as Mike came into the kitchen.

"I hope this is okay. I'm really starved," she said. "Becky, this is great. You're awesome. I might just keep you around. I'm starved too." Rebecca pointed toward the sliding-glass door that led onto the patio. "Out there?"

"My favorite place for an early lunch or brunch. Umbrellas will keep us dry. Looking kind'a like rain."

Watching Rebecca work Mike found himself feeling happy. It was good to have a companion for the moment. Lunch with a pretty girl suited him just fine on this somewhat dreary atmosphere morning that had been promising not more than solitary gloom.

On the patio Rebecca put down her sandwich and sat looking at Mike's beginning of a new sculpture.

"That's beautiful, Mike." Becky whispered. Mike looked around at his work. "Thanks Becky, but it has a ways to go. If you hang around a while I'll take you to see *'Lovers,'* the one I did for a friend."

"Lovers," Rebecca said. "I like that name. I can't wait to see it."

"According to Mario Lucca *Lovers* is destined for Krista's grave." Rebecca looked away. "Krista would like that."

"Yeah, I was just finishing it when she went to Santa Fe. The damn thing kept me from going with her." Rebecca smiled. "I'm glad you didn't go."

"I'm not so sure," Mike whispered.

Rebecca pointed at the sculpture. "It's marble?"

"Yeah, Carrera from Italy."

"I'd love to be able to do something like that," Becky said, "but I'm not very creative."

"How do you know?"

"I just feel it. Writing and sculpture and stuff like that are kind of intimidating to me."

"You won't know until you try," Mike said. "Someday maybe I'll try something," Rebecca said. "How about sculpture?" Mike said. "Huh?"

"How about sculpture?" Mike repeated. "I don't know," Rebecca said. "That's kind of scary."

"I'll teach you," Mike said. "I couldn't afford anything like that," Rebecca said. "For God's sake Becky, I wouldn't charge you. And Krista would love it."

"I'd have to live around here," Rebecca said. "Where are you living know, Becky?" Rebecca looked away and shrugged her shoulders. "Rundown trailer park up in Santa Rosa. It's full of dopers and party people."

"Job?" Rebecca looked away again. "Oh God, Wendy's."

"Well we can get you a Wendy's kind'a job down here in Monterey or Carmel and my friend Mario Lucca has rentals. I'll twist him to get you something to live in. And cheap."

Rebecca shook her head. "Why would you do that for me?"

"Well, because my Krista loved you and that's good enough for me. Krista would approve, don't you think?"

"Yeah, I guess. I kind'a loved her too. She was kind'a mom-like."

"I still do and always will," Mike said, looking away. "She loved you too, Mike, she told me on the phone…just before she went to…"

"All you need to say is, *yes.* In the meantime you could live here at Casa Viejo…no strings attached. Well…you might have to make sandwiches. You could apprentice to me and become a master sculptor…not that I'm a master by any means of the word."

Rebecca nodded. "Yes! I'd love that." Mike looked at Rebecca. "Boyfriend, fiancé?" Rebecca shook her head. Mike thought she looked sad and wished he hadn't asked. "Nope! I had a boyfriend but he found a blond he liked better." Mike shook his head. "Men! How can you girls even stand them?"

"Isn't easy sometimes," Rebecca laughed. "Well then, with that settled, why don't we talk about your Dad while we finish these super sandwiches."

"You called your house Casta-something?"

"Casa Viejo. It means old house."

"Is that Spanish…or maybe Italian?"

"Spanish was Krista's favorite second language. She pretty much named it." Rebecca put her ice tea down and looked away. "Becky," Mike said, trying to get her attention. Without looking at Mike Rebecca said, "Did he try to kill Krista?"

"Becky, it won't help."

"I know he was a bad man but…he was my Dad…no…he was my father, he was never a dad."

"Did he try to hurt Krista?"

"Yes he did. He hit her once that I know of."

"He did it to her before. Many times," Becky said. "She never told me much about that," Mike said. "Mostly she tried to forget."

"A policeman had to kill him?" Becky asked. "He was at Krista's house with a gun. He was there at night trying to get in. Yes a policeman shot your Dad…father."

"Why?"

"Because he shot at the policeman."

"Can I talk to the policeman?" Mike shook his head. "Bobby Duncan has passed away."

"Because my father shot him?"

"Bobbie had a heart attack. He was my friend and he was Krista's friend."

"I'm sorry. My father caused it, didn't he?"

"I'm sure it caused Bobbie some stress, but he was in poor health. He suffered trauma residue from his job and smoked and drank too much."

"Where is my Dad...father buried?"

"The county has been holding his ashes for the next of kin."

"I guess that's me."

"If you want to Becky, I'll help you get them." Becky looked away. "I don't want them."

"Okay, I'll let the county know."

"Can we take flowers to Krista's grave?"

"Yes, she'd like that."

# CHAPTER 34

## *Lessons*

Ten days after arriving on Mike Zorka's doorstep Becky Coleman moved into his guest room and in a sense became the lady of the house; fixing meals, cleaning and doing the essential shopping. She'd found a part-time job working some evenings at the Bicyclette Restaurant and had quickly became good friends with the two older Lucca girls. Mike found himself enjoying her company and slowly began to feel better about life. Rebecca had frowned on his still too frequent need for alcoholic comfort causing him to rethink his approach to grief and slowly slacked off and eventually quit drinking in her presence. He discovered this novel *sea-change* in his life comfortable and easy. In his heart he knew that Krista would approve of his unconditional and *sort of* adoption of Rebecca Coleman.

Carolyn Stewart gave Becky a few hours' work a week at the Changing Paths Gallery. At the gallery she soon discovered she had a certain creative thirst she'd never known. Bright, quick to learn, and full of energy she'd eagerly adopted several of the Bicyclette's best recipes and soon put them to work in Mike's kitchen. Mike having recently completed less than three weeks recovery in a Big Sur Monastery found himself feeling better about life than he had in a long time and had even began daydreaming from time to time about Mona Lisa Bartalucci. Surprisingly he'd discovered that the toughest part of spending three weeks at the the monastery was that he truly missed Becky. However, he'd recently heard about Mona Lisa's engagement via Annabella Lucca to a very successful Florentine architect and so began making conscious efforts to put her out of his mind. But then during some rather sleepless nights she would crowd into his semi-conscious state and keep him tossing and turning until dawn's early light. However, on occasion, and somewhat against his better judgment, he did find himself entertaining Becky about this incredibly beautiful Italian woman he'd once been in love with and so fittingly named, *Mona Lisa.* The first time he'd talked about Mona Lisa Becky had grinned while quipping, "Did she have *that* Mona Lisa Smile?"

Mike and Becky were sitting on his flagstone patio at six thirty on a slightly chilly morning; the pink sunrise was just appearing in the east. A pot of coffee and two cups sat in front of them. Becky poured from the French Press. Mike sipped and smiled.

"I may have to keep you around young lady; you make the best coffee I've ever tasted."

"Stop being nice Michael."

Mike smiled. "Well okay, it's not the worst."

"That's better."

"Okay," Mike said, "lesson time."

"I'm all ears and eyes, Professor," Becky said.

"That is exactly the first thing I want to talk about Miss Becky, eyes, that is. Well…ears too."

Becky was nodding. "And?"

"I've heard about too many one-eyed marble sculptors to not start your training with safety."

Mike sat his coffee cup down and laid both arms out flat on the table. "See these little white spots on these magnificent arms of mine?"

Becky grinned. "I see the whites spots but the…what? Magnanimous arms?"

"Okay, so-so arms. But those white spots are scars from marble splinters sky-rocketing off my sculpture points. If they do that to my arms just imagine what they'd do to those very beautiful eyes of yours."

"Hmmm!" Becky said, frowning.

"Get the picture?" Mike said.

"Could you been suggesting goggles or glasses?"

"Goggles. Eye-protection. Never ever strike a point to marble without eye protection. My protective glasses have nicks out of them from being pitted by faster-than-light splinters."

For the next couple of hours until Becky retreated into the house to whip up scrambled eggs and bacon Mike clarified the differences in marbles and sculpting tools. He put ample emphasis on using imported Italian tools assuring her that they were the best available and that Italy was virtually the birthplace of marble sculpture (which he knew it wasn't).

After breakfast on the patio while basking in a warming ten o'clock sun, Mike furthered Becky's instructions by telling her that the nose and ears were also subject to sculpture damage.

"Do you still want to learn this most precarious art of marble sculpture?" he asked her.

Becky nodded. "Mike, for sure."

"When we get to the use of power tools such as side-grinders, sanders, etcetera, you'll need to wear a face mask in order to keep the silicate dust out of your lungs and ear-guards to save your hearing. This stuff can be uncomfortable, but...in time you'll get used to it."

Becky responded to this safety lecture while grinning impishly, "Did Michelangelo and Donatello use all this safety stuff?"

Mike had scowled and shook his head. "Becky, go to your room!"

Becky grinned. "Well?"

"Only with battery operated tools," Mike kidded. "Home Depot was in its infancy at that time with electricity unheard of because Benny Franklin hadn't invented kites yet."

"Did he invent kites?" Becky asked with feigned innocence.

"Naw, I think it was the Wright Brothers."

"Frank Lloyd Wright?"

"Someone like that. Frank and Orville, maybe."

"I thought they invented gunpowder," Becky grinned.

"I think that was the Romans," Mike laughed. "Enough! Now back to school."

A week after Becky's introductory lessons in the art of marble sculpture she began shaping a one hundred pound block of Portuguese Rose. Mike had expressed that he rather regretted starting her out on Portuguese Rose because it was a tough marble and particularly resistant to the tools. However, he assured her, that *the* Rose is unbelievably beautiful when finished. "The sanding and polishing part will be a pain in the…,"then he stopped himself short of saying what he was thinking.

Becky struggled with the tools while encumbered in dust mask and goggles. There were those moments when she would turn toward Mike with total exasperation written on her face and throw her hands up in the air shaking her head no. At those times Mike would simply point at the marble and say something like, "Back to work young lady. Masterpieces don't carve themselves." And she would reply with something like, "Michael, this ain't gonna be no masterpiece." He would laugh and correct her by saying," Miss Becky, don't say ain't."

"Well it ain't," she'd respond.

However, as the weeks at the marble bench wore on Mike began to see a sense of growing talent in Becky's efforts while the piece began to take a very recognizable and pleasing form. He knew it was only a matter of days or weeks before he would have to introduce her to power tools and the finishing process. He looked forward to this effort because the finishing process; grinding, sanding and polishing, had always been his favorite part of finalizing a sculpture. Even if it could be a pain in the…"

While Becky struggled with the unfamiliar tools Mike worked nearby on the 400 pound block of Carrera marble he planned to call *Ode to Krista.* But at the same time keeping a wary eye on his eager student. Becky would accidentally hit her thumb or suffer a marble splinter to the arm or cheek and curse almost in a whisper. Mike would respond with, "Daughter, that doesn't help, the tools can't hear you." And Becky would come back with something like, "But it makes me feel better, Professor."

# CHAPTER 35

## *Mona Lisa*

"Hello," Mike growled into the phone while glaring at the ceiling annoyed that his morning's work had been interrupted. Outside in an early mist Becky continued to chip away at her Portuguese Rose. No answer. More agitated now by the silence Mike barked into the phone, "Hello out there. Anybody home?"

"Michael I know about Krista." Mike took in a deep breath. "Mona?"

"Yes, Mike."

"Mona, I'm so happy to hear your voice. It thrills me…I'm shaking." More silence. "So am I," Mona whispered. "How do you know about Krista?"

"Mario called me."

"Mario Lucca?"

"Yes, when Mario and Isabella were in Florence six months ago they looked me up. He remembered that you and I were once… friends…well lovers…and he remembered where I worked. I showed them around on my day…days off. I showed them our old haunts but it kind of hurt. I hadn't been back to them since we…parted."

"Good old Mario," Mike said. "Isabella and I really hit it off," Mona said. "Her Italian is perfect."

"Isabella is a pearl."

"They told me how badly you were suffering over the loss of Krista."

"They've been so good to me. Mario threatened to kick my ass if I didn't snap out of it."

"They thought it might help a little if I talked to you."

"It will...is," Mike quickly interjected. "He told me about the tough time you were continuing to have and about the Zen Monastery he took you to. God bless them."

"Saved my life."

"I know," Mona whispered. "Mario paid the bill?"

"Every penny."

"He's Italian...that speaks for his concern and generosity." Mike took in a deep breath. "Mona." Long silence. "Yes Michael." On an sudden impulse Mike blurted. "Can we be together again?" In his heart and mind he hadn't envisioned ever saying anything like that, but it had simply surfaced out of his subconscious. Silence followed. Quickly he felt that he'd blundered badly.

"Michael I can't replace Krista. I wouldn't even try. I think, no I really feel, that Kristy would be a hard act to follow."

"Friends first and then lovers?" Mike whispered. Then he thought, "Shit, I'm begging." Becky came in and refilled her coffee cup and then turned toward Mike and raised her eyebrows. "I'm out of here," she said, taking her coffee and scooting back outside. "Did I hear the name Mona?" he heard her say through the sliding glass doors. He turned quickly and nodded yes with a broad smile on his face.

"Michael Zorka stop this," Mona whispered. "Well?"

"Well we were pretty close in those days," Mona Lisa said. "What happened to your architect friend?" Mike asked. Long silence. "Who?"

"Mona, you know, the builder guy." Silence again, then, "You mean as you might say in English, *what's-his-name?*"

"Yeah, what's-his-name." Michael, his hands were all soft, pudgy and cold. He's skinny and he can't drink wine...makes him sick. Can you even imagine an Italiano that can't drink wine? You're hands are big and strong...kind'a scarred...but warm. He was a sloppy kisser... and smelled like an ashtray...he chain-smoked."

"You kissed him?"

"Of course, dummy."

"Did you think about me while you kissed him?" Mike whispered.
"Nope, I thought about your movie guy Roberto Redgrave."

"Mona, its Robert Redford."

"That's what I meant. I loved him in Butch Cassidy and the Sundown Kid."

"Sundance Kid. He's married now."

"His loss," Mona said. "Miss Mona, your ego is showing."

"Just kidding."

"But your sloppy-kisser is an artist."

"No, he's a pencil-drawer of stuff."

"Such as?"

"Bridges, buildings, apartments. He is definitely not an artist. You are an artist."

"I'm no Michelangelo."

"Yeah but you are an Auguste Rodin."

"Rodin was a womanizer. I'm no womanizer," Mike offered. "Yeah?"

"Yeah! I thought you loved him. You were engaged weren't you?"

"I rebounded with him. You left me feeling worthless and unloved. When Mario and Isabella arrived in Florence they talked about you and suddenly I couldn't stand whats-his-name for another minute."

"Miss Mona, flattery will not get you back in my arms. Well actually it might."

"What makes Mr. Michelangelo think I want to be back in his arms?"

"Because you do," Mike ventured. "Who's ego is showing now?"

"Well?"

"I gave him his ring back the very next day…at Traitoria Donatello. He cried. Poor man!"

"I don't blame him."

"Oh hell Michael I wanted you back and I told him so. Isabella offered to pay my way to Carmel, but I told her absolutely not. I do have some pride."

"You should have come."

"Oh sure Michael. Little sad Italian girl running and begging…
love me…please love me."

"Oh, you'll take what's-his-name back."

"Mike."

"Yes Mona."

"Go to hell."

"Will you be there?"

"If you will be," Mona Lisa whispered. "When do we head that
way lonely little Italian girl?"

"Not soon enough lonely big American man."

"Well then?"

"Michael."

"Yes Mona."

"Please come."

"Mona Lisa mi Bella, I'm on my way." Mike turned around and
Becky was standing in the kitchen smiling at him "Yes Mike, go. Go
get Mona Lisa and bring her here."

"Soon as I can," Mike said. "You'll love her."

"I can guess," Becky said.

"I'll be gone a while."

"I'm a big girl and I have Carolyn and the Changing Paths Gallery
to keep me busy."

"Yeah, and I've heard rumors of a boyfriend," Mike said.

"Oh just rumors," Becky said smiling.

# CHAPTER 36

## *Changing Paths Gallery*

Carolyn Stewart had agreed to show Becky Coleman's first attempt at marble sculpture. Becky had spent weeks carving, sanding and polishing and making a pedestal for a small bird figure she began calling *Lonesome Dove*. With great pride but with some hesitation she had helped display the sculpture in a very prominent area of the gallery with a striking photograph of herself at her work-bench serenely toiling with tools in hand; sans goggles and dust mask.

However, the show had not been arranged for Becky but for a Mexican artist named Juan Garcia showing his new collection of colorful abstracts very much in the Jackson Pollock genre. Becky Coleman secretly felt that the show was in her honor. It was Carolyn's second showing of Garcia's work and in each show they had sold out. Garcia had done so well for Carolyn that she had paid for the shipping of his works from Mexico City to the Changing Paths Gallery and had arranged to pick him up at the airport. Early the previous morning she'd met Garcia at the airport and driven him to Carmel by the Sea where she had previously earmarked an expensive suite for him at the beautiful and elaborate Highlands Inn. A dinner in his honor with eight guests had had been arranged that evening at the Cabello Blanco Restaurant. Becky Coleman and Michael Zorka had been a select fragment of the dinner entourage. The dinner had gone exceptionally well with Mario Lucca buzzing about pouring his best wines and expounding about the vintages and those so-evasive nuances one should look for in taste, smell and color. He'd eagerly spent most of the evening diligently monitoring and urging the waiters and bus-people to stay on their toes while making this an exceptional evening for...as Mario began calling him...Maestro Garcia. Clint Eastwood, the former mayor of Carmel, and his wife had been invited but they'd begged off as Clint was leaving early the next morning for a film project somewhere in the Texas Pan Handle. The Changing Paths Gallery glowed in an air of festivity with an array of colorful balloons hovering outside the double-front glass door highlighting a life-sized poster of Juan Garcia at work painting in his Mexico City studio. Garcia was delighted when he noticed that the balloons were all the national colors of Mexico; red, green and white. Upon being introduced to Garcia for the first time Becky had unwittingly and embarrassingly blurted out," You look like Anthony Quinn." Garcia had merely smiled giving her a little hug while saying, "My old friend Tony Quinn was much better looking and talented than me."

Becky Coleman stood near the wine and hordourves table holding the hands of a tall young man and a little girl of three or four years old. She had just finished enduring the praise of several guests one of which was showing a sincere interest in purchasing her *Lonesome Dove* sculpture. Mike Zorka, while moving about the room and greeting people he knew and a small mix of tourists, was keeping an eye on Becky and wondering who the young man and small girl were. Carolyn Stewart was staying close to Mike and joining in his conversations with the others. Carolyn had found herself becoming quite attached to Mike since Krista's death. They had spent some time together and had even enjoyed a picnic on Pfeiffer Beach in Big Sur where Mike had regaled her on the legend of the Japanese shipwreck of the freighter, the Honda Maru and the untimely Scuba diving death of *Carmel's Man of Letters,* Mike Swain, in the jaw-like clutches of a Great White Shark. Carolyn had shivered and stayed close to Mike hoping, no, actually praying, that they wouldn't hear the strains of that mythical Japanese music stemming from the area where the doomed ship sunk taking nearly all hands but one to the bottom.

Mike adored Carolyn and enjoyed her company tremendously but was thinking of her in terms of a young sister or an emerging best friend. Becky Coleman, ever observant of Mike and Carolyn, quite often could be perceived encouraging the paring of the two. Mike consistently assured her that he and Carolyn were just good friends and nothing more. Becky often quipped with something like," Yeah but you two look beautiful together." Becky Coleman had become a big part Mike Zorka's life and he had readily learned to love her like a daughter.

Mike excused himself from a fading conversation and walked over to Becky. She saw him coming, smiled, and put her arms around him for a hug. Mike kissed her on the forehead and then turned to the young man and child.

"Becky I don't believe I've met your friends."

The young man put his hand out to shake. Becky moved close to him and took his elbow. "Mike, please meet my friends Zackary Dickson and his little sister Melody. Zack this is Mike Zorka, my knight in shining armor and finest friend. Mike took the proffered hand and shook. Then he reached down and took the little girls hand. She blushed and then moved over to Zackary and hugged his leg.

"I'm so happy to meet you too, Melody."

"Zackie and Becky call me Mellie," she said.

"How old are you Mellie?"

"Four going on seven."

"Going on five," Zackary corrected. "She's in a hurry to grow up."

"Yes you are Becky's best friend," Zackary said. "She talks about you a lot."

"All good I hope."

"For sure," Zackary said.

"Zack wants to write," Becky offered.

"A man with a name that starts with Z can't be all bad," Mike joked. "I'm happy to meet you and Melody."

"I admire your work Mr. Zorka. I've always loved sculpture, especially marble."

"Thank you," Mike said," and what about your writing?"

"Oh nothing much yet," Zackary said. "A couple starts on novels and one or two short stories. I've sent the shorts stories out but then you don't hear from the magazines for months on end. However, no one seems to want my stuff. And heck, writing a novel is a test of endurance and will-power. I guess I've got to learn to stay with it."

"It'll come if you're really serious," Mike said. "You've got to really want it. Mike Swain told me a writer needs to work every day rain or shine, feel good or feel terrible. Swain always said that the writing business was a tough one."

"I do, Mr. Zorka. I really do."

"You can call me Mike."

"Zack is a great writer, "Becky said. "He lets me read his stuff. It's only a matter of time. His latest story called *Death of a Dancer* made me cry."

"That's promising," Mike said.

"Becky, Mellie and I are going Saturday night to see one of Swain's movies."

"Which one?"

"*Islands in the Mist.*"

"That one ends violently," Mike said. "Might be a little rough for Mellie."

"Mellie will be asleep during the first half hour," Zackary said.

"No I won't, Zackie," Melody said, "I love movies."

"We'll see, "Zackary said.

"What kind of work do you do, Zack?" Mike asked.

Zackary let out a deep breath and shook his head. "Oh gosh Mike, I'm just a bank clerk. Sure ain't nothing exciting."

"Well it's an honest job so stay with it until you start to make money with your pen. I know of a former great writer who earned his keep as a postal clerk. And another who was a secretary and wrote when the boss wasn't looking. So…stick with it."

"That's the plan."

"Are you and my Becky an item?" Mike said smiling.

Zackary looked down at Becky. "You'd better ask Becky."

Becky took Zackary's hand and then tip-toed up and kissed him on the cheek. That's for sure."

"How about your folks?" Mike asked.

Zackary looked down at Melody. "Mellie lives with me because our mom and dad went away on a long…trip."

"A…permanent trip," Beck whispered looking down at Melody."

Mike nodded. "I understand."

"Saffron stays with Mellie during the day while I'm at work." Zackary said.

"I love Saffy," Melody said. "We play tea and we dress my dolls all up real pretty. Saffy thinks that the dolls can hear us talk so we have to talk real nice to them."

"Saffron is an African-American lady with six kids of her own ranging in ages from 10 to 19," Zackary said. "She gets her kids off to school and then comes over and stays with Mellie. She's a wonderful lady. And…reasonable. She fits into my meager budget."

"Well I bet they can hear you, Mellie," Mike said. "A pretty lady named Barbara used to live with me and she collected dolls. When she went away she left a few in my closet. One of these days you and Zackary will have to come over to my house and see them. Maybe you'd like to have them."

"We'd love to do that wouldn't we Mellie?"

"Can we go tonight?" Melody said.

"Not to tonight honey," Zackary said.

"How about tomorrow night?" Mike said. "I'm sure Becky would cook us a great meal."

"Yes come over tomorrow night," Becky said.

"Can I have a doll?" Melody asked.

"Yes you can," Mike said. "Those dolls are as pretty as you and Becky."

Melody moved over and hugged one of Becky's legs. Becky bent and pick her up and hugged her. Melody kissed Becky on the cheek.

"I love Becky," Melody whispered.

"So do I," Mike said. "Becky is my little girl."

"Becky and me are big girls, "Melody said. "Becky is gonna be my new mommy."

"Zackary looked at Becky and then at Mike and shrugged his shoulders. He appeared a bit embarrassed.

"I'd love to be your new mommy," Becky said.

"How did you guys meet?" Mike asked.

"At a book signing in Monterey," Becky said.

"Beck and I both love books, "Zackary said. "And lucky for me I went to that signing."

"And me," Becky added.

# CHAPTER 37

## *Leaving*

"I'm glad you're going," Becky said while pouring coffee for her and Mike. "I'll miss you but I do hope you aren't gone long and that you'll bring Mona Lisa home."

Mike tasted his coffee and nodded smiling. "I'll miss this…and you. Coming here to live will be up to Mona Lisa, I expect."

"Michael, use your powers of persuasion."

"I'll try but I'm not so sure our relationship will resume as it was before. A lot has happened to me and I still think about Krissy…fact is I'm still in love with her."

"I know Mike, but Krissy's gone. Mona is alive and well. I think she'll love you even more than before. After all, she's missed you, dreamt about you, dumped her architect boyfriend because he wasn't the man Michael Zorka is…and…called you with condolences over Krissy. But I'm a girl and I know that call was partly to get your attention. And don't tell me it wasn't."

"You think?"

"Michael, I know. I'm a woman. Mona wants you back and soon."

"Will you be alright alone?"

"Michael, I've got Zack and Melody. I've got the Lucca's and I'm great friends with their daughters. Carolyn and I are close and I'm gonna live with her…probably."

"Yeah, I guess I won't have to worry too much about you."

"You won't have to worry at all. Zackary and Melody won't let me be lonely for even one minute."

"Is Carolyn okay with what I'm doing? She and I have gotten pretty close," Mike asked. "Well," Becky said grimacing "Carolyn is going to hurt a little. I think she's fallen in love with you. She talks about you all the time."

"Ouch!" Mike said. "Really? I didn't know that. Didn't guess! Look I think the world of Carolyn but I'm not in love with her. I love her like…I love you."

Becky took a sudden breath and her eyes dampened. "Mike…you love me?"

Mike got up from his chair and went to Becky and wrapped her in his arms. "Yes Becky I do. I've think I've loved you since that first day when you nervously showed up on my door."

"That's the nicest thing anyone has ever said to me," Becky sobbed. Tears were flowing down her cheeks.

Mike laughed. "Now Becky, I'm sure Zack has told you that."

Becky wiped her yes and smiled. "Not yet. But he shows it. Anyhow it wouldn't be the same as hearing it from you…Dad."

"He will," Mike said. "I see love blooming. Didn't your dad… father ever tell you that?"

"Nope!"

"Your mom?"

"Nope!"

"Well I do and I always will. Becky you know my love is unconditional."

"Thank you Mike, I love you so much. But I've been kind of afraid to say it. I didn't want to put any kind'a trip on you. You're the only father…family…I've ever really had."

"Well we are a family and if Mona Lisa will have me she will be a part of our family."

"And Zack and Melody?"

Mike smiled and kissed Becky on the forehead. "And Zack and Melody."

"Mike."

"Yes Becky."

"I don't remember when I've ever been so happy."

# CHAPTER 38

## *Flight*

Mike Zorka sat on his flagstone patio drinking his late morning coffee. It was one of those frequent cool days in the Carmel Valley with the fog off the Pacific Ocean lingering on past noon. Probably one of those days when the fog would hang on until around two in the afternoon and then drift back out to sea temporally and then roll back in around four or five just in time to build a fire in the living room fireplace and pop the cork from a honest bottle of good wine. Although anxious to see Mona Lisa Bartalucci and Italy he was having various nagging qualms about leaving the Carmel Valley and the new surrogate daughter he'd quickly and easily learned to love.

Scattered here and there around his courtyard were a myriad of potted plants Krista Coleman had place, nurtured, and loved. Her *Joy* roses where his favorite. He would miss them. Those plants were in some ways the living embodiment of Krissy. There were days alone on the patio when he spoke to the plants as he would have had Krista been there. On the kitchen counter just through a window Mike could see the toaster Krista had happily and characteristically named Mr. Pop-up. The early morning tone of her happy chirp as she spoke to Mr. Pop-up encouraging him to hurry up with her morning toast, was, in Mike's so-melancholy memory, like the echo of a sigh. He remembered how Krissy had always been starved in the morning and had been able to out-eat him regularly without ever having gained so much as an ounce. Breakfast with Krista had always been a joyful event; an event he deeply missed.

Mike was sincerely lamenting leaving the Carmel Valley and everything he knew and loved and dreading the thought of the red-eye flight he'd booked from San Francisco International airport to Florence, Italy. In another hour or two he'd stow his suitcase and carry-on in the trunk of the rental car and drive down the Carmel Valley Road and turn north on Highway One toward San Francisco and a very undefined future. His Jeep Wrangler (that Jeep-Thing) was safely stowed in a locked garage along with his trusty, but still untested, and somewhat rusty, Colt Forty-five automatic pistol his father had covertly shipped home from Danang, Vietnam just a few days before his death. The pistol was in its customary hiding place within the jeep's interior; a hiding place that was readily accessible should it be needed quickly. Having a gun handy for self-defense was frowned on as neurotic by some folks but one of Mike's beliefs had always been that *"God helps those who help themselves."* A partially finished marble sculpture sat abandoned on his outdoor work bench covered securely with a waterproof canvas while his tools were now cleaned, sharpened, lightly oiled, and stowed.

The morning was too quiet and unsettling. He felt alone; an abysmal loneliness. Becky and Carolyn had left the day before on a two day get-away driving south for 90 picturesque miles through the Big Sur country to visit the historic and magnificent Hearst Castle near Cambria, California. They had said their goodbyes the evening before the trip with a quiet dinner at Mario Lucca's Cabello Blanco. Becky had cried at the end of the evening and clung to Mike ardently before she and Carolyn went off to sleep at Krista's Tara so they could get an early start in the morning. Carolyn had been taciturn and left Mike with a thin hug and quick guarded kiss on the check. She was very aware that he was leaving to join a former lover with great hopes for his future. Acutely chagrined she went home that night and went straight to bed fully knowing her chances of having a life with Mike Zorka were nil. Becky Coleman, while suffering her own loosing Mike

Zorka blues, had covertly perceived a certain wetness in Carolyn's eyes as they had gloomily bid each other goodnight.

Within the next two or three hours Mike would bid his Casa Viejo goodbye, stow his suit case and carry-on in the trunk of the car and leave the Carmel Valley for what? Forever? Would he and Mona Lisa regain their former passion for each other? Would they abandon Italy and return to live in the Carmel Valley? Would he always stay in touch with Becky? That quasi-orphan he had learned to love and care for. He sat remembering a song he'd heard about someone singing something like happiness was Lubbock, Texas in the rearview mirror. Would he feel that way about Carmel by the Sea and the Carmel Valley? No he wouldn't.

At four o'clock he loaded the car and headed north toward San Francisco. He rode along remembering a hippy song that went something like *"when you go to San Francisco, wear a flower in your hair."* Mike looked in the rearview mirror and shook his head. "Ain't no flowers in my hair," he whispered. Hours later as he made the turn-off into the San Francisco International Airport toward the International terminal he was surprisingly feeling a fresh eagerness to get the flight over with and see Mona Lisa Bartalucci and Florence, Italy for the first time in nearly four years. Where did that formerly nagging hesitation go? He asked himself, and then laughed while looking in the rearview mirror.

# CHAPTER 39

## *Return to Mona Lisa*

A mostly miserable jet-ride later Mike stepped off a jet at Florence International Airport and took a cab into the heart of the city, however choosing to walk the last few blocks toward Traitoria Donatello hoping to settle his quivering nerves before seeing Mona Lisa for the first time in years.

The familiar facade of Traitoria Donatello loomed ahead of Mike. He was jet-lagged and feeling protracted jet-ride muddy, but real anxiety sat heavily on his stomach. Mona Lisa knew he was coming. For several weeks since her first phone call they had been working out the details and now that he was on the street half a block from the restaurant, he felt edgy; would their relationship be the same? Would it be dulled by their absence from each other? Or by Mike's love for another woman. Would Mona feel the same about him? Feel the same ever again? After all he had changed during those three years? He was older, a bit grayer, and a couple pounds heavier due to his year or two of boozing after Krista's death. Maybe Mona had become a heavy peasant woman and her hair had grayed some? Maybe she had cut those beautiful tresses? He was happy now that he'd spent those life-saving three weeks in a Big Sur Monastery thanks to the love and kindness of Mario and Isabella Lucca. Without that interval of rejuvenation based on nutrition, exercise and meditation, Mona may not have recognized him due to his previous appearance following those alcoholic months of neglect and depletion.

"C'mon Zorka" he whispered aloud, "it's hasn't been quite four years." At the door to Donatello's he paused and took a deep breath. Today was one of Mona's work Days, otherwise, she had told him, she'd have been there at the airport with bells on. He went in and was thrilled to be in Donatello's Traitoria once again. The old familiar cooking aromas were there; Pasta, cheeses, wines, pastries, the pizza and bread oven glowing in a corner, the wood-smoke smell. He felt a surge of joy as he walked to his favorite table and sat down, but his heart slowed when a waitress he had never seen before came out of the kitchen toward him. She was an older woman, fiftyish, and rather heavy. She was Mike's impression of a very settled peasant woman of Italian origin.

"May I help you?' she said with a slight scowl and in very broken English. Mike answered her in Italian and made it clear he wanted to look at the menu for a while. She huffed and disappeared back into the kitchen. Mike heard her say something about "An English bastardo." A male voice reprimanded her. Leonardo sounded angry.

Moments later the kitchen door opened and Mike took in a quick breath. Mona Lisa walked toward him with an order pad in hand. She looked absolutely beautiful in her flowered knee-length skirt, lace blouse belted at her tiny waist. Her hair was piled in a bun at the back of her head and supported by a colorful headband. She wore a red rose planted skillfully in the hair-bun. She was not smiling. Mike felt the back of his neck tingle and his breath became restricted.

Mona Lisa walked up to Mike's table and flipped open her order pad. "Can I help you?" she said in English.

Mike looked down at the menu, thinking "Okay, I'll play that game."

"Do you have Sour krout?"

"Yes, in a can, where it belongs."

"That's what I'd like."

"You can't have it."

"And why not?"

"We lost the can opener."

"Well then do you have a special?" Mike asked. "Yes."

"May I ask what it is?"

"Fried frog in a lemon sauce," Mona Lisa said while pretending to scribble something on her order pad.

"Then I'll have that."

"You can't," Mona Lisa said. "And why not?"

"Because if you want that you have to sleep with the cook." She was trying desperately to suppress a grin.

"That can be arranged. What's her name?" Mike asked. "The cook is a he and his name is Leonardo. You wouldn't appeal to him."

"Isn't there someone else I can sleep with?"

"Yes."

"Who might that be?"

"Margarita, the other waitress."

"You mean?"

"Yes...that Margarita."

"Gee, aren't you available?"

"I'm working."

"So is Margarita."

"Do you ever get off work?"

"At four."

"What will it cost me?"

"You can't afford it big lonely American man."

"Are there any other arrangements?"

"Yes."

"What will it cost me Little Lonely Italian girl?"

"You have to beg." With that Mike slid off his chair and dropped to his knees in front of Mona Lisa and put his hands in the prayer position. Mona looked around startled. Other customers were looking.

"Michael, not here you idiot, tonight. You can beg all you want tonight." Mike slid back onto the chair. "How long will I have to beg?" Mona seemed to think about it for a long moment, and then grinned. "Long enough for me to get my clothes off," she whispered. Then she bent and kissed him on the forehead. "Now get lost until four, Big Lonely American Man."

Mike reached for her, she pulled away frowning. "Michael, you're gonna get me fired."

"Not a chance. Leonardo loves you. But Miss Mona, I have to eat." Mona rolled her eyes and flipped open her order pad. After spending his lunch time trying to talk to Mona Lisa and furtively trying to touch her as she waited tables and then needing to kill time until she got off work, he decided to take a walk around the historic City of Florence reuniting himself with those so-memorable haunts of yesteryear. The city seemed to be welcoming him home. The aromas, the echoes, and the people seemed to be emanating a vibrant ambiance that he felt deep in his heart and soul. He found himself smiling as he ambled along.

However, as he strolled through those once familiar streets of Florence he found himself absurdly in one of his all too *au fait* self-dialogues where he strained to settle an inner-conflict that was weighing profoundly on his mind and conscience. During these infrequent mental confrontations he frequently found one side of his feelings that toiled greatly to justify his desires, while the other hemisphere ruthlessly became the *Devil's Advocate* throwing curves into every timorous belief he reached. These dialogues were ceaseless and rarely provided answers. He knew very well that he was feeling guilty about returning to Mona Lisa. He dreaded the thought that he might merely be rebounding with Mona. Was Mona only a known source? Was Mona making herself too available? Was he being true to himself and Mona? Was Mona simply feeling sorry for him? Was Mona just a well-known comfort?

As he walked he felt the haunting presents of Krista Coleman and deep down feared that she might be condemning him for his all too seemingly sudden reversal of affections and his hasty flight toward the arms of a former lover. Had he forgotten Krista? Does love fade that quickly?

Is there no loyalty in Michael Zorka? Did he not truly love Krista Coleman? Why was he so ecstatic to hear Mona Lisa's voice? He had grieved Krista's loss, spending months in a morose and highly destructive state of mind. His sculpting had faded to dark while his tools had dulled and rusted lying untouched. He had drunk whisky at night to cloud his loneliness and with any luck, find a modicum of slumber.

In time Mario Lucca had practically kidnapped Mike and hauled him away to a Zen Monastery high in the hills of Big Sur where he remained for several days monitoring Mike's daily activities, and putting a temperate halt to his imminent self-destruction. Mario had returned to Carmel only when he was satisfied that Mike would stay at the monastery and had developed a daily routine that would, in a couple weeks, hopefully restore him. The exercise, the vegetarian diet, and hours of yoga and meditation had worked wonders for Michael Zorka. By the time he left the monastery three weeks later he had come to reasonable terms about Krista's death. A week later he ordered a 400 pound block of Carrera Marble from Renaissance Stone in Oakland, sharpened his tools and began a sculpture he planned to call *Ode to Krista*.

And now walking the streets of Florence some of the old uncertainty and depression returned. He thought he had to come to terms with this specter of guilt. However, that Devil's Advocate lurking in his head gave dispute to his what he really knew was common logic. In his mind the conflict carried on much against his will:

"Zorka, you're cheating on the memory of Krista."

"I'm not, Krista is gone forever."

"In your mind?"

"No, in my heart."

"Yeah, don't lie, you've forgotten her already."

"No, but my love for her is like a dying ember, only the ashes remain."

"How poetic. Quit kidding yourself, you've forgotten in less than a couple of years. Admit it, you've always loved Mona Lisa. Krista was just a pastime."

"That's bullshit. I'll never forget Krista."

"Yeah, but the first time Mona called you would have run to her without a moments haste. Why don't you face the truth? You always loved Mona. Again, Krista was an interlude for a lonely man. Yeah, big lonely American man."

"Yeah, I still loved Mona, but I was not in love with her."

"But this girl Mona will help."

"Yeah, hell I'm not dead."

"Do you think Krista knew that you still loved Mona Lisa?"

"She knew all about Mona. Krista had a big heart."

"That's not what I asked. How do you know what Krista thought?"

"Because she has come in the night and I felt her warmth. She's happy for me."

"Alcohol dreams? Wishful thinking? Delusion?"

"No, it happened while I was at the Zen Monastery. I was sober and had been for two weeks. She even touched me. I could even smell her perfume...scent."

"Paranormal delusions? Meditation dreams? Oh Zorka my friend you can always dream what you want to. I think you are sociopathic, justifying yourself."

"That's bullshit."

"Must be that Mona Lisa smile. You've heard the song by Nat King Cole."

"Mona is love personified. It has nothing to do with that so-called *Mona Lisa smile.*"

"Well Zorka, you just can't toss love around. You know, here today, gone tomorrow. Remember, *love loves a masquerade.*"

"For God's sake drop it."

"Answer my question about tossing love around."

"If you insist on that terminology. Krista is gone."

"Have you even taken flowers to Krista's grave?"

"Once!"

"Ha, why only once?"

"Because it makes me sad."

"Ha, well then go run to Mona Lisa big lonely American man. Isn't that what she calls you? That girl with the...you know...*devilish smile.*"

"Thank you I will. An hour later and with his *Devil's Advocate* basically silenced for the time being he sat in a familiar sidewalk café sipping a hot latte and people watching. He had found no real answers to this emotional impasse but knew beyond a doubt he was ready for a life with Mona Lisa Bartalucci. Krista Coleman would always remain in his heart sensibly locked away in those *wind mill memories* of another time.

Watching the Italians and the myriad tourists strolling or hurrying by on their important what-ever business and being once again in this historic city thrilled him. After Krista had died he'd felt like his life was over but on this day he sensed a powerful renewal of the *life-force* clutching his heart. Considering that his life's work was devoted to sculpture his thinking easily shifted to those great master sculptors of the Renaissance, Michelangelo and Donatello. These two ancient icons of the artistic world couldn't have been more disparate. It had been during Mike's original stay in Florence while visiting a museum that a curator had enlightened him to the dissimilarity between the works of these two personalities. His original desire, in an adolescent sort of way, had been to emulate these two masters. At first he was chagrined of himself for not having grasped and scrutinized this foible. Since that day he had not been able to compare Michelangelo and Donatello without experiencing a certain degree of distress for his former, and first-most champion, Michelangelo Buonarroti.

The curator had pointed out a disturbing departure between the two. The oddity was that Michelangelo's female sculptures were masculine and unrefined while his male figures, David for instance, embodied the very virility of the male physique. Conversely his female figures presented breasts that more often resembled soccer balls than a woman's bosom and failed sadly to exhibit the eminence of feminine beauty. Contrariwise Donatello's females were slender, beautiful and the very embodiment of the fairer sex. His males were lean, attractive, and carried with them a natural degree of manliness. This Michelangelo idiosyncrasy had led many art historians to question his sexual orientation. Mike Zorka recognized that the bottom-line was, did it really make any difference?

Mike couldn't help but smile at himself remembering the trouble he'd suffered after climbing over the guard ropes near Michelangelo's David sculpture and brazenly reaching out and touching one of his unfinished marbles. Were the guards upset? Yes, about one hundred dollars' worth. Mike remembered a certain sense of electricity running through his body as his hand caressed the marble just short seconds before a museum guard bellowed at him. Then the handcuffs had come out and a trip to the local Carabinieri headquarters followed. There the remainder of his meager and much coveted traveler's checks had quickly evaporated sending him to an international phone call in a desperate hunt for funds. A former pal, following excessive moaning and groaning, had wired him a hundred dollars based on a *death-threat* promise that it would be paid back immediately, *'if not sooner.'* The next day Mike sold his deep-sea diving watch, Kodak camera, and gold school ring; life was good again.

As a sculptor and having conversed with dozens of other contemporary artists about a somewhat universal, but marginally paranormal, conviction that Michelangelo must have had *Devine Intervention* from a higher source in order to accomplish what he had. Mike and most other modern day sculptors worked with a myriad of specialized tools operated by either electricity or air. Michelangelo had none of these benefits, and yet produced masterpiece after masterpiece that still remain unparalleled in modern times. When today's contemporary sculptor stands mesmerized while contemplating Michelangelo's *Pieta* or his *David* he or she is usually mystified as to how these masterpieces could have been created without modern power tools, electricity and lighting. Master sculptors like Auguste Rodin and Constantin Branscusi, although great artists in their own right, had not been able to rival Michelangelo's unfathomable accomplishments.

Florence during Michelangelo's time was very likely the largest city in Europe. Had he lived during the 1300's in Florence during the *Black Death Plague* he would have undoubtedly died along with the sixty-thousand plus Florentines that perished from that raging cataclysm. This historical recollection set Mike to wondering how many great artists and writers have died from wars, accidents, and pestilence without ever having discovered their inherent talents for art, literature, medicine, or statesmanship. This question of lost talent echoes an illimitable loss to the cultural and art world of human existence.

# CHAPTER 40

## *Beyond This Place*

"But Mona Lisa Sweet, "Mike pleaded, "I remember you saying something about taking your clothes off."

Mike and Mona were having their coffee after finishing dinner in a Traitoria near the Arno River. The evening was cozy warm with just a hint of breeze off the river. The traitoria doors and windows were open. Just down the river from the restaurant the chapel bells at St. Patrick's Duomo Del Fiume (St. Patrick's Chapel on the River) were ringing in seven o'clock.

"Michael," Mona said without looking at him, "have you even looked at the river? The city lights are sparkling like diamonds on the water."

"Miss Mona, you are avoiding my question."

Mona looked back at Mike. "Oh, what was the…question?"

"At noon today, while I was begging to merely touch you, you said something about me only having to wait long enough tonight for you to take your clothes off."

"I did?"

"Yeah, you did," Mike confirmed.

"Oh, I did?"

"Yes, you did."

"I meant my work clothes," Mona said without looking at Mike.

"So?"

"So we could go for a long walk and get...well...you know, reacquainted."

"Huh?"

"Michael it's been almost three years."

"And so?"

"And so I'm nervous."

"So am I frightened little Italian girl"

"Michael, I'm not frightened but what about...you know...Krista?"

"I'm here because of you. Krissy Coleman is just an affectionate memory."

"You loved her?"

"Well, yes."

"Would you be here with me now if Krista hadn't died?"

"Well if Krista hadn't died you wouldn't have called me with condolences and, I assume, we wouldn't have become reacquainted."

"Nice answer big lonely American man."

"Will you at least stay with me tonight," Mike asked? "Heck, I'll even sleep on the floor."

"Mama will not like it."

"She doesn't have to sleep on the floor with me."

"Michael, you're being an ass."

"Jerk, is the American term."

"Whatever you call it but you are being one."

"Kidding."

"So where?" Mona asked while looking back toward the river."

"I rented an apartment, well sort of an apartment, over-looking our Piazza."

"Already?" Mona Lisa's eyes widened.

"Mona sweetheart, I'm staying in Florence forever so I might just as well have settled in. I had to do something with this afternoon."

"Furnished?" Mona Lisa asked.

Mike grinned and took Mona Lisa's hand. "It's got a bed. What else do we need?"

Mona Lisa shook her head a Mike. "Oh Michael."

"Okay," Mike said," a mini-kitchen with microscopic fridge, bathroom with no tub but a shower, tiny-weeny bedroom with a view of the piazza...sort of."

"Why take an apartamento so soon?" Mona asked without looking at Mike.

Mike reached and turned Mona toward him. "Because Florence, or Firenze, is where my Mona Lisa lives. You know, that incredible girl with the Mona Lisa smile."

"Incredible? What does that mean in your American lingo?"

"It means incomparable."

"Huh! What does incomparable mean?"

"Mona, you're being difficult."

"Am not."

"So does this mean you'll stay with me tonight?"

"Hmmm...maybe," Mona said still looking toward the river.

"Why maybe Miss Mona?"

"I'm worried."

"About?"

"Am I, what do you Americans call it, slave for a broken heart?"

"The word is salve," Mike corrected.

"Is it salve?"

"No it isn't salve. It's...love."

"You haven't seen me in years but you already love me?" Mona Lisa asked.

"I never really stopped loving you," Mike promised.

"Really?"

"Sweetheart, spend the night with me like in the old days. No strings attached. Tomorrow is your day off and we'll spend the whole day getting, as you say, getting re-acquainted."

Mona, while still looking at the river. "No strings?"

"Not even one little string."

Mona turned back to Mike and reached and took his hand and smiled. "Deal!"

"Mona."

"Yes Michael."

"Not even one little kiss?"

"We'll see."

"What happened to that Italian Siren I used to know?" Mike whispered.

Mona grinned and took Mike's hand. "She got smart."

Mike and Mona slept together that night in his hastily acquired apartment one story above the Piazza. Over coffee in a sidewalk café next morning Mike said," Mona, we made it through the night without...well you know."

"By the grace of God and my willpower," Mona said.

"Well honey, after all, I'm not a monk."

"In time," Mona said. "Be patient."

"Devil woman!"

Mona finished her cup of coffee. "Time to go."

"To where?"

"To see Sister Teresa at the..."

"Convent?" Mike interrupted.

"Well she is a nun."

"About?"

"Our...reunion," Mona whispered.

"She's a nun," Mike said, "What could she possibly know about boy-girl love?"

"Wouldn't you be surprised," Mona grinned.

"Oh yeah, I remember. You taught her all about the birds and the bees."

"Birds and bees?" Mona said wrinkling her nose.

"Boy and girl stuff."

"Another of your American ways of avoiding talking about...sex? Mona Lisa asked.

"Yeah."

"She'll bless our life together."

"She cute?" Mike said while grinning.

"Michael, don't be an ass. But yes, she is."

"Okay," Mike said, "I guess I can handle Sis Teresa."

"And Mama."

"Excuse me," Mike said. "Your Mother?"

Mona grinned. "Of course Mama will be there…and maybe Father Peter."

"Oh shit," Mike said, "I ain't going."

"Mama will be mad. It'll remind her of how irresponsible you are."

"She probably hates me anyway."

"For?"

"For not coming back to you."

"More than that," Mona whispered.

"More?"

"Yes, you left me with child."

Mike jumped up off his chair. "Mona Sweetheart…what?"

Mona laughed. "Had you worried didn't I?"

"I'll get even with you for that. You scared the hell out of me."

"I bet you will."

During the week that followed the meeting with Sister Teresa, Anna Bartalucci, sans Father Peter, *and a painful meeting for Mike Zorka*, he and Mona spent every spare minute together. During Mona's work hours Mike lunched every noon at Traitoria Donatello and was waiting for her at the door at quitting time. Each evening they dined at different bistros followed by walks along the Arno River and enjoying the gaily lighted streets of Florence. Midnight found them in Mike's apartment living more or less like brother and sister. Mona still refused anything more serious than kisses and hugs. Activities that were usually followed by Mona telling Mike to "Calm down Michael." Breakfasts of coffee and croissants were often in the apartment with an occasional celebratory breakfast at an early morning sidewalk bistro. Mona's workday at Donatello began at 10 leaving them time to sleep in a little and enjoy mornings. Mike's oft heard complaint was "Mona Sweetheart, I'm living like a Nepalese Monk. Can't do this forever." A complaint that was each time followed with silence and moments of eye rolling by Mona.

On her day off during the second week of Mike's return they packed a picnic lunch of Traitoria Donatello sandwiches, a bottle of Chianti wine donated by Leonardo, a bag of pastries and in a borrowed car drove to one of Mike's favorite places in all of Italy, the "Michelangelo stone quarry near Arezzo. The same quarry where Michelangelo's step-father cut stone and marble for many of the magnificent buildings in Florence, Rome, and many of the surrounding cities.

There in the shade of an over-hanging excavated wall, while listening to the quiet gurgle of the ancient quarry spring, they made love for the first time in more than three years. Afterward Mona quipped that "Michael, it's about time." Mike followed with "Sweetheart, I've been trying." Followed by "Michael, you haven't been trying hard enough." With that Mike scooped Mona up off the blanket, carried her over to the spring and gently laid her in the water. She laughed and pulled Mike down for a kiss but instead jerked him into the water. For next half hour they played there in the water splashing, laughing, and acting like children.

# CHAPTER 41

## *The Girl Mona Lisa*

Mike and Mona were sitting in a sidewalk cafe beneath a large umbrella shielding them from a steady drizzle. The cobble-stone streets of Florence glistened in the subdued mid-afternoon light. They were finishing a bottle of Chianti and had just ordered a demitasse of coffee. In recent weeks they had developed the happy routine of whiling away Mona's day off afternoons by lingering for hours in side-walk cafes, visiting museums, window-shopping, and strolling the streets planning their future together. Mike reached and took both of Mona's hands in his and sat staring into her eyes. She blinked and shook her head in question.

"Miss Mona Lisa Bartalucci," Mike said, "I don't really know you…but I do love you…anyway."

Mona Lisa sipped the last droplet from her wine glass and squinted at Mike.

The demitasse arrived and the waiter poured cups of coffee. Mona sipped hers, frowned, and then added sugar, tasted again, smiled, and then said, "My name is Mona Lisa Bartalucci and I'm five feet two inches tall and l weigh…well never mind what I weigh, and I'm 34 years old, and I'm in love with a big lonely American man. What else do you need to know?"

Mike grinned. "Were you a…virgin when we met?" Mona shook her head. "Hell no! I gave that nonsense up when I was sixteen. And you damn well know it."

Mike laughed. "Gosh Miss Mona, don't get mad."

"I'm not."

"Mi Bella," Mike said, "I know all that, what I mean is what has your life has been like before we met…fell in love."

"If you'll quit being an ass I might tell you."

"Deal! As of this moment my being an ass days are over." Mona squinted. "Yeah, I bet."

"Scouts promise."

"Were you a…what do you American's call them? Boy Scouts?"

"Nope, they wouldn't have me."

"Too much of an ass?"

"Something like that."

"Well, I guess you mean the Teddy-Bear stage of my life?" Mona said. "Yeah, the Teddy-Bear stage and forward. You can leave the virginity part out."

"Michael, you're being an…"

"Ass?"

"You said it. How about the Michel gone to Krista period? Will that do?" Mona Lisa said. Mike hummed and hawed. "More or less. But, you know, more details."

"Like?"

"Well…were you a homely baby…fat…bucked toothed? Stuff like that."

"Well I, as you already know, was born into a very happy family. Hard working Papa and very loving Mama. Dozens of aunts, uncles, cousins and grandparents…good Catholic families with absolutely no idea about birth control. Daddy and all our family loved the Pope and would have never done anything that would cause their *Poppolo* to frown.

That is we were very happy until my three year old brother died of pneumonia in my Mama's arms. Mama and Papa were devastated and things were very sad for many months but eventually life had to go on, but it was never the same again in the Bartalucci house."

"See Sweetheart, there are those things that I don't know about you and your family."

"Those things are past and can't be changed," Mona Lisa said. "I know but I want to be a big a part of your life. I can understand you better when I know what it has been like."

Mona nodded. "Well, moving on with the history of Mona Lisa. When I was six Papa enrolled me in a Catholic school in Florence run by an order of Nuns called *The Holy Order of the River.* The priest, Father Paul, was usually too drunk to administer the day to day stuff so Mama Superior basically ran everything. Sister Kathleen was the meanest woman I have ever known. Kathleen would slap a girl's face just because she didn't look happy at the moment and the revolting and demeaning punishments flowed like the River Arno. Father Paul was a kind man but was too weak to stand up to Sister Kathleen. Father Paul eventually drank himself to death but that was a year or two after Papa had pulled me from the school. Sister Kathleen always said that Father Paul was queer and couldn't live with it and that is why he drank. She hated him and made no bones about it. Our Florentine Bishop had removed Father Paul from the Order a few weeks before he died. I think that is why he died...of a broken heart."

Mike raised a hand. "We civilized folks usually call that *gay*."

"You American's are weird. Do you like gay people?"

"To each his own." Mike said. "Now back to you."

"There was one Nun that was sweet and kind; Sister Teresa. Yes, she was a sweet lady but she was also strong. She was the only sister that would stand up to Mother Superior. Teresa would go nose to nose with Kathleen...and in front of the students. Therefore Teresa was soon transferred to a different Florentine order, the *Sisters of Redemption.* Father Paul tried in his way to fight it but lost without a whimper. Sometimes I think the Bishop was afraid of Kathleen too. But Teresa and I have kept in touch and we see each other often as possible. You'll meet Sister Teresa."

"That's good," Mike said, grinning, "I like Nuns...I think they're sexy."

"Michael you dope. But yes Teresa is very pretty. When we meet she sneaks out without her habit. Big trouble if she's caught. I bought her a wig and designer sunglasses and lipstick. She loves that stuff...

Notices the good looking men, too. Great big eyes for guys that are, what do you American's call it? Hot!"

"That's a dirty *habit*," Mike quipped. "Michael, don't be a moron."

"She notices good-looking men, well that lets me out," Mike said, grinning. "Ha, she'll steal you away...your heart anyway." Mona paused and looked away with a slight smile on her face. "What?" Mike said. "Oh nothing."

"Oh nothing, what?"

"Sister Teresa."

"C'mon Mona, what about Sister Teresa?"

"Well one time I met Sister Teresa for coffee. She was in her *'young woman shopping disguise'* and as we sat and sipped she asked me a very private un-Nun-like question."

"Hmmm," Mike said grinning, "the plot thickens."

"Well Teresa blushed quite red and after mumbling and stumbling, asked me what it was like to be with a...man."

"Surprised I said something like...you mean? And she said yes, that's what I mean."

"Did you tell her?"

"Well yeah, gently at first, but she kept pushing; urging me on."

"And so?"

"And so I gave her the full red, white, and blue."

"I like your Sister Teresa more and more."

"Trust me, she'd be fried in grease if her Mother Superior ever found out," Mona Lisa said.

"Yeah, but you can bet Mama Superior would be very interested in the details." Mona laughed. "That she would."

"Wait just a minute Michael Zorka, you asked me about my virginity. How about yours, big lonely American man?"

"None of your business."

"Michael!"

"Well, let's see. When I was about sixteen there was this twenty something gal that lived next door and she used to have me over once in a while to listen to music."

"And?"

"And well a couple of times we did more than dance to the music."

"Such as?"

"Mona, do I have to draw you a picture?"

"How many times?"

"How many times a day, or total?" Mike grinned. "Mike, you dog."

"Let's say more than once."

"Yeah, well every sixteen or seventeen year old boy needs an older woman to break him in and teach him the tricks," Mona Lisa said.

"I couldn't agree more," Mike said. "Well there is a difference," Mona said. "Yeah."

"Yes, I thought I was in love. It wasn't just sex when I...you know?"

"I thought I was in love with Irma," Mike said. "I certainly loved what we were doing."

"Not love," Mona shook her head. "So what happened to lover-boy? That beast that seduced you and left you a broken-hearted child?"

"He went away to school in Roma, fell in love with another girl and forgot me almost overnight...for a...blond."

"You still miss him?"

"No! Not since I met this American guy named Michael."

"You sure?"

"Oh God damn Michael, what do I have to do to convince you. Crap, I practically wasted away waiting for you. I took whats-his-name on just to get even with you for that Krista thing."

"Enough! So you were Daddy's girl?"

"Papa was my hero, and still is...along with this Mike guy I know."

"Why did you love him so? And still do?"

"Because he loved me and I knew it. And he wasn't afraid to show it."

"How did that ride with your mother?"

"Oh, a little jealous now and then but she always got over it. He doted on me and that annoyed her...a little."

"Did he leave you anything when he died?" Mike asked. "Well he couldn't have known it was coming, but yes, he'd provided something for me just in case."

"Such as?"

"Papa left enough money in a trust to put me through two years of design school and enough extra to set me up in a shop with basic equipment and supplies."

"And why didn't you do that?"

"After I finished the classes Mama became very ill with a breast tumor and I had to go to work. She recovered thank God, but Papa's start-up money had gone away to pay bills and feed us. My job at Traitoria Donatello didn't pay nearly enough." Mona grinned, "Of course I stole food and that helped."

"And wine?"

"Of course."

"Get caught?"

"No, but I think Leonardo knew. He knew we were struggling. He's a good man. Besides, he and Papa were pals."

"Good man."

"He is a good man! How about you and your mother?" Mike looked away. "Well after Dad was killed in that *useless war* Mom grieved for months and couldn't seem to shake it, began drinking to cauterize the wound. The night-life soon followed on the tail of the drinking. Yeah, night after night, kind of looking for, what was the name of that book? *Looking for Mister Good Bar?* She wasn't necessarily being bad; she was looking for love in all the wrong places. She was on her way down when she met Precy Zorka at a meet *the author* thing at our local library. I took her, insisting that she get interested in reading again; find another outlet other than grief and self-destruction. He saved her life. They hit it off and were married three months later. Precy adopted me and became a real father to me. Precy wasn't rich but he'd done okay in real estate and had the money so he and mother could eat out occasionally and do a little travel from time to time."

"That's wonderful," Mona said reaching over and taking Mike's hand. "It's kind of, what would you Americans call it? A Fairy-tale?"

"Yeah, I guess you're right," Mike agreed. "What did your Dad think about all this while looking down from Heaven?" Mona Lisa asked.

"He'd be happy for Mom and he'd be happy for me. He wouldn't have wanted Mom to be alone. Fact is Mom received a letter he'd written from Vietnam three days before he was killed. It arrived the same day two Marines showed up at the door looking for the NOK, *next of kin* with the details that Dad had been killed."

"That's so terribly sad," Mona said with tears in her eyes. "That letter must have torn her heart nearly out."

"Just about," Mike said. "Thank God I was there at the moment. Ten minutes later and I'd have been off to football practice."

Mona slid her chair over closer to Mike. "Do you remember the letter?" Mike grinned. "Yeah, Dad was always pragmatic. His first line of that letter stole a quote from General Douglas MacArthur used during his retirement near the end of the Korean Conflict. MacArthur said something like *'Old soldiers never die, they just fade away.'* So Dad used it to tell Mom to move on in case something happened to him. He wrote, 'Young *soldiers never die, they just go AWOL.'* Then he added, I'll always be around like a feather in the wind, or a single drop of rain, but Sweetheart, I will always remain."

"Mike, your Dad was a poet."

"Yeah, he was very creative guy. Could fix anything, too."

"I would have liked to have known him. Will I eventually meet Precy and your Mom?"

"Can't be too soon. They know all about you. They live in New York but I write to them and call often…even though I hate telephones."

"Yikes! They do?"

"Yeah…well before Krista."

"And now?"

"They're happy I'm with you. Now back to Mona. How about the clothing design?"

"Not much. Kind'a hum-drum. I've bought material from time to time and made and sold a few dresses in Florentine shops but haven't ever really got going. Working six days a week at Traitoria Donatello and helping Mama on my days off doesn't leave much time or energy for Mona."

"We need to work on that," Mike said. "I've seen your work. You are very talented. Besides I need someone who can earn enough money to let me live in the style to which I'm accustomed."

"Yeah, and what might that be?"

"Pasta and red wine on a daily basis with an extra-large serving of Mona Lisa Bartalucci."

"You've seen my designs?"

"Oh duh Mona, I know you make all your own clothes."

# CHAPTER 42

## *Stone Quarry*

Mike Zorka walked alone through a stone quarry on the outskirts of Florence. Mona was at work and after eating his lunch under her care at the Traitoria Donatello he'd driven a borrowed car out to a different stone quarry a few miles outside of Arezzo. He'd learned about this ancient quarry while studying Michelangelo and the craft of sculpture. This particular excavation held extraordinary meaning not only in Michelangelo's life but also for Michael Zorka. His study had indicated that Michelangelo was raised in a family of simple means but with a father who was basically a public servant and never one to have an abundance of money. After his mother had died when he was nine years old his father had sent him to live with a 'nurse-maid' and her husband, a stone-cutter. It was in this very stone quarry that his so-called *god-father* earned a living cutting stone and marble for a myriad of building and sculpting projects in Florence and Rome. It was speculated that Michelangelo's exposure to this man had shaped his life-long passion for cutting stone and sculpture.

Mike felt a pervading sense of deja vu as he walked through the ancient jumble of broken stones and marble fragments. Was it a bit of nostalgia? Had he been here before? The smell of the quarry was present; a smell that was difficult to define. It was an ancient pong, one that he'd experienced before? When? In his outdoor sculpting studio? Or was this an ancient source of memory? He sat on a broken stone and thought about this mood; he so hoped he had been there before. He desired that he had been there during Michelangelo's time; during Donatello's time; during the Renaissance.

As he sat thinking he saw chisel cuts on the surfaces of broken stones and marble fragments, were these left by Michelangelo's Godfather? Had Michelangelo been here and made cuts? Were some of these cuts made by Donatello? Mike could only hope as he ran his fingers over the ancient chisel and mallet wounds.

Gazing around the quarry he saw things that he felt he'd *seen* before. Directly across from him on an edge of the pit water seeped out of the cut-bank and ran freshet-like into a puddle near the center of the excavation. He got up and walked over to the pool, knelt down and with cupped hands tasted the clear, cool water. The water was sweet and fresh. He tasted again and then nodded his head. "I've drank here before," he said aloud, letting the water dribble through his fingers. Then he sat back and looked up at the sky and said aloud, "This is the same sky."

# CHAPTER 43

## *Saint Peter's Square*

"Michael, why are we sitting in the Saint Peter's Square at the Vatican," Mona asked while squinting her yes and nodding at Mike.

"Huh?" Mike said, avoiding her eyes while pretending to admire the architecture.

"Mike, I've been here before. I love Roma but I'm almost too Catholic now."

Mike continued to look away. "Up there on that balcony is where the Pope greets folks."

"No shit, Michael, I didn't know that."

"Mona, be nice."

"I'm being honest. So now, why are we here? I'm hungry, let's go eat."

"You love it here," Mike whispered.

"I do but I'm hungry."

"Mona honey, I'm trying to learn to be a Catholic."

"Why?"

"So your mom will love me."

"She already does, but I don't know why."

"Mona."

"You don't have to become a Catholic, Michael."

"I know but will Father Peter marry us if I'm not Catholic?"

Mona looked at Mike and shook her head. "Who said anything about marriage?"

"Huh?" Mike whispered.

"Shit Mike, you are confusing me."

"Mona, you shouldn't be swearing in the Vatican. Gosh, the Pope might hear you."

"Poppolo probably swears," Mona said. "Heck, some of the ancient popes had wives or concubines and boozed a lot. Some even went to war."

"Mona Lisa Bartalucci that's blasphemous."

"I'm a blasphemous broad."

"You're not a broad. You are the incredibly beautiful Mona Lisa."

Mike put his arms around Mona; she gave him that quizzical look he loved. "I bought you something in the gift shop while you were peeing."

"Michael don't be crude and you very well know I don't like touristy trinkets."

"Well," Mike said, "you can at least look at it. You don't like it, I'll return it and get my two Euros back."

Mona shook her head. "Two Euros might buy me a glass of decent red wine."

Mike handed Mona a gift shop bag. Mona looked at it and shook her head, and said, "If I must," and opened it and peered inside.

Mona inhaled sharply and looked up at Mike. "Michael?"

"Yes Mona."

"Michael is that what I think it is?"

"That's according to what *you* think it is."

"I think it's a ring box."

"Smart girl. Very observant."

"It is?"

"Are you going to open it or are we going to lunch?"

"I'll open it and then we'll…go to lunch."

Mona's hands were shaking as she opened the box. Tears filled into her eyes as she lifted a sparkling diamond engagement ring out of the box. She was shaking so that she nearly dropped the box.

Mike put his arms back around her and kissed her forehead. "Well don't cry about it for God's sake."

"Michael it's beautiful."

"Love it? If not I can take it back to the gift shop, but it's worth a little more than two Euros."

"I love it and I love you and the answer is yes, yes, yes."

"Now you know why the Vatican."

"Now I love the Vatican and I love Roma and I love the Pope and I love life."

"Typical Italian wench," Mike said while slipping the ring on her finger. "Now kiss me before I change my mind and head back to the gift shop."

# CHAPTER 44

## *Baby Bump*

"It's about time," Anna Bartalucci said, smiling and hugging Mona Lisa, "you've failed to cover that belly up very good. Is it what the Americans call a *baby hump*?"

"Baby bump, Mama," Mona Lisa corrected. "Honey, I noticed a month or so ago," Anna said. "Mothers are hard to fool." Mike grinned and hugged Anna. "Yes Mama, we dawdling aliens call it a baby bump. She's beautiful isn't she?"

"I think he will be a wonderful grand baby," Anna ventured.

Mona laughed and hugged her mother. "Mama, he just might be a she."

"Then she will be beautiful just like my baby Mona Lisa. Your daddy would be so happy for you…and for us."

"I know he would Mama."

"But your daddy is in heaven and looking down and smiling at my daughter's beautiful baby hump."

"Bump!"

Anna put her arm around Mike. "So that is why the ring?"

"No," Mike said, "I love your Mona Lisa with or without her baby…hump."

Anna smiled up at Mike. "I told my daughter to be careful with you Americans and now look what you've done to her."

"It's all her fault Mama, she chased me until she caught me."

Mona Lisa punched Mike on the arm. "Yeah, right. Who chased who?"

"Whom," Mike said.

"Who, whom, who or whom cares?" Mona said.

"I forgive you my little daughter, this Michael is irresistible. You better hang on to him."

"She's nothing to worry about Mama."

"We'll name him Joseph just like your daddy," Anna said.

"Funny name for a baby girl," Mona Lisa said.

"If he's a girl we'll name her Josephina," Anna said.

"Mama, Michael and I might have something to say about his or her name."

"No, no, let his grand mama names him."

"Or her."

Suddenly tears began streaming down Anna's face. "My little girl is going to have a baby. I'm a so happy."

"I'm happy too Mama," Mona Lisa said.

"Oh and please let Father Peter marry you," Anna said.

"Yes Mama," Mona Lisa said," Michael and I will talk to Father Peter."

# CHAPTER 45

## *Father Peter*

"C'mon Michael," Mona pleaded, "at least see Father Peter and let him get to know you. After all he might marry us and you're not Catholic. It'll be tough at the least. He is a very old school Catholic…a no nonsense priest."

Mike scowled. "So how long have you known this Father Peter and what makes you think he'll go against the canons of his faith to marry a heathen like me?"

"Father Peter baptized me a week after I was born. Trust me he knows me well. And…Zorka my friend…you are not a heathen, so shut up about that."

"You have some kind of twist on Father Peter?"

"No, but he has often told me that if he'd had children he would want me for his daughter."

"He loves you. Horney old man!"

"Michael, stop."

"Just kidding, but I'm sure he thinks you are incredibly beautiful and…well…sexy."

"No!" Mona warned.

"Well he is a male," Mike said. "I've always wondered how celibate young priest handle having gorgeous young girls in their flocks. Must be difficult."

"He loves all his flock equality," Mona Lisa offered. "The word is equally," Mike corrected. "Yeah, he couldn't help but dream about a beauty like you."

"Michael you moron, he's a priest. Priests don't think like that."

"Yeah?"

"Yes."

"What make you think so?"

"His faith."

"Yeah, well his holiness is, again, a male."

"Enough Mike Zorka."

Mike and Mona were finishing a lunch at a sidewalk café. Mike swirled his cappuccino cup and finished the remains. "I'm a religious nothing. The only time I've ever been in a church is for funerals or weddings. I was never baptized."

Mona Lisa frowned. "Michael, that means you can't go to heaven."

"It's Purgatory for me," Mike said.

"That doesn't mean you don't believe in God."

Mike grinned. "Has anyone ever seen God?"

"No but has anyone ever seen air? But Michael it is all around us, as is God."

"Where?"

"Where?" Mona asked. "You know damn well where. The Cathedral!"

"You mean that church place?"

"Yes, that church place. The Cathedral of Saint Patrick's of the River."

"The river?"

"Yes dummy, the Arno."

"That where Father Pete hangs out?"

"Michael, you're being an ass, and don't ever call him Father Pete."

"Well people call me Mike."

"You are a Mike."

"But I like Michael."

"I call you Michael...most of the time."

"Do you think Michelangelo was ever called Mike?"

"Michael, you are being dumb. But he was probably called Maestro."

"Maestro?"

"Yes…master."

"You can call me maestro any time you want. You know am your master."

Mona scowled and gave Mike a playful shove. "Dream on… maestro."

"Maestro…I like that."

"I'll call you something nasty if you don't go with me right now," Mona warned.

Father Peter Dominique was sitting in the Cathedral garden, sipping tea and smoking his pipe. He looked up and sprang to his feet with a huge smile on his face, his wooden Cross of the Crucifixion swinging wildly from a leather tong around his robed neck. He moved quickly to Mona and with his arms encircled her in a powerful bear hug. Mona caught her breath and grinned at Mike.

"Mona Lisa my daughter," he said, then leaned away and beheld her eyes. He shook his head and turned to Mike," This girl is so beautiful that at times I question my commitment to celibacy."

Mike stood thinking, "I might like this guy after all."

"Father Peter," Mona said, "you're embarrassing me."

Father Peter laughed. "Let us pray the Pope did not hear me, but priest or not, I am a man and exceedingly fond of feminine charms."

Father Peter unwrapped his arms from Mona and turned to Mike reaching out his hand to shake. "I've heard so much about you Michael from this lovely child."

"Thank you Father," Mike said, "I'm sure she exaggerates."

"Not at all. She tells me you put Michelangelo to shame with your fabulous sculptures."

Mike scowled and shook his head at Mona Lisa. "Not at all."

"Sit down children, I've been expecting you for days. "I've a fresh pot of tea here and cookies. Please enjoy."

Father Peter reached across the table and took one of Mona's hands in his. "You love birds want me to marry you here in my Cathedral."

"Yes, very much so, Father," Mike said, "but I'm sure you know that I'm not Catholic."

Father Peter nodded his head, released Mona's hand and picked up his cup of tea and sipped. He sat thinking for a long moment and then turned back to Mike and Mona. "That is a problem."

"Insurmountable I presume?" Mike said.

Father Peter nodded and reached and retrieved Mona's hand again. "I've been a priest for 40 years and in the name of love and the Holy Father, I will find a way. Of course, if I do this, the Pope may very well put me out to pasture. If not burn me at the stake."

Mona got up and moved quickly around the table and gave Father Peter a hug and a kiss on the cheek. He clearly blushed and laughed. "For a hug and a kiss like that even the Pope would find a way."

"So Father we can, I mean you can...do it?" Mona Lisa pleaded.

Father Peter looked toward the sky and placed his hands in the prayer position. "Yes daughter, but we must move quickly." Then he smiled, removed his Cross of the Crucifixion from around his neck and with his right hand reached and placed the cross gently against Mona's swollen belly.

Mona blushed and patted her belly and the cross. "Father, this is a love-child with or without matrimony."

Father Peter kept his hand and the cross against Mona's belly and said a prayer for the baby, Mona, and Mike. Then he looked up, smiled at them both and said, "I think I should say a prayer for myself."

# CHAPTER 46

## *The Belfry*

"Look Michael," Mona said as she stood at the Cathedral belfry port window looking down at the flowing Arno river, they had just gazed down to see Father Peter in his favorite place puffing on his pipe apparently absorbed in profound thought. "It's beautiful. I've never loved that river before but I do now. The garden where we planned our wedding and pleaded for Father Peter to marry us is right below the tower."

Mike stepped up behind Mona and put his arms around her, looking down over her shoulder to the river. "It is our river," he said," so maybe our baby's middle name should be Arno."

"Wouldn't that be lovely," Mona whispered, and then she turned to Mike. "What will our baby's first name be?"

Mike thought for a moment. "How about Anna?"

"Mama would be thrilled but what kind of a name would that be for…let's say…a little Michael?"

Mike turned Mona Lisa back to the window and put his arms around her again. "Well it won't for sure be Michael."

"We'll see," Mona said.

Mike kissed Mona on the back of her neck. Mona sweetheart, do you know something I don't?"

Mona turned back to Mike. "First off don't kiss me on the back of my neck, you know what that does to me."

"Yeah I know."

"Yeah, it inflames me. Wait until tonight," Mona Lisa said.

"Mona you are not answering me. Are you avoiding something?"

"Nope!"

"Well then?"

"It is a beautiful river, isn't it?" Mona whispered.

"Yes but it has trash floating in it," Mike said.

"Does not."

"Pizza boxes."

"Leaves and grass."

"Looks like trash to me."

"Michael stop."

"Mona, you are still not answering me."

Mona turned, rose up on her toes and kissed Mike. "Well I did see Doctor Della Valle this morning."

"Mona, stop," Mike pleaded. "What?"

"Well just maybe a little Michael."

Mike wrapped his arms around Mona. "How so?"

Mona turned back to the port window. "Well there is something called a sonogram."

"Mona sweetheart, what did Della Valle say?"

"Well he thinks that he could see a little...boy thing."

"Mona...and legs and fingers and toes and all that?"

"Seems so," Mona said.

Mike scooped Mona up in his arms and kissed her. "I've just decided," he said."

"Decided what?"

"What we'll name him."

"Yeah?"

"Yeah."

"What?"

"Peter."

"After Father Peter?" Mona said. 'Why not Pietra?"

"Yes for Peter and no for Pietra."

"Do I have anything to say about it?" Mona said.

"None what-so-ever."

"Well I had something to do with it," Mona protested.

Mike grinned. "Yeah, but I had the tough part."

Mona gave Mike a playful shove. "Yeah right, poor boy."

# CHAPTER 47

## *Home is Where the Heart Is*

"Home is where the heart is," Mike said as he examined the tiny kitchen refrigerator. He was down on his knees exploring the interior of the small appliance. "We won't be able to store much in this silly thing."

"So what's wrong with it?" Mona said.

Mike smiled up at Mona. "Well a quart of milk and half a dozen eggs will fill it."

"So?"

"So in the U.S. our friges are huge. You can store a month's supply of food in them."

"You American's are extravagant," Mona said, "you always want more than you need. In Italy we shop each morning for the day's meals. That way everything is fresh."

Mike reached up and grasped Mona's leg. "That's why I chose you, Sweetheart. I wanted so much more woman."

Mona rolled her eyes and brushed Mike's hand away. "You didn't choose me, I chose you."

"Yeah, right," Mike said. "Who started this flirtation business at Traitoria Donatello? You know, extra wine and bread...followed by a not asked for desert. Hmmmm!"

"Huh," Mona said, "you did. I was just a poor innocent little girl doing her job...trying to earn a living for herself and her widowed mother."

"Ha," Mike said," Italian wench on the hot prowl."

"Weren't not."

"Yeah, innocent big lonely American tourist was taken advantage of by Italian wench."

"You loved it."

"Still do," Mike said standing and kissing Mona on the forehead.

"And what's this home is where the heart is thing?" Mona said. "One of your American colloquial thingies?"

"Wow! Mona is using big words," Mike kidded.

"Glad you notice," Mona said.

"It's a known truth," Mike said, "in America our hearts are in our homes."

"Hmmm..."Mona said," I like that."

"Yes," Mike said, "in the U.S. we go the whole nine yards."

"There you go again Michael. What does that mean?"

"Well basically it means we go all the way."

"Why don't you just say we go all the way?" Mona asked.

"It's kind of talking in circles," Mike said, grinning.

"There you go again. How does someone talk in circles?"

"Just like this. I'm talking around the subject."

"Oh, the whole nine yards of it," Mona added.

"Yeah."

"Okay, why nine yards? Why not five yards, or six feet?" Mona asked.

"Because the whole nine yards is historical."

"Historical?"

"Yeah, during World War Two, while you Italians were cuddling with the Nazi SS...,"

"Stop right there Professor," Mona raised her hands. "El Duce was cuddling the Germans, not we true Italians."

"Mona sweet you weren't even born then. You weren't more than a twinkle in your Daddy's eye. How can you be so sure?"

"Michael don't be crude about my Papa's eyes and my grand mama and grand papa told me all about that awful war. My great uncle Markos died fighting for the Americans."

"After they got smart and coalesced."

Mona squinted at Mike. "What does that mean?"

"Change your mind and agreed. Something like that."

"They learned to hate the Germans."

"Yeah, after Mussolini was shot and hung upside down in a gas station."

"The Italian people were sick of Mussolini's war mongering too. He was a monster."

"Yeah my great Uncle Michael died at Anzio during the beach landing. He was only 19."

"Michael, the whole nine yards?"

"Oh yeah, World War Two. Well the American fighter planes held machinegun belts with nine yards of bullets in them. Sometimes it took the whole nine yards of bullets to bring down an enemy fighter plane in a dog-fight."

"A dog-fight? Why don't they call it a cat-fight?" Mona asked.

"Mona don't be difficult, you know what I mean."

"Mona laughed. "Go on Professor."

"So this little colloquialism became a standard comment when someone wants to say it took all they had to accomplish something or they use all of something else to get a little done."

"What's a coll...thingy," Mona asked.

"Oh God," Mike said," how do I describe a colloquialism? Well using a different term to describe something other than the way you would normally use."

"Huh?" Mona said, shaking her head in misunderstanding.

"Never mind," Mike said.

"Is there gonna be a quiz on this, Professor?"

"No but you'll pay for it."

"I bet I will. You Americans are all crazy, you know that?" Mona said.

Mike shook his head. "Nope, I'm part Italian now, and you are part American."

"What makes you think so?" Mona said.

"What is it we did to produce your present state? You did have *some* American in you."

"Michael your being crude again."

"Ain't not. But you are part American now because you've got that little American-Italian guy in your tummy. He's probably mostly American."

"Dream on big lonely American man."

Mike followed Mona Lisa through the apartment as she made her plans for a few perfunctory renovations. Mike noticed that her eyes sparkled as she talked and was so excited she failed to complete some sentences before starting the next. Mike laughed, shook his head, and took one of her hands as they continued through the little apartment.

"This will be the baby's room," Mona said, waving her hands about the tiny room.

Mike raised his free hand, "Wait, this is our bedroom. The only bedroom."

"Yes," Mona said, "but we'll call it the baby's room."

"Yeah, but when he's older are we still gonna be able to...you know...here?"

Mona shook her head no. "No Michael we won't be doing it anymore by then."

Mike put his arms around Mona, picked her up and laid her gently on the bed. "In that case we'd better start making up for the time we'll lose."

Mona laughed and kissed Mike. "Michael, we'll always manage to find a place to...do it."

"Can we use this place right now?"

"Practice makes perfect. Isn't that one of your America collo... qual...issys?"

"Ha, that was close," Mike kidded. "But will it hurt the baby?"

"Silly boy."

"What would Della Valle say," Mike asked.

"He doesn't have to know." Mona said. "Besides...it is doing the comes natural. Isn't that one of your..."

"Colloquialism!" Mike interjected.

# CHAPTER 48

## *Something Happened*

"What's wrong Mona?" Mike asked while watching Mona gasping for breath. They were eating dinner at Traitoria Donatello. Leonardo was watching Mona from the kitchen with an expression of concern on his face.

Mona sat quite still shaking her head and not answering Mike. Both her hands were pressed tightly against her stomach. The color had drained from her face and she began breathing hard, taking in quick little gasps of air and then holding it.

Leonardo came out of the kitchen and walked to their table. He looked at Mike and shook his head.

"Mona?" Mike said again.

"Daughter?" Leonardo said in English placing his hand on Mona's shoulder.

Mike reached and took Mona's hand. "Honey, what's wrong?"

Mona managed a smile and reached up and put her hands on Leonardo's.

"Nothing at all," she whispered.

"Mona Lisa Bartalucci?" Mike said.

"Daughter?" Leonardo repeated.

"Indigestion, I think," Mona whispered.

"From my food?" Leonardo said. "Never!"

"Try again," Mike said.

Leonardo stood nodding. "It'sa the baby, no?"

Mona nodded yes.

"Why the pain Honey? Tell us," Mike begged.

Mona looked up at Leonardo. "There's a little pain when I...bleed some."

"Then we're going right now to find Doctor Della Valle," Mike said starting to get up.

Mona grabbed his hand. "No, this is common. Lots of women have pain and bleeding when they're pregnant."

Leonardo stood shaking his head no toward Mike. "It's not so. Mi Carla has make'a five babies and no bleeding."

"Yeah," Mike said. "Now listen to Leonardo."

"I'm better," Mona said. "We can see Doctor in the morning. But it's nothing."

"Let's go home and I'll put you to bed. I'll call Della Valle tonight and get an appointment for first thing in the morning."

"Right after coffee," Mona managed a smile.

"Okay, right after coffee," Mike promised.

"And breakfast."

"And breakfast, for God's sake."

"And let's take some of Leo's wonderful pastries home for breakfast," Mona begged.

"Honey, you don't need pastries. You need eggs and milk and fruit," Mike countered.

"Michael!"

"Yes Mona."

"Mama will know what to do about the bleeding. We don't need Della Valle."

"Mona Sweetheart, Mama is a wonderful lady but this is a concern for Doctor Della Valle."

"No!"

"Yes. Mona this is my baby too and you are my baby too."

"I know. Leo, can we take some pastries home?"

# CHAPTER 49

## *The Wedding*

Anna Bartalucci looked rather young and pretty in the dress Mona and Mike had bought her a week before the wedding ceremony in the *Chapel on The River*. The basilica was fixed in a Florence Cathedral called Saint Patrick's in a lovely venue on the banks of the Arno River; a watercourse that graciously smote the City of Florence nearly in half. On this soft early afternoon Anna Bartalucci had tears in her eyes as she turned to see Mona and her Uncle Savo Bartalucci beginning the walk down the aisle toward Father Peter and the Catholic alter. Savo had begged to be the one to give his favorite niece away. Anna resisted at first thinking only of her deceased husband and Mona's father but eventually relented feeling that Joseph Bartalucci would have been pleased that his brother would step in. Father Peter Dominique had jumped through dozens of Vatican hoops to convince his bishop that Michael Zorka was in the process of being confirmed in the Catholic Faith and that God, and the Pope, would not frown on this union. The evening before the wedding he had knelt alone in the chapel praying passionately that he was not committing a sinful act in the eyes of the Father, the Son, and the Holy Ghost. Very privately he'd recalled the feeling of a warm hand on his shoulder just at the moment he said amen. Now feeling that Jesus Christ had just blessed him he arose, smiled into the chapel dome, and went to bed feeling that he was doing God's work by blessing Michael Zorka and Mona Lisa Bartalucci in matrimony.

Michael had hoped that the organ music would be the traditional Wedding March used mostly by anglophiles and then as its heart-thrilling descant commenced he felt his stomach constrict, he began to tremble fighting back what could have easily been tears of joy and happiness. He stood there thinking about how was it possible that an American could come to Italy and discover, mostly by chance, the woman he would love and spend the rest of his life with? Was it fate? Was it fortuitous? Was it God's plan? Was it an accident? It didn't matter to Michael Zorka because he was here in Florence, Italy in the Cathedral of Saint Patrick of The River standing next to Father Peter, and he was about to take Mona Lisa Bartalucci as his wife. Michael thrilled at the thought that not only was he marrying the woman of his dreams but that she was also carrying their love-child snuggled tenderly and very much loved in the warmth and affection within her perfect body.

Momentarily Anna stood, kneeled and made the sigh of the Holy Cross toward the alter, then rose up and turned toward her daughter and brother-in-law as they approached her pew. She smiled and threw her daughter a kiss. Tears were streaming down her cheeks. Mona's free hand reached out and lightly touched her mother's as she passed her mother's pew. The congregation was now standing looking toward Mona and her Uncle. Mike sensed a quiet joy throughout the cathedral.

Behind Father Peter Mike could see the remains of a severely weathered Cross of the Crucifixion with the body of Christ pinioned through feet and hands with paths of crimson blood seeping from the stigmata of the *Crown of Thorns.*

Mike had never given much credit to the off and on reports of people throughout the world of Christianity suffering the Stigmata, however recent reports and historical records had boosted his acceptance. His and Mona's visit to the Cathedral at St. Francis of Assisi and having learned that St. Francis himself suffered the Stigmata accompanied with Mona's undying faith had convinced him that this portent was real. Having always considered himself a religious nothing he'd begun to feel *'the presence'* in his life and having lived with Mona Lisa and becoming enmeshed in her faith and love of the Catholic

Church. Father Peter of the Cathedral of the River had convinced him that altruism existed in the hearts and souls of certain people. Mike had not consented or acquiesced to becoming a Catholic but had had assured Mona, Anna, and Father Peter that he would always respect their beliefs without question. Father Peter had received him 'cautiously' into the *Family of the Lord* without demand or disapproval. However, the Bishop and the Pope had been nefariously led to believe that Michael Zorka was in the process of conversion. Father Peter had confessed his little fabrication to God during his evening prayers hoping that the Angels of Wisdom would turn their pious heads.

Mike stood stiffly beside Father Peter and his best man, Mario Lucca, who had flown in from Carmel by the Sea to be with them on this wonderful day. Isabella Lucca and two of her daughters walked as bridesmaids for Mona. Mike's tuxedo was too small for his large frame and the collar of the shirt had failed to button properly leaving the bowtie askew and a source of embarrassment. He had discovered that the rental of an appropriate tuxedo in Florence was akin to buying Texas-style cowboy boots; neither was to be easily found. He had obviously seen Mona on this halcyon morning as they had always spent the nights together since the day of his return to Florence. However, within minutes she had disappeared in the company of Anna Bartalucci and the Lucca girls. Now, radiantly dressed in a flowing white gown holding an exquisite bouquet with a lengthy wedding-train being carefully monitored by the Chelsea, youngest Lucca girl.

Mona and her Uncle approached the priest both kneeling and making the sign of the Cross. Father Peter cleared his throat and began the ceremony in Italian. Mike had learned enough of that romantic language to understand most of what was being said. He stood there thanking Mona Lisa for her insistence that he begin speaking Italian often. In the beginning he struggled but as time had gone on he'd found it easier and easier.

Mike watched as the two candles were lit symbolizing that at this moment he and Mona were still two individuals. He already knew that when the marriage vows were complete a center candle would be lit to symbolize their love and life together from that day on.

Father Peter began the ceremony with a warm smile toward the two lovers. "Although life is a gift given to each of us as individuals, we also learn to live together in harmony. Love is a gift to us from family and friends. Through these gifts of love we learn on behalf of ourselves to give back. Learning to love and live together is one of life's greatest challenges and is the shared goal of a married life."

Mona looked toward Mike and smiled. He nodded faintly. Father Peter went on.

"As you Mona Lisa Bartalucci and Michael Zorka travel through life together, I caution you to remember that the true measure of success, the true avenue to joy and peace, is to be found within the love you hold in your hearts. I would ask that you hold the key to your hearts very tightly."

Mike chanced a hurried look at Mona Lisa and saw she was smiling and nodding in agreement with Father Peter. Mona's Uncle Savo seemed to be squinting at Michael as if to endorse something like "You had better treat my niece well or else." Mike smiled at Savo and nodded. Savo didn't smile back. In her seat on the isle at the front Anna Bartalucci was crying openly and dabbing at her eyes with a handkerchief.

"And so today," Father Peter continued, "is truly a glorious day which the Lord hath made, as today both of you are blessed with God's greatest of all gifts, the gift of abiding love and devotion between a man and a woman. All present here today and those in heart wish both of you all the joy, happiness and success the world has to offer."

The ceremony continued with all the traditional Catholic tenets and ended with Father Peter's closing prayer and cheerful blessing.

"Let us pray with confidence to the Father, in the words he gave us: Our Father, who art in heaven, hallowed be thy name, thy kingdom come, thy will be done on earth, as it is in heaven. Give us this day our daily bread; and forgive us our trespasses; as we forgive those who trespass against us, and lead us not into temptation, but deliver us from evil. Amen."

With Father Peter's offer Michael kissed Mona Lisa and turned back to the priest. Father Peter reached out and took each of their hands. "God bless you both and I pray for your long, happy, and successful lives together. I am pleased to present to those gathered here, Mr. and Mrs. Michael Zorka."

A cheer went up throughout the congregation as organ music suddenly filled the chapel. Mike and Mona Lisa, hand in hand, turned and retreated back up the isle to the courtyard where they were to greet family and the members of the congregation.

# CHAPTER 50

## *Wedding Reception*

When Mona and Mike walked into Traitoria Donatello they were delighted to see the jubilant greeting they were receiving from Mona's employer, Leonardo Bonicelli. Leonardo, called Leo by everyone who knew him, had closed the restaurant for the day and decorated extravagantly with Silver bells strung from colorful red, white and green ribbons, the colors of the Italian National flag. At the back wall several dinner tables had been pulled together, draped in the same flag colors and set with several uncorked bottles of red and white Italian wines. A similar table nearby was set with an assortment of Leonardo's finest desserts. The traitoria sparkled with elation and joyfulness. Leonardo quickly tossed his jacket and tie aside and disappeared into the kitchen where a three course meal had been prepared for the wedding revelers; several pastas, fish dishes, and red meats. A giant wooden bowl of Italian-style salad appeared immediately across the counter where dishes, forks and knives were stacked in ready. Several loaves of heated garlic bread stood piled on a wood table next to the salad bowl. Leonardo's wedding gift to the newly-weds was this overgenerous reception. Earlier that morning while smoking a cigar in his and Joseph Bartalucci' traditional piazza he had looked up into the sky where he knew his old friend would be and said, "Joseph my friend I will take care of your Mona Lisa."

Twenty-five members of the wedding congregation filed into the restaurant behind Mona and Mike. The food and wines were consumed amidst a raucous prattle not unlike most Italian restaurants. As the bottles of wines dwindled the chatter rose in direct proportion to the enthusiastic consumption of wine and food. Mario and Annabella Lucca and their children were introduced as special wedding guests from the United States and were happily ordained by Father Peter as true Florentines. Father Peter had ended this so tangible honor by saying that he would have given Mario and Annabella the key to the city but he couldn't find it and related it to "what you Americans call, *a senior moment.*"

Finally it was time for Mona's uncle Savo to speak. Mike had been told that it was very traditional for an immediate member of the bride's family to give a speech. In light of the fact that Mona Lisa's father was dead the honor advanced to Savo. Savo stood shakily at his table, hanging somewhat precariously to the back of his chair. His face was flushed from his profound consumption of Chianti. He spoke in English:

"In the beginning, when this G.I. Joe Americano began chasing my beautiful niece Mona, I had a notion to...well...kick his ass, but in time he won me over...a little. But I still think he's a prick...but an okay prick."

At this time Mona interrupted her uncle. "Uncle Savo...please stop."

Savo raised his hand to quiet Mona. "I'll go on. The reason he is a good and acceptable prick is because of him we are going to have a new Bartalucci in the family."

Mona stopped him again. "Uncle Savo...our baby will be a Zorka."

At this point Savo walked behind Mike's chair, leaned down, and kissed him on top of the head. "Welcome Michael to the Bartalucci family."

Mona again. "Zorka...it is Mona and Michael Zorka...not Bartalucci."

"Yes I know that my beautiful niece, but your little guy will always be a Bartalucci."

Mike got up and gave Savo a bear hug. The two men traded European kisses in the traditional style. Savo pushed Mike back. "Welcome brother...however, if you ever mistreat my beautiful..."

Mona again. "Savo...stop."

"Savo mi brother in law, then I will kill you," Anna Bartalucci interrupted.

"Sister?" Savo pleaded.

# CHAPTER 51

## *Leonardo Bonicelli*

Leonardo Bonicelli watched from the kitchen of Traitoria Donatello and was more than elated watching the wedding party eating, drinking wine, and prattling Italian-style about the happy couple and the joy the future held for them and the soon to arrive baby boy. Leonardo was proud that he had footed the entire cost for Mike and Mona Lisa's wedding reception. Leo loved Mona like a daughter but had learned early on that she could be contrary and challenging. He and Mona's father Joseph had been best friends since childhood.

Sundays for Leonardo and Joseph had always been reserved for Bocce Ball at a local park and then, after several hard-fought games, cigars on a bench near the fountain at Piazza Santa Croce. In the beginning of their Sunday excursions they'd usually ended the day with a bottle of wine or two in the park but when the two controlling wives discovered their tipsy husbands wobbling home they quickly put an end to the Piazza wine-bar. Both men took turns providing the cigars and they were never the cheap ones you could find in the local tobacco shops. Joseph and Leonardo refused to settle for less than Partagas, Monte Christos or Romeo and Juliets; cigars that cost them in the neighborhood of ten or fifteen Euros each. This extravagance was easily hidden from their wives by arriving home with a pocket bearing one or two of the two dollar cigars you can get in some local tobacco shop. This habit forced both men to watch their extra change all during each week.

Afternoons in Piazza Santa Croce with cigar smoke billowing around their heads Joseph and Leonardo argued about politics, money, and women, while jokingly demeaning one another. One of Joseph's favorite digs at Leonardo was why he had named his restaurant Traitoria Donatello and reminding Leonardo that Donatello was one of those kind of guys that liked men better than women. Leonardo always said that he was an art lover and Donatello was a master sculptor. "Are you one of those kinds of men?" Joseph would joke. But at the end of the day they always exchanged affectionate hugs and the tradition Italian two-cheeked kiss and parted as surrogate brothers.

Weekdays Joseph never missed his morning cups of coffee at Traitoria Donatello while walking to work and of course Leonardo refused to accept one cent in payment. However, Joseph always left a small tip for which-ever waitress attended him. In the early days Leonardo would often beg Joseph to bring his beautiful daughter Mona Lisa with him, but Joseph always retorted that the couldn't risk his daughter around a *snake* like Leo Bonicelli.

When Joseph died Leonardo wasted no time in helping Anna and offering Mona a job at the Traitoria. There had been those days when Leonardo nearly regretted his decision to give Mona Lisa a job; she could be difficult, but on the other hand, the customers loved her attention and she was hard working and very good at what she did. Leonardo had even let her display some of her clothing designs in one corner of the restaurant. A number of women had admired her work and on several occasions made purchases. The extra money had helped Mona and her mother endure. Mona often ruminated that if her father had not died; she wouldn't have gone to work for Leonardo and would not have met Michael Zorka. Mona was somewhat of a mystic, and she'd decided that it was meant to be. The fact that Michael had gone back to the United States and fallen in love with Krista Coleman, and then returned to Italy, convinced Mona Lisa that she and Mike's life together was meant to be and that their forthcoming child had been merely biding his time somewhere out there in Nirvana. It was now, as it had always been meant to be. Mona believed that each person's life was written in the big book and that it would go that way without effort or evasion.

# CHAPTER 52

## *Remains of the Night*

"Mona, are you okay?" Mike had just walked into their bedroom and found Mona doubled up on the bed.

"Yes," Mona whispered, without looking up from where her face was buried in a pillow.

Mike sat on the edge of the bed and put his hand on Mona's arm. "You're hot."

"It's nothing."

"Honey, what's wrong?"

Mona kept her face in the pillow.

"Honey?"

Mona drew her face out of the pillow and there were tears in her eyes. Her face was flushed. "I'm bleeding a little. I'm sure it's nothing."

"You are in pain. I can see that."

"A little. No…badly."

"Come on, we're going to the hospital," Mike ordered.

"No Michael, don't make me. I can't face Doctor Della Valle right now."

"We need to go, Honey."

"All I want to do is sleep. I'm so tired," Mona whispered into the pillow.

"Honey, the bleeding."

"It's has stopped…I think."

"You aren't sure."

"Yes, I'm pretty sure."

"Can I look?"

"No you can't."

Early the next morning Mike drew in a deep breath when he saw the huge splotch of blood on the sheet between Mona Lisa's legs. He lay back down and put his arms around her. He realized he was trembling.

Mona stirred. "Michael why'd you wake me up? I was sleeping so well. I was having this lovely dream about our baby."

Mike kissed Mona on the back of her head. "Sweetheart, we need to go to the hospital now. You need to see Doctor Della Valle."

"Uh ah, I'm all better. I don't hurt anymore."

"You're still bleeding," Mike whispered.

"How do you know?"

"I looked."

"You didn't?"

"Five minutes ago."

"Michael, mind your own business."

"You and our Baby are my business," Mike whispered.

"Okay," Mona said, "but first I want a cup of coffee."

"I'll make it right now."

"And then boiled eggs and toast."

When Mona said *toast* Krista Coleman's Mr. Pop-up toaster flashed through his mind. "Shit, he thought, an omen? No!"

"Mona Lisa you're being difficult. You're stalling," Mike said.

"I'm not. I just don't want to bother Doctor Della Valle over nothing. I'll be all right, you'll see."

"C'mon, honey. We need to go."

"No Michael."

"We'll see Doctor Della Valle right away even if I have to tie you up and carry you."

"Michael, I didn't know you were into, what do you American's call it, binding?"

"*Bondage,* and I never have been and never will be."

"Sounds scary."

"It is," Mike said, "now I need to change the bed."

"Coffee first."

Mike went to the kitchen and brewed coffee, filled two cups and returned to the *'Baby's Room.'* Mona was asleep curled into a ball, her legs drawn up around her belly. Mike went back to the kitchen and called Doctor Della Valle's office.

# CHAPTER 53

## *That Mona Lisa Smile*

Michael," Dr. Della Valle said in English, "I'm afraid there are some complications with Mona's pregnancy."

The Doctor stood quietly waiting for Mike's response. Mike stood very still staring straight into Dr. Della Valle's eyes. Then he shifted and looked out a large hospital window into a grove of trees supported by a frost-bitten yellowing lawn. Fall leaves buried much of the lawn and a myriad of birds fluttered about scattering leaves and competing for the first unlucky worm.

"Is my English okay?" Della Valle asked. "Do you understand me?"

Mike looked back at Della Valle and drew in a deep breath. "Oh… yes Doctor."

"And?"

"What are Mona's problems? I know the bleeding and pain are not right," Mike whispered.

Della Valle Shrugged. "There's a possibility she'll miscarry the child…but she'll survive."

"Why did you say that? Is there a chance she might not?"

"There is always a chance…a slim chance…but Mona is a healthy young, strong girl…I see no real danger. And Michael, if she loses the child she'll still be able to have babies…I'm certain."

"And exactly what is the…prognosis…problems?"

Della Valle shrugged again and turned to the window. "Well…"

"Doctor?"

"Mona has a uterine cyst, or maybe several cysts. We don't know exactly at his moment."

"Oh shit," Mike said. What about cysts? I don't know anything about them."

Della Valle came back to Mike from the window. "Most cysts are benign and create no problems. However, there are cysts that cause profuse bleeding, extreme pain and anxiety. Occasionally they become malignant and yes...can be fatal."

"Are there different kinds? "Mike asked.

Della Valle nodded. "Yes, a variety."

"And what are...or is Mona's?"

"Well for a better name...and one used often by your American doctors...*Chocolate Cyst of the Ovary.*"

"And?"

Della Valle shrugged again. "Well not the worse. There is no sign of cancer."

"Might cancer develop? You will remove the cyst, or cysts, right away?" Mike pleaded.

"Not right away," Della Valle said. "She's lost a lot of blood and she's a bit weak right now. Of course you must understand removal of the cyst is fatal for the child."

"Doctor Della Valle, I love that child but I love my Mona...even more; far more. Please save her life."

"I'm doing everything I can for Mona right now. I've called in other obstetricians and internists for advice and support. And I've assigned nurses to her 24 hours a day."

"Would it help Mona if you induced...the miscarriage?"

"We may have to do that soon. Do I have your permission?"

Mike was fighting back tears, his voice gone hoarse. "Yes, of course."

"Mona is a little delirious at the moment and if we proceed with an abort...induce the miscarriage, we'll need you to sign the papers. However, if that happens it won't be until tomorrow. You should get some rest. You'll need it."

"I need to see her first."

"Yes, you should," Delle Valle agreed.

"When this is over and she's home again?"

Della Valle shrugged. "Bed rest, plenty of good food, and lots and lots of love and understanding...and patience on your part."

"Give her back to me Doctor and I'll do everything I can...and more."

Mike thanked Doctor Della Valle and walked slowly into Mona's hospital room. A nurse sitting near the bed nodded to Mike. "I'll be right outside," she said.

Mike walked to the side of Mona Lisa's bed and softly laid his hand on her bared arm. The arm felt unreasonably hot. He closed his eyes, blinking away tears, and thought that it was time he learned to *pray*. The stuffed animal he had brought her was cuddled against her breast with both arms. At the sound of the door opening behind him Mike turned and saw Anna Bartalucci hurrying in with her cheeks tear-streaked and eyes red rimmed. At the sound of her mother's voice a faint smile touched Mona Lisa's pale façade, although her eyes remained closed. Anna saw the smile and nodded reaching and putting her hand on Mona' forehead.

When Mike and Anna left an hour later Mona was still sleeping. Mike walked Anna home and returned to his and Mona's apartment. The apartment seemed cold and unfamiliar. Mike went into the Baby's Room and lay down on the bed. He placed his head on Mona's pillow and breathed in her scent, then he began to sob and cry out her name.

Mike returned to Mona's hospital room later the same day. She was awake but her skin appeared opaque and her face looked thin and her beautiful dark eyes sunken and unresponsive. The nurse excused herself and Mike sat on the bed next to Mona and held both her hands in his. The stuffed animal was tucked in next to her baby-like, Mona turned toward him and smiled almost imperceptibly.

"My Michael," Mona whispered.

"Stay quiet honey, I just want to sit with you. Don't try to talk."

"I...need...to talk."

"Okay, but go slow."

"Michael, you will take care of our baby won't you and love him forever? This...is not his fault."

Mike turned his head slight away from Mona, fighting back tears. "Sweetheart...we will take care of our baby and love him together."

"Michael."

"Yes?"

"Do you think I'll go to Heaven?"

"Yes Honey, you will, but not for years and years and years."

Mona reached and touched Mike's face. Her hands were fire hot. "If I do go to Heaven I'll watch over both of you all the time."

"Honey, you aren't going anywhere but back to our apartment."

"When I'm gone you can still talk to me. I'll always be listening. You can talk to me at night when you're lonely...if you are lonely."

Mike held Mona's hand and sat with her until she fell asleep. Mike went out and told the nurse to please call him immediately if Mona's situation changed. The nurse assured him that Doctor Della Valle was staying at the hospital and sleeping when he could, in an unused room. Mike walked slowly back to their apartment dreading the emptiness he would find there.

The phone was ringing and pulling Mike out of a troubled slumber. He opened his eyes to a lighted bedroom; he'd fallen off while trying to read an Italian newspaper. Mike's wristwatch indicated three in the morning. The phone was on the bed next to him and with his heart pounding he picked it up and answered. Dr. Della Valle's voice came through weakly and with palpable exhaustion.

"Michael, "Della Valle whispered, "You had better come now."

Less than 20 minutes later Mike was standing in the hallway outside Mona's room. Dr. Della Valle was standing in front of the room door. Mike sensed that the doctor was in effect, blocking the door. Della Valle stood silently looking at Mike with a hint of moisture invading his red-rimmed eyes. Mike grasped the doctor's 'shoulders. Della Valle shook his head and stared down at the floor.

"Too late," he whispered. "I did all I could. I've been with her all night."

Mike stood shaking his head. "No! No Doctor, you're wrong."

Della Valle nodded his head and looked back up at Mike. "Not wrong."

"Our baby?" Mike whispered, looking past Della Valle at the closed door.

Della Valle began to weep openly. "With his mother in Heaven."

Della Valle stepped aside and nodded toward the door.

Mona was lying peacefully with the stuffed animal clutched in both arms. Mike sat on the side of the bed and took one of her hands and held it to his lips and then began to cry. He was all too aware that Mona's small baby-bump was gone. Later he sat stroking her hair as it splayed out across the pillows. Over and over he tried to talk to Mona but words would not come.

At 5:45 a nurse came in and told Mike it was time for him to leave.

Mike wiped his eyes and stood up. "May I have a few more minutes with my wife?"

"Yes, of course," she said and went out closing the door.

Mike sat for a while and then laid down next to Mona and put his arms around her, kissed her and told her good-bye. "I'm not leaving you Sweetheart," he whispered, "because you have already gone up there to Heaven."

At 6 o'clock Mike walked out of the hospital just as the six o'clock bells were ringing from the belfry of the Cathedral of St. Patrick of the River.

# CHAPTER 54

## *Missing Mona Lisa*

The streets of Florence had darkened. The lights were dimed; *or were they?* The evening was cold; an empty cold as Michael Zorka walked slowly and without destination. He walked past side-walk café's, the same one's he and Mona had haunted for their lunches on her days off and patronized during their casual evenings when they wanted to be out and about in this ancient renaissance city. He recalled a favorite past-time of theirs; watching the locals and the tourists, and comparing the actions of both genres. Mona had frequently giggled at the so often tangible confusion of the tourists while the natives always seemed to know where they were going and usually in a hurry.

Michael felt that he cherished those cafes; deep in the memory of how it had been and the details of some of those halcyon times; things like how the weather had been and how Mona had looked and how he had felt her love, and how they'd always chose to sit under umbrellas on the side-walk on those sporadic rainy days rather than be isolated inside. And now, as he walked, places began to call to him; store fronts, flower shops, bakeries, and wines shops, beckoned for him to "come in, come in and see if Mona Lisa is here; she is not gone, she is merely out shopping for your dinner or breakfast; come in and see her; she'll be here." Mike resisted that ensnaring and cruel voice in his head and finally and with deep regret, turned in the direction of he and Mona's apartment. He remembered that she had learned to imitate him and say, *"Home is where the heart is."*

# CHAPTER 55

## *Father Peter*

"Son," Father Peter said softly, "the Lord giveth and the Lord taketh away. He gave you and me and Anna and Joseph, Mona Lisa for a short time, but how lucky we were to have known her for that time. As you already know, I've often thought and said, had I been a father I would have wanted Mona Lisa as my daughter."

Mike and Father Peter were sitting in the garden of the Chapel of St. Patrick of the River. They were sitting at the same table where they had sat planning the wedding. Occasionally Mike's eyes would drift upward toward the belfry, remembering that perfect day when he and Mona had stood up there gazing down at the river and she telling him that "there just might be a little Michael Zorka growing inside her baby bump."

Mike had made the decision to see Father Peter one last time. He would spend his last night alone in he and Mona Lisa's apartment, finish packing and fly back to the United States in the morning. He had also decided that he would never see Florence again; nor Italy. To return to this city of heart-break in the future would be too much. Italy was gone now forever.

"Mona Lisa was worried that she wouldn't go to Heaven," Mike whispered. "She thought maybe because our baby was conceived out of wedlock that God and the church would frown on her."

Father Peter smiled and shook his head. "Do you remember what she said here in this very garden when we were discussing your wedding?"

"I'm not sure."

Father Peter reached and took one of Mike's hands. "She said that your baby was a love-child with or without matrimony. Be assured son that God and Jesus love children and yours is no exception."

"Thank you Father," Mike said.

"So you can rest assured that God and his Angels love and welcome...welcomed Mona and the child into Heaven."

Mike sat fighting back tears. "Father, I want to be with Mona. If I could only find...a way. I feel that my life is over. What is the reason to get up in the morning? What is the purpose of life now? Why should I feel motivation to do anything? I'd like to lie down and die."

"Son, God frowns on suicide. And so would Mona and your child."

"I know."

"Michael, go home and get on with your life. Mona is safe with Jesus now and she'd want you to go on. She has released you to love again."

Mike shook his head. "No, I'm through with that part of my life."

Father Peter nodded." So be it. Can we pray?"

Mike looked up toward the belfry. "Yes Father."

Mike left Farther Peter sitting alone in the garden and began his solitary walk back to his and Mona Lisa's apartment. He again dreaded facing the emptiness there; seeing the things Mona loved and once again, and for the last time, trying to sleep alone in the *baby's room*. As he walked that formidable 'Devil's Advocate' voice began invading his consciousness; questioning him and rebutting his vague or weak rebuttals. He stopped at a sidewalk café, one that he and Mona had not frequented, ordered a café and sat trying to drive the demons out of his head. However, it seemed that this mental tyrant had to have its say before relenting and letting his mind settle back into that recently acquired state of semi-consciousness.

"Go ahead and run home little boy," the voice whispered.

"I'm not running," Mike disputed in his head.

"Yes you are. You're leaving aren't you?"

"There's nothing here for me."

"Yeah, how about Anna Bartalucci?"

"She hates me."

"She doesn't. Time will heal her wounds."

"Yeah, I think time wounds all heals. Besides, she thinks it's my entire fault."

"It isn't."

"She thinks so. But hell, Mona wanted that baby just as bad as I did. Anna was no exception, she wanted to be a grandma."

"Yeah but she's still your mother-in-law. You owe her."

"Owe her what?"

"For God's sake Zorka, how about loyalty?"

"I am loyal but she hates me."

"Anna will realize that in time."

"Well I'm going home. Anna hasn't spoken to me in a month. Hasn't spoken or acknowledged me in any way since the funeral."

Stick around and give her a chance to heal. Look Zorka, she loved that girl and now it'll take time for her to heal. Hell, can't you remember? You became a drunk after Krista Coleman was killed."

"That was yesterday and this is today."

"Gonna become a drunk again?"

"No, I wouldn't do that. My friend Mario Lucca saved my life. I can't let that happen again. Besides, Mona sure as hell wouldn't approve."

"Well Zorka, you're right on that account."

"No matter, I'm leaving on a jet plane in the morning."

"You gonna have to face Krista's death again. You know she's buried nearby."

"I've settled that in my head. All I have is memories of Krista, sort of like smoking ashes."

"You should have gone with her to Santa Fe."

"I know that. It would have saved me a lot of heartache."

"You're a selfish bastard, Zorka."

"I know that too."

"You are nothing but a wasted stone-cutter."

"Yeah, that's what Krista used to tease me about."

"Yeah, so run on home, Stone-Cutter."

"Thank you, I will."

"Wait, who's gonna put flowers on Mona Lisa's grave?"

"Anna will take care of that. Anna and Leonardo and her uncle."

"I guess it's okay; you never took flowers to Krista's grave."

"That's right."

"Why not?"

"It makes me sad."

# CHAPTER 56

## *Dust, Wind and Dreams*

That evening he finished packing Mona's favorite things, having arranged for Savo to pick up those thing he would leave behind, those things that her family would like to have for remembrance's sake. One box was marked *for Anna*. Anna Bartalucci now felt that Mike had caused Mona's death and had verbally disowned him. He had not seen her since the funeral and wouldn't before leaving. The things he'd packed for her would be irreplaceable for Anna.

In Mike's suitcase were those intimate things that had been a part of their life together; Mona Lisa's broken handle Vietri coffee mug that she always held in both hands while sipping her morning cup. Her bible and prayer book were packed as was her pictures and memorabilia album chronicling their life together; photos of their wedding, their trip to the Basilica of Saint Francis, and a myriad of *things* she had picked up during their travels; ticket stubs, colorful napkins, and even the label off a bottle of wine they'd enjoyed the night before their wedding. Mike had discarded some of his own clothing and personal items in order to take more of Mona's things with him. The one item he would have liked to have kept was the stuffed animal she'd held tightly in her arms as she died. But he'd soon realized while making the arrangements for her burial that the little stuffed animal belonged with her and the baby. All three were buried together in the same coffin and it gave Mike some, if little, comfort to know that Mona Lisa and their baby, and the little stuffed animal would be together into eternity. The morning before his last visit with Father Peter Mike had taken the small duffle of the lovingly purchased baby clothes and left with heavy tears at a charity shop near Piazza Croce. He'd retained one small flowered infant sleeper as a tender memory of happier times and what might have been. While packing he'd told himself that he was taking these things *home*, but then the odd notion struck him right out of his subconscious…home? Then he'd had to admit to himself that this renaissance city of Florence, Italy was now, and always would remain, his home; *a home-place* that he would never return to.

# CHAPTER 57

## *Becky*

Becky, Zackary and Mellie were waiting for Mike as he drove into the driveway at his Casa Viejo. The sight of the three young people standing in his driveway gave him a sense of home and for the first time since Mona Lisa's death he felt an aspect of joy. The three were smiling and waving. Suddenly the thought *"this is home now"* entered his emotions. He felt ready to be home and the thought of Florence, Italy and that rather imagined life seemed alien and dreamlike. Had he ever actually gone to Italy? Had he really ever known and loved a girl named Mona Lisa? Was he truly the father of a baby boy now gone to Heaven with his mother? At that moment as he climb out of his rented car he wasn't sure about any of it. But the happy vision of his house carried with it rushed memories of Krista Coleman. Krista had not subjugated his thinking since before his reunion with Mona Lisa, and he was now where Krista had walked, played, and loved.

Straightaway Becky broke away from the other two and ran to Mike wrapping her arms around him and kissing his cheek. Mike felt tears well up in his eyes. Pulling back and looking at her he saw that she was crying. He laughed and hugged her again. "Look at the two of us," he said, "crying like babies."

"Mike, you're home...finally."

"Yes Becky, I am, and I'm here to stay."

Zackary walked over to Mike with his hand outstretched. Mike took the proffered hand.

"Well Mike now I won't have to listen to Becky moaning about missing her…Dad."

Mellie stood next to Zackary with an arm around his leg. "Can you say welcome home to Mike?" Zackary said. Melody stood quietly staring up at Mike. He knelt down to Mellie. "How is that doll I gave you doing? Is she behaving?"

"Ah huh," Melody whispered. "Becky made new clothes for her."

"I bet she's very pretty in her new clothes. I can't wait to see her again. Did you ever give her a name?"

Becky drew in a breath and looked at Zackary.

"Her name is Krissy," Mellie whispered. I'm six now."

Becky locked arms with Mike as they walked toward the house. She looked up at Mike and held him to a momentary pause. "Mike… Dad…I'm so sorry about Mona Lisa. I know you loved her…and the baby very much…and I would have too. I dreamed about when you might bring them here to live with us."

"Wasn't meant to be," Mike said.

"Fact is,' Becky said, "I'd already felt very attached to her via her letters…in difficult English, that is, and her phone calls to me, and of course the photos of you two together. She was incredibly beautiful, or well, *bella.* Heck, I'd already started studying Italian. But gosh, those Rosetta Stone CD's are expensive."

Zackary and Mellie were chasing lizards in the courtyard while Becky and Mike were in the kitchen putting together a lunch of sandwiches, potato salad, chips and ice tea. Mike's jet-lag was nagging but he'd felt a surge of energy just being with Becky and feeling the ambiance of his much-loved Casa Viejo.

"Mike, "Becky said without turning from the counter," I polished up your sculpture tools s and washed off the marble. I hope you'll get right back to work. Carolyn and I are desperate for something of yours to show in the gallery."

"How is Carolyn…and how's the gallery doing?"

"Quite well…both."

"And your sculpting?"

"Ugh! I haven't been very good about it. Too busy with Zack, Mellie and the gallery."

"First things first."

"Yeah," Becky said while turning to Mike. She grinned and then held up her right hand. A diamond ring flashed in the kitchen lights. Mike took her hand and examined the ring.

"You didn't tell me. When?"

"I couldn't have told you, "Becky said, "it just happened last night. We were having dinner at Cabello Blanco while Saffron was watching Melody. I should have known something was up. Zack can't really afford Cabello Blanco. However, that wonderful Mario Lucca comped the bill. Turns out he knew what was up"

"That's our Mario for sure. So…when?"

"Not until June. We've gotta have time to get our finances in shape and so on."

"I'll do a piece for you and Zack's house."

"Mike, you might?"

"Might is the right word actually. I'm not so sure at the moment that I'll ever get back to sculpture."

"You will in time. I know it," Becky assured.

Mike hugged Becky whiles saying "Congratulations Sweetheart. That Zack is one lucky guy. I'd better get out to the courtyard and congratulate my future son-in-law…and granddaughter." Then he turned to go.

"Mike," Becky said, "wait a minute."

Mike turned back. "What honey?"

"You will give me away…won't you?"

# CHAPTER 58

## *Etched in Stone*

Mike got out of a sleepless bed after a Purgatory-styled night of visions of Krista Coleman's body laying cold and alone in the Santa Fe morgue, combined with images of Mona Lisa in death still cuddling the stuffed animal in place of her lost baby. He wobbled into the kitchen, put a pot of coffee on and sat at the table waiting for it to perk. With coffee in hand he wandered out onto his flagstone patio and sat in one of his well-worn Rattan chairs. Looking back through the kitchen window he could see the toaster sitting on the work-space counter. He smiled and looked toward the sky and said, "Krista Honey, your little Mr. Pop-up misses you. And so do I."

He sat in the morning sun sipping his coffee and trying to remember what Krista Coleman and Mona Lisa Zorka had looked like; trying over and over to picture them but the images failed him. "Why is it" he thought aloud, "that I cannot remember their faces? Is this some kind of a defense mechanism?" Probably, he decided. But odd how the faces of two women I loved more than life its self-have escaped me. Before getting up off the chair he thought that it would be a noble idea to pray for the souls of Mona Lisa and Krista, but he didn't, after saying aloud, "For all the good it would do."

After half an hour he took the remains of his coffee and walked to his long-abandoned sculpture bench. A two hundred pound block of Portuguese Rose marble sat abandoned and slightly mossed from months of rainstorms and neglect. He'd ordered the marble after returning from Italy during one of his "Mike Zorka get over it" moods, but then spent days into weeks ignoring it. He brushed several inches of fall leaves off the marble and stood examining the stone. "Weather and pollution not good for marble," he said aloud. Then he chuckled and said," Yeah, just look at some of the ancient stuff that's been left to the elements. Disastrous, that's what. "Shame on you Zorka and you call yourself a sculptor? You're nothing but a stone-cutter, Zorka. Misters Michelangelo and Donatello would laugh in your face. And how about August Rodin? Yeah...he too."

On a sudden impulse he threw his coffee cup onto the flagstone patio, watched it shatter into dozens of minute fragments, took a quick notice that the remaining coffee stain on the stones resembled Abraham Lincoln, and then picked up his sculpture mallet from the ground where it had lain in neglect and rust for weeks after his return from Italy and raised it high above the stone, then hesitated.

"Easy does it, Zorka," he said aloud and then lowered the mallet. "Might as well test it for fractures and faults. Hell, I could get you nearly done and then watch you cleave right in half at the mere tap of my mallet and point. Huh, happened before Zorka. Yeah it did!" Then He looked around and said, "For Christ sake I'm reduced to talking to a rock...well stone."

He began tapping the marble lightly at various places while listening carefully for the tell-tale signs of a fault or fracture. Satisfied that the marble was sound he put the mallet down and turned toward the distant faint gurgle of the Carmel River. "Rain has brought her up some," he mumbled.

He lay his hands on the cool surface of the stone and said, "Yeah, you're sound alright but it ain't likely I'll soon carve you into anything. However, if something or someone is hiding in there it might have to wait awhile, years maybe, before I release it...set it free that is... maybe never. But you know, there could be a baby in there curled into a bundle of blankets. Yeah, maybe. Something like that would please Becky for sure. Bless her heart she keeps encouraging me to get back to work but hell, it ain't likely to happening soon. Too much dust of loss to ever focus, maybe never focus again on anything as meaningless as my feeble efforts. "But then again…" he said aloud.

Five weeks later Mike finished his morning coffee on the flagstone patio while ignoring a light, misting rain and then walked over to one of Krista's neglected rose bushes and picked several well-aged flowers. Then, while sucking his thorn-pricked thumb, walked slowly toward the sound of the river. He stopped only once during his passage to look back.

A week after Mike vanished Becky, Zackary and Melody drove to Mike's Casa Viejo to begin the settlement of his belongings. It was their first visit after losing contact with Mike. Near the flagstone patio Zackary and Becky pulled a canvas cover off Mike's sculpture bench and discovered a beautifully completed sculpture of a newborn baby swaddled in blankets asleep on a bed of flowers.

"Look Zackie," Melody said," a baby sleeping on some flowers."

# End